Till the Cows Come Home

Till the Cows Come Home

Judy Clemens

Poisoned Pen Press

Copyright © 2004 by Judy Clemens

First Edition 2004

10 9 8 7 6 5 4 3 2 1

Library of Congress Catalog Card Number: 2003117124

ISBN: 1-59058-082-6 Hardcover

Poisoned Pen Press
6962 E. First Ave., Ste. 103
Scottsdale, AZ 85251
www.poisonedpenpress.com
info@poisonedpenpress.com

Printed in the United States of America

For Steve, Tristan, and Sophia,
who make the world a better place.

Acknowledgments

My thanks must first go to the farmers. Without them, this book would never have made it past my imagination. Don Chapman, who sent me the article which planted the seed for the plot, and who spent countless hours answering questions and reliving his years as a dairyman; Tom Halteman, who let me tag along on work days, providing me with hands-on experience to fill my book with detail; Marilyn Halteman, who answered every question I threw her way, and never begrudged my drop-in visits; Paula Meabon, Stella's real-life counterpart, who showed me that dairywomen have what it takes, and more; Randy Meabon, a director of Dairy Farmers of America, who gave me the lowdown on milk distribution and the dwindling numbers of family farms; and John and Norma Hockman of Penn View Farm, who didn't even blink when I showed up in the early morning hours to observe as they processed the milk from their farm.

Many others gave freely of their time and knowledge, and I thank them: Dr. Sarah Ward, Associate Professor of Plant Breeding and Genetics at Colorado State University, for giving of her valuable time and knowledge, showing me a side of science I never imagined; Judy Harrington, Dr. Ward's research assistant, for her enthusiasm, knowledge, and speedy responses; Detective Randall Floyd of the Telford Borough Police, for carving time out of his insane schedule to make sure I got Willard on the right track; Assistant Chief George J. Fielden, Jr., of the Radnor Fire Company, for answering my questions about arson; Chris Zink, DVM, PhD, who helped make the book's animals and veterinarian real-to-life; Dr. Doug P. Lyle, who answered my medical questions with speed and detail; Dave Smucker, who taught me how to mess up a combine (which I of course would never attempt); and Ralph Smucker, who set me straight on insurance issues. Any mistakes in this book reflect not on these resources, but on me. Of course, I may have just slipped them in to accommodate my story. I'll never tell.

I also could not have gotten this book on the shelves without the support of many other friends: Caroline Todd, my mentor and friend, who guided me through every aspect of the submission and publication process; the best writer's support group ever, my on-line buddies at AandP (members past and present); Daryl Wood Gerber, Marjorie Merithew, Sandra Parshall, and Elizabeth Zelvin, who generously read and critiqued the book; the lovely women of Delaware Valley Sisters in Crime; and the Indian Valley HOG chapter, who proved to me that bikers are so much more than just leather and loud pipes.

I am fortunate to be working with a wonderful publisher. A special thank you to Monty Montee, who believed in Stella from day one; Jennifer Semon, who sweated with me over re-writes; Rob Rosenwald, for his generous and welcoming attitude; and Barbara Peters, who kept at me until the book was where it needed to be.

Finally, I thank my family for being my biggest fans, supporters, and readers of multiple drafts. Mom and Dad, Jim and Angie, thanks so much. My wonderful husband Steve, thank you for watching the kids, listening to my ramblings, helping me with motorcycle and painting details, and for telling people I was a writer before I even did. Tristan and Sophia, thank you for bringing such joy to my life. And for taking naps so I could write.

Chapter One

"It's a boy! It's a boy!" Zach shrieked.

"Oh no. Really?" I slumped to the floor, my elbows resting on my knees. "All that work for a boy?"

Carla grimaced. "Sorry, Stella."

"Stop. It's not your fault."

"Poor old cow," Howie said.

I sighed and leaned my head back against the wall. It was only mid-morning and already the temperature was in the high eighties. I wiped my forehead on my sleeve and looked at the mother, never one of my favorites. She'd just had a calf cut out of her side and now she stood there, dumbly chewing her cud, as if nothing had happened. I made a face at her.

"What now?" I asked.

"Now we sew 'er up," Carla said. "Give me a hand."

Doctor Carla Beaumont waded through the straw to her med kit and pulled out a hook-shaped needle and long pieces of thick thread. Her biceps-high gloves made the work cumbersome, but she handled the instruments with the deftness of an experienced veterinarian.

"Come on," she said. "Hold this while I stitch. Keep the two sides out far enough I can get to them."

I grabbed hold of the cow's uterus, visible through the gaping incision in the side of the cow. It was slippery and warm, covered with blood and who knows what other kind of slime. I held on the best I could and Carla started closing it up, pushing the needle through the thick flesh and bringing the two smooth sides of the cut together.

Zach, my fourteen-year-old farmhand, sat on the floor with the bull calf, his first very own Holstein. Since I'm a dairy farmer, bull calves aren't much use to me, lacking the necessary udders, and I'd promised Zach the next bull calf would be his. I usually sell them to a neighbor who raises them for beef cattle or veal, but one less sale this month wouldn't be too much of a loss for either of us.

Wendy, the cow, lifted up her hind leg below the incision, and her uterus slipped out of my hand.

"Whoops," Carla said.

I grabbed the uterus more firmly, and Carla had just found her place when Wendy lifted her leg again.

"Oh, stop it, cow," Carla said. "I should've numbed more than her tail, poor thing."

I got hold of the flesh and once more Carla started stitching. She had gotten a couple of inches down when Wendy started to shift.

"She's going down!" Carla shouted. "Keep her up, keep her up!"

I leaned into the cow with all my weight, pushing her in the opposite direction until she got all four legs under her. The last thing we needed was for her to lie on her side and fill the incision with straw and afterbirth from the floor.

"Dumb cow," I muttered.

"It's okay, Wendy," Howie said, patting her head. "Here, drink some water." Howie, my family's farmhand of twenty-some years, moved the bucket closer to her. She lifted her leg and the slippery muscle slid out of my hands.

"Stop kicking, you stupid animal!" I yelled.

Blood spurted over my shirt and face. I closed my eyes and spat.

"Come on!" Carla said. "This vein's gonna bleed all over the place!"

I got a good grip just in time for Wendy to kick again. I grabbed at her uterus and squeezed it.

"For Pete's sake, Carla," I said. "Hurry up. My hand's cramping."

"Shut up, Stella. And hold on tighter."

"Yelling at Wendy isn't helping, either," Howie said.

"Fine," I said.

Zach wisely kept his mouth shut.

We had a few quiet moments and Carla got to the bottom of the incision. "Okay, I have two more layers to go. You don't need to hold them together, but stay here in case I need you."

I tried to wipe the blood off my face, but my gloves were too messy and my shoulders were covered, as well. I looked down at my boots and they were hidden beneath birth muck and manure.

"She's goin' down!" Carla said.

I jumped forward and pushed against the cow, all of her five hundred pounds pressing my legs into the floor.

"Come on! Come on!" I yelled. "Stay up, damn you!"

She suddenly righted herself and I slipped and fell face first onto the floor.

"Oh, great." The front of my overalls now sported a mixture of blood, afterbirth, and straw, just like the rest of me. "I knew there was a reason I didn't like this cow."

Carla tried not to laugh, and I pointed at her with a slimy glove. "Don't you laugh, Ms. Vet. You're looking way too clean."

"Sorry," she said, not meaning it.

"Are you about done? Or am I going to get covered in something else yet?"

"I'm on the last layer. If she doesn't try to lie down anymore we should be fine. And she hasn't kicked for about three minutes."

"Stupid cow," I said again.

"Why don't you go clean up," Howie said. "I'll make sure she doesn't go down."

"No sense in your getting messy, too. How's your calf, Zach?"

"He's great!" Zach's face lit up the room. "Thanks. Thanks a lot. His name's Gus."

I grunted. "Just make sure you get him colostrum as soon as his dumb mother can give it."

"Oh, I will, I will."

I knew I didn't need to tell him about the mother's first, and most nutritious, milk. I couldn't use her first three milkings after delivery, anyway, so we'd save it for this and any other calves we had out in the hutches.

Zach continued using a towel to wipe down the calf, even though it was completely dry. I had a feeling Gus was going to turn into the farm stud. The way Zach's face looked, there was no way the calf would ever be sold for beef.

"There's a hutch all ready for him out back," I said. "You can move him into it when you're ready."

"Do I have to? Can't he stay in the barn?"

"You know he'll be safer out there. It's clean, there aren't any big cows to step on him, and besides, there are two chick calves out there to keep him company."

"Okay, Stella, she's all sewn up." Carla stepped back from the cow and stripped off her gloves. She threw them on the ground and felt around in her med kit until she came up with a can of antibiotic spray. She covered the incision with several yellow coats of medicine.

"This should kill whatever happened to get in there," she said. "But I'm going to leave you a can to spray on tomorrow, too."

"Great. Thanks a lot, Carla. I appreciate your coming out so quickly."

I had awakened earlier than usual that morning to Wendy's keening. Cows usually moan when they're giving birth, and since Wendy is one of our more dramatic cows I figured she was just playing it up. Unfortunately, after several hours of her wailing and me rooting around in her uterus, I knew there was no way she was having the calf without the help of a vet. That's when I called in the pro.

"Hey, it's my job," Carla said. "Besides, I only get to do three or four of these a year, so I got some variety in my day."

I put my hands on my waist and rolled my head forward, trying to loosen my tight shoulders. A very pregnant barn cat sat on a bale of hay, watching.

"You'd better have an easier time of it, girl," I told her. "I ain't going through this with you, too."

She stared at me, unblinking.

"It looks like you've had some happenings this morning."

Another voice entered our conversation and we all looked to see who it belonged to.

My stomach turned. "Well, well, if it isn't our local land poacher."

"Stella," Howie said softly.

Hubert Purcell put up his hands. "Hey, now, I came on friendly terms."

I heard a threatening, guttural noise and realized Queenie, my dog, had followed Hubert into the barn. Hubert jerked back against the wall, and I smiled. Not many people are afraid of collies, but Hubert is one of them. Of course, it didn't help that my dog disliked the man, and she was baring her teeth.

"It's okay, Queenie," I said. "He's leaving now."

Hubert Purcell, owner of CHP Properties, was a little man in every sense of the word. He stood about five feet five, even with the cowboy boots he liked to wear, so at five nine I towered over him. I probably outweighed him by thirty pounds, too, and I'm not even close to fat. Hubert made his living by buying out farmers and putting as many cheap houses as he could over the entire acreage. He's been after my farm since the day my father died when I was three.

His "communities," as he liked to call them, all looked pretty much the same—full of white bread yuppies and money. Hubert loved Republicans as much as he feared everyone else—blacks, Koreans, bikers. All in all, he was a pretty pathetic specimen.

Queenie growled again, and I enjoyed the pale fear on Hubert's face. But I'm not cruel. At least not much.

"It's okay," I said. "Sit."

Hubert looked around at the bales of straw.

"I meant the dog, not you. What do you want, Hubert? You can see I'm a little busy here."

He smiled. "I brought someone to meet you. That's all."

I felt a quiver of unease. It couldn't be that simple, I knew, because Hubert wouldn't waste his time coming to talk with me unless he had a reason. I'd told him in no uncertain terms he would get my farm when the world ended or everybody else in the world, including me, was dead.

"I'm not exactly in my hostess gear," I said.

"She's not going to care. Besides, you don't look that much different from usual."

I scowled at him.

"Should I bring her in?" Hubert asked.

"No. I'll come out there." I wasn't going to discuss anything with him in front of Carla and Zach. Howie knew everything that happened at the farm, but the other two didn't need to be subjected to Hubert's crap. Besides, I didn't want Hubert, let alone his friends, invading my barn. "I'll be out in a minute."

Hubert smiled again, setting my teeth on edge, and went outside.

I peeled off my gloves and grabbed a paper towel, rubbing it over my face. I wouldn't look beautiful for his friend, but I didn't care. I stomped out of the stall, and Howie gently grabbed my arm.

"Stella. Don't do anything you'll regret."

I shook off his hand. "Stop mothering me, Howie. I promise I won't kill anyone."

His face closed and he turned away.

I sighed. "I'm sorry. You know how he gets to me."

Howie nodded but didn't look at me. I told Queenie to stay, and walked outside.

The sun beat down on the farmyard, and I shaded my eyes with my hand. Hubert and a woman were standing over by Carla's truck, peering into her Port-a-Vet. Her F250 sparkled amidst the dust of the farm, and the large storage cap on the bed was open, revealing her medicines, syringes, and other tools. I was sure she wouldn't have appreciated the scrutiny her property was getting.

"I hope you're studying to be vets," I said. "I would hate to think you're snooping."

The woman spun around at the sound of my voice, and I grinned. "Pam Moyer. Since when are you back in town?"

She held out her hand. I held mine up to show her the filthy condition of it, and she laughed.

"Wait a minute," Hubert said. "You ladies know each other?"

I snorted. Ladies, indeed. Wouldn't my mother have laughed at that one. Howie, too.

"Of course we know each other," Pam said. "Stella used to defend me from the white collars on the bus."

"And the playground," I said.

"Oh, God," she said. "Don't bring up that time on the jungle gym."

"You mean when Jacky Landis ended up with his shorts wrapped around the bars?"

Hubert grunted, reminding me of his presence.

I gestured to him. "So, Pam, what are you doing traveling around with *that?*"

"Hey," he began, but Pam shushed him. "I somehow let the town council drag me into duty. Well, more like Sonny Turner talked me into it."

"The council president? Isn't he the Turner Enterprises guy?"

"And the richest man this side of Philly. Can't hurt to listen to his advice and jump on board. So here I am. The *Agricultural Liaison.*" She waggled her eyebrows.

"Sounds fancy."

"Eh. Anyway, I'm supposed to be 'reacquainting myself with the farming community.' Hubert's on the council and volunteered to drive me around."

"Who else have you seen?"

"Actually, you're the first."

"Figures. Hubert can't seem to get me off his mind, can you Hu?"

Pam grimaced. "And I'm not sure who else we're visiting."

I opened my mouth to make another smart comment but was interrupted by a large milk truck rumbling onto the driveway and backing up to the milkhouse. The truck stopped and the driver hopped out of the cab. He looked from Hubert and Pam to me, then smiled.

"Howdy, Stella."

"Wayne. You're looking cool today."

He had on a uniform of a red shirt and shorts, with the trucking company's emblem of a happy milk-drinking cow on the left breast pocket. He wasn't even sweating.

"You betcha," he said. "And you're looking…especially attractive. Hard calving?"

"C-section. Carla's just finishing up."

"Hope it was worth it."

"Bull calf."

"Oh well. Better luck next time."

I glanced at my watch. "Running a little late?"

He rolled his eyes. "Got tied up at one place. No biggie. Just means I'll have my lunch a little later. I haven't decided if you're my favorite or least favorite farmer, since you're right before lunch."

He pretended to tip a hat, and got on with the business of getting the milk from our tank. Our milk gets collected every other day, sometime in the late morning. Wayne was responsible not only for collecting our milk, but for procuring samples and measuring how many pounds of milk we had that day. He'd been our milk hauler for about ten years.

I turned back to Pam, noticing she looked a lot the same as she had fifteen years before on the school bus. About a head shorter than me, but not a weakling. Brown hair, tan skin. Her years at school had done nothing to turn her farm girl muscles into fat.

"So what's your real job these days?" I asked her. "Or is the council a full-time gig for you?"

"Yeah, right. I'm working part-time at the University of Penn. Crop research. I only have to go down a few days a week, so I'm helping Dad on the farm, too."

"You graduated from Penn, didn't you?"

She put a hand on her heart. "My dear alma mater."

"And your degree is in what, exactly?"

"You sure you want to know?

I shrugged.

"I have a Ph.D. in Genomics and Computational Biology. It basically means messing with DNA and computers.

I raised an eyebrow. "So do I have to call you *Doctor* Moyer?"

"Only if you want to send me into a fit of giggles."

"Don't knock it," Hubert said. "You're our town's only Ivy Leaguer."

She wrinkled her nose. "In a sense. I was just a scholarship kid."

"Doesn't matter how you paid for it," Hubert said. "You're still one of them."

Irritation flashed across her face, to be quickly replaced by a tight smile. "Well, Hubert, I'm sure Stella has better things to do than stand around yakking with us all day." She turned to me. "I guess officially I'm the one you call now if you have any concerns or questions about farm stuff."

"You know me," I said. "As long as I'm left alone to run my place and take care of my herd, I'm happy as a pig in shit."

Pam chuckled and they turned to go. I touched her elbow. "How's your dad doing?"

Her face dropped, and her eyes swiveled toward Hubert.

"Give us *ladies* a few minutes, Hu," I said.

He put out his hand. "No problem, no problem. I'll see you soon, Stella. I wait with anticipation for the day you call me."

"Then you live for disappointment. Get lost."

He dropped his hand and stalked to his car.

"So what's up?" I asked Pam. "Your dad's still farming, isn't he?"

"Turning the ground over every year. I swear one day he'll die sitting on top of that damned combine. If the vultures don't run him out first."

I grunted. "Developers?"

"If that's what you want to call them. Hardly a week goes by he doesn't get some kind of offer. Wouldn't you know I have to put up with the worst of them driving me around today."

We glanced over at Hubert's Lincoln Town Car, where he was feigning disinterest.

"Your dad holding up okay?"

"He'll keep the farm if it kills him. Every day I see him grow older and more determined. Breaks my heart. If Mom were still around he'd be living off Social Security by now."

We watched a cow meander up to the paddock gate and sniff at the lock, turning her lip up at the smell.

"You?" Pam said.

"Same old, same old. I drive Hubert away every chance I can. I won't sell, either, but I can't say my checkbook's happy about it."

She shook her head. "Dad goes into debt deeper every year. Has a bad crop, has to borrow to make up for what he didn't make. Then the next year the bank won't lend him as much because his profit was so low. In fact, we have an application in at the bank as we speak. Should be hearing any day. Not that I expect anything."

I sighed. "I'm right there with him."

We stared at the cows some more until Pam shook herself. "Guess I'd better crawl back over to the Devil's car. Can't believe I have to spend the day with him."

"You're a strong woman. You can handle it."

She smiled. "I learned it all from you."

I laughed and jutted my chin toward the car. "Just don't sign any papers he gives you."

"Don't worry. He gives me papers my dad'll run him over with a tractor."

Now that was a pleasant vision.

Pam smiled again and trotted over to Hubert's car.

I crossed my arms over my chest, then regretted it when I felt more slime from my coveralls transfer to my skin. I stayed that way, however, and watched while Hubert and Pam drove off in the Town Car, kicking up a cloud of dust. The CHP design on the door looked incongruous with the expensive vehicle. CHP, meaning Communities of Hubert Purcell. I thought of it as CHeaP.

Queenie came running, barking at the departing car, and I went back into the barn, musing over Pam Moyer and hoping she wasn't being played for a fool by Hubert Purcell.

By this time, Carla had packed up her tools and was squatting on the floor, checking out the calf and talking to Zach. Howie was gone, off to do some other chores. Wendy stood lazily munching some hay Howie had put out. I glared at her, then grabbed a pitchfork and started cleaning up the mess around her feet.

Carla pushed herself up and gathered her bags. "Isn't it about time you got ready for lunch?"

I poked the fork into a cake of sticky straw. "I want to get this cleaned up first. Why? What time is it?"

"It's already noon. Weren't you supposed to be there by now?"

"Be where?"

She looked at me with exasperation. "Your birthday dinner, you dope. Ma Granger said we'd eat as close to noon as possible."

I smacked my forehead with my hand, which was a mistake, given the spray it produced. I had forgotten all about the dinner. I had forgotten all about my *birthday*.

"Well, I've gotta get this taken care of—"

"Stella!" Zach yelled. "Watch out!"

Before I had a chance to react, Wendy lifted her tail and sent a stream of urine gushing out, splattering off of the floor and onto my legs and arms. I jumped out of the way and slipped on a pile of manure, Wendy's other most recent gift, and fell right into the pouring stream.

Zach and Carla stood open-mouthed and silent as Wendy's tail lowered and the river stopped flowing. I opened my eyes and took a deep breath through my nose. If either one of them showed a hint of laughter, I was going to have to deck them. Luckily for them, their eyes showed not a flicker.

We all looked at each other without moving.

"Well," Carla finally said. "I guess we'll tell Ma you're going to be a little late for dinner."

Chapter Two

Carla was gone, headed over to Ma Granger's with Zach in the passenger seat, itching to tell his family all about his new calf. Howie was in his apartment, located above my garage, and I stood in the lane, watching Wayne and the tanker truck disappear.

Only when I realized I was standing in the full sun and the filth on my body was starting to dry did I make a move toward the house. Ma would understand my lateness and would go ahead and get the Granger clan fed while I took a much-needed shower. I really wasn't looking forward to a birthday party, anyway. The only reason I had agreed to any kind of celebration was that Ma was throwing it, and that meant a family get-together. There would be a few people there who weren't actually family, including Howie and Carla, and even me, but as far as Ma was concerned, we were all family.

The Grangers and Howie are all the family I know. When my father died in a farming accident when I was three, my mother was bound and determined to keep the farm and make it work. Howie Archer was our farmhand at the time, and my mother made it clear he was welcome to stay. He had stayed, and had been living in an apartment above the garage for almost thirty years. There were times I was sure he would have liked to exchange his bachelor's quarters for the farmhouse and my mother's bed, but he never brought it up, and by the time I was sixteen my mother was dead from breast cancer and Howie was still alone, living above the garage.

I wasn't a typical sixteen-year-old, having lost both parents and being a farmer to boot, and Howie made sure nobody, including Hubert Purcell, got anywhere close to taking anything from me. In fact, if it hadn't been for Howie, who knows where I'd be by now. I glanced up at the garage and hoped Howie hadn't been too hurt when I'd snapped at him that morning.

I took off my boots outside the back door and shook out my hair the best I could. Stopping in the mudroom, I stripped down to the skin, loading the clothes into the washer and starting it right away. The smell was already invading the house, and it would have been too much for even me.

Upstairs, I went into the bathroom and started the shower, stepping in only when I was sure the water was cool enough I wouldn't suffocate on this hot July day. I washed my hair twice and scrubbed as hard as I could with the Lever 2000 bar, and the water running down the drain eventually cleared.

I was pulling on my underwear when I snagged a callous on my finger. I looked at my hands, chapped and dry, and thought if anything showed my twenty-nine years, it was them. The rest of me was holding up pretty well.

I never was one to win beauty contests. Not that I tried. But my body is hard and angular where other women are soft and round. I may not fill up a swimsuit the way other women do, but I can throw bales of hay five feet up into the hayloft and wrestle a cow to the ground, if I have to. The sun's done its best to age my skin, but fortunately I have my mother's olive tones, and I can't burn if I try.

"You about ready, Princess?"

I looked out my open window, hiding behind the curtain, and Howie peered up from the yard.

"I'll be down in a minute."

I threw on some jean shorts, a black T-shirt, and some tennies I dug out from the back of my closet, and ran a brush through my short dark hair. I keep my hair short partly for the fact it's wash-and-go and partly to show off the cow skull tattooed at the base of my neck. The horns reach around to the front so you

can just see the tips of them when you're looking at me head-
on. Howie about *had* a cow when I came back with it, but he's
learned to ignore it. He wasn't so appalled when I came home
with "To thine own self be true" scripted around my left biceps,
but he didn't acknowledge it, either. Zach is constantly after me
to get "Got milk?" engraved on me somewhere, but so far I've
managed to put him off.

I glanced in the mirror, decided I looked presentable, and
ran down the stairs to meet Howie.

"You want to drive?" he asked.

"How soon do you need to get back?"

"The milking parlor's ready for tonight, and I got the feed
set to give out. I can stay away a few hours."

"All right, we can go together then. It's too hot to take the
Harley, anyway. C'mon, Queenie."

The three of us hopped in my truck, an older version of
Carla's, and headed to the Grangers'.

Howie give a big sigh and settled back into his seat. Queenie
stood behind us and stuck her head out the back sliding window.
Her tongue flapped in the wind and made splatter marks on the
window panels, but I didn't care. I'd gotten her when she was
two months old, and that little ball of brown and white fluff had
turned into one of my closest friends. Man's best friend? Make
that "Woman's," and we've got an agreement.

I took my companions' cue and relaxed, too, trying to fend
off the feelings of hopelessness that had been brought about by
Pam's visit. The ride to Ma's would take ten or fifteen minutes,
and it was mostly a pretty one. We had to pass several packed
developments that had popped up, but eventually we came to
more open countryside. I had to wonder how soon that would
be gone, too.

A few miles from home, Howie turned to me. "Time to
place your bets."

I grinned. "How 'bout one of those new Hummers?"

"Oh, good one." He rubbed his chin. "I'm feeling sophisticated today. I say a Cadillac Sedan DeVille. Black."

We approached the bed-and-breakfast, and I slowed. Das Homestead, a family home dating back to the 1700s that housed General Washington during war years, pandered to the elite, and it was a game for Howie and me to guess what vehicles would be gracing the parking lot on any given day. The more expensive we guessed, the better chance we had.

I smacked the steering wheel when the parking lot came into view. "Damn, I'm good. Look at that thing." The Hummer sat in its spot like a huge toad. An armored one.

Howie grunted. "Birthday luck. What do you want to bet my Caddy's there on the way home?"

"Sore loser."

About half a mile from Ma's I had to slow down to negotiate some curves that took us almost perpendicular to the road we'd been traveling, and then back again—a regular S curve. I had to shift down to get the truck around them, and I wished I was on my bike. Those curves were fun on the hog—maybe because they were a little scary. The right angles and the menacing gravel along the sides of the road, not to mention the steep ditch leading down to a creek, made for exciting riding.

Once we were out of the curves, we could see Ma's house in the distance.

The party was in full swing when we got there, with numerous Grangers seated under trees and at picnic tables, and kids running around with water pistols. The crowd seemed smaller than usual, though, and I wondered about it.

I parked along the lane amidst the other trucks and cars, and hopped out. Queenie jumped out behind me, wagging her tail furiously.

"Whose little toy is that?" Howie asked, pointing to a shiny red Volkswagen Beetle.

I stared at it. "I have no idea. None of the Grangers would be caught dead in it."

Howie chuckled at the thought.

"Well, well, if it isn't the birthday girl finally making an appearance." Jethro Granger, father of Zach and oldest of the Granger eight, enveloped me in a bear hug.

"I was busy giving your son a new pet," I said, extricating myself from his huge arms.

"Don't worry, we've been hearing all about little Gus. Now come on and get some barbecue before Ma throws a fit."

Queenie stood looking at me with expectation, her eyes bright.

"Go ahead, girl," I said. She gave a little yelp of excitement and ran ahead of me.

I waded through children and adults, shaking hands and getting lots of hugs, until I finally reached the kitchen, where Ma stood over the sink.

"Aren't you going to sit down and take a break even when the guest of honor's here?" I asked.

"Oh! Here you are at last. Let me fill you up a plate of meat, then you can get the rest out on the picnic table. I've been keeping this warm in here for you."

"Thanks, Ma. You spoil me."

"Nonsense. Your mother would have done the same, so I figure she's watching from heaven to make sure I'm taking care of you."

She handed me a plate with a slab of beef, and I gave her shoulders a squeeze with my free arm. "Whatever. I sure appreciate it."

"Now get on out there and eat up. You need your energy."

"Yes, Ma."

The picnic table was full of all the usual goodies: cole slaw, baked beans, deviled eggs, and potato chips. All very healthy, I'm sure. I put a forkful of Ma's homemade potato salad into my mouth and closed my eyes, savoring the flavor.

"Hey, birthday girl."

I opened my eyes and looked into a pair of beautiful hazel ones. I forced myself to swallow through my suddenly tight throat. "Abe. What are you doing here?"

"What kind of a welcome is that? I was due for a long week-end, so I came home. Wouldn't have missed your party."

I grinned. Abe was the youngest of the Granger clan, about six months younger than me. He was also the only son whose name was something other than a Biblical "J" name. Ma somehow knew from the point of conception that Abe was going to be different from the rest of the gang, and had named him accordingly. How right she'd been.

I had been instituted as the "adopted" Granger daughter when I saved Abe from drowning at the age of ten. My mother and I were picnicking at Lake Nockamixon when this dumb kid had fallen out of a boat minus a lifejacket. Without thinking I had dived into the water and dragged him out, kicking and screaming. How humiliating to be saved by a girl. He eventually got over the embarrassment and we'd been the best of friends ever since. We may have been more, but we were both too stubborn to admit it.

But just then, on my twenty-ninth birthday, my insides began tapping out a little line dance they hadn't done before. Abe was looking awfully good.

"Well," I said. "I'm glad something can bring the black sheep home again."

"Hey, just because my collar's a different color doesn't mean I'm not my mother's son."

"Tell it to the judge."

A hand snaked around his elbow. "Abie? Aren't you going to introduce me?"

My line dance froze. "*Abie?*"

Abe smiled uncomfortably. "Missy, this is Stella. Stella, Missy."

"How do you do?" the little brunette said, sticking out her hand.

I looked at it a moment before taking it.

"I've heard so much about you," she said. "It's wonderful to finally meet you."

"Bug," I said.

"I beg your pardon?"

"You own the VW Bug."

She smiled. "That's right. How did you know?"

I looked at Abe, but he avoided my eyes.

"Lucky guess," I said. "I'm going to go eat now. Nice to meet you."

I found Howie sitting at a table with Jethro and his wife, Belle. She looked a little pale, but I didn't think it would be polite to comment on it.

"Who's the co-ed?" I asked.

Jethro laughed. "I thought you'd be surprised. Ain't she something?"

"How come nobody told me about her?"

"Aw, they just started goin' out. Anyway, we figured you'd meet her whenever she showed up. Why does it matter?"

I shrugged and kept my eyes averted. "It doesn't."

"Great barbecue," Howie said. "As usual."

"Don't worry," Belle said. "It probably won't last."

"The barbecue?" Howie said, concerned. "Is it almost all?"

Jethro laughed again. "Abe's new girlfriend, she means. But I don't know. He's pretty sweet on her. And she's smart. Works in his accounting firm and all."

Belle looked at me and I shrugged again. "It's his life. How's she getting along with Ma?"

Belle grinned. "Okay, except for when she tried to put her luggage in the same room as Abe's. Ma made it very clear there was to be no fornicating under her roof."

This pleased me an uncomfortable amount.

"Hey, Stella!" Zach came running up. "Grandma wants to know if you're about ready to open presents."

"*Presents?*"

"Of course presents," Belle said. "We can't have a birthday party without presents."

"Oh, all right. Remind her I just got my food. Let me at least finish my lunch."

Zach ran off, and Jethro slapped Howie on the shoulder. "Told you she'd hate presents."

"Where's Mallory?" I asked, to take the attention off myself.

Mallory is Zach's older sister, baby-sitter extraordinaire. Usually at these occasions she would be herding the smaller tikes, but I didn't see or hear her today.

"Oh, she's got that flu," Belle said. "Just came down with it last night and feels something awful. I wanted to stay home with her, but she insisted I come. Said the baby-sitter didn't need a baby-sitter."

I laughed. "Sounds like her." I pushed my plate away and leaned my elbows on the table. "What is this flu? Aren't lots of kids getting it?"

Jethro nodded. "Just the last couple weeks. Must be some new strain. Haven't found a medicine to beat it yet, so it must be viral."

"And it's just kids?"

Jethro shrugged. "Pretty much. Not many adults have gotten it, except ones who're already sick with something, or real old folks. That could change, though. They say it might just take longer for grown-ups because of our immune systems or something."

"Any of the other cousins have it?"

"Joseph and Joshua each have a sick one," Belle said, talking of Granger sons number two and seven. "Jacob" (number five) "says Nina is keeping a close eye on their two. She wouldn't even bring them today, in case someone here was contagious."

Jethro rolled his eyes. "Like a kid's gonna die from a little cold."

"Come on, Stella!" Zach stood about thirty feet away, the still-healthy kids around him, anxious for presents even though they weren't theirs.

I pushed myself away from the table. "I guess this is it."

"You make it sound like going into battle," Jethro said.

Howie laughed. "For her, it is."

I made a face. "Bah, humbug."

Finally we were all gathered in one general area under some trees so I could do the embarrassing thing and open presents.

Gifts ranged from flannel shirts to chrome knick-knacks for my Harley to a Stevie Ray Vaughn CD. Quite a haul.

With my thumb and forefinger I picked up a gift bag, decorated with flowers and overflowing with pink tissue paper.

"That's from me," Abe said.

I looked at the gift and then at him.

"Well, from us. Missy wrapped it."

I stuck my hand in the tissue and came up with a variety of shower gels and lotions and one of those puffy washing things. I looked at Abe. He turned a bit pink, making him a match with the gift.

"Um, Missy picked it out."

She smiled. "I figured with all the work you do on the farm you could use some good smelling things. You know, to pamper yourself."

"Sure," I said. "Thanks a lot." I put them back in the bag. They wouldn't see the light of day until I could find someone else to give them to, but she didn't need to know that.

"Okay, here's the last present," Jethro said. He lumbered over, carrying a large flat package. He was grinning from ear to ear.

I ripped open the paper and caught my breath. It was an aerial photograph of my farm.

"Oh, wow," I said. "It's beautiful." I ran my fingers over the glass. Everything was there—the milkhouse, the heifer barn, the farmhouse, and a little of the fields surrounding it all. There were even dots of cows in the pasture.

"It gives a good look at the manure lagoon," Jethro said, laughing.

Belle elbowed him in the ribs. "We thought you'd like it. Jude and Marianne pitched in, too. It's from the four of us."

I looked at Jude with surprise. Jude was number six of the Granger boys, five years older than me. His wife, Marianne, was my age, and not from a farming family, which she was always quick to point out. Jude worked my land and planted crops on it. The Granger acreage wasn't enough to support them, and mine made up the difference. In return, he kept my cows in hay and silage from his harvest.

"We thought you'd like a picture of your most prized posses-sion," Marianne said. Her snide tone of voice made me wonder why she allowed Jude to even give me a present, but I wasn't going to let her spoil the moment.

"It's great," I said. "It's going up in my office tonight."

A baby wailed somewhere in the mess of people, and Mari-anne flinched, then looked down and started picking up the wrapping paper I'd thrown on the ground. I was surprised how much there was.

"Thanks, everybody, for all the great stuff."

I don't know if anybody heard me. Their attention was diverted by Queenie, yelping happily as the kids decorated her with cast-off ribbons and bows.

People started to get up and walk off. I turned toward Abe to see if we could do some more catching up, but Missy's hand looked permanently grafted to his elbow. I ditched that idea and went over to give Ma a hug. "Thanks for a great party."

"I thought you'd come around and enjoy yourself, eventu-ally."

"Want me to put this in the truck?" Howie asked. He held up the photograph.

"Sure, why don't you—"

"Stella!"

Jethro lumbered toward me, a look of fear on his face. My heart skipped a beat.

"What is it?"

"You seen Zach? Where is he?"

"Over there." I gestured toward the side yard where Queenie and the boy were wrestling, ribbons and bows flying. "What's wrong, Jethro?"

Instead of answering, Jethro hustled over to Zach, hauled him up by the arm, and started pulling him toward his truck. Queenie leapt up and stood in front of them, teeth bared.

"Queenie!" I yelled. I ran over and grabbed her collar before Jethro could do something stupid. "Jethro, what the hell is the matter with you?"

Queenie quieted, but didn't sit.

"Out of my way, Stella. The dog, too."

"What did I do, Dad?" Zach said. "You're crushing my arm!"

Jethro's face changed suddenly and he looked down at his huge hand, encircling Zach's elbow. He dropped Zach's arm and ran his hand over his face. "Sorry, son."

"Jethro—"

"Just shut up, Stella, and let me talk, okay? Belle just took a phone call in the house. We have to get home to Mallory." He stopped and swallowed.

"What? What was the phone call about?"

"You know little Toby Derstine?" he said. "Lives just down the road from you? He came down with flu symptoms three days ago. Now he's dead."

Chapter Three

The party cleared out in a heartbeat. Moms, dads, aunts, uncles, all headed home to make sure their sick ones weren't sicker and their healthy ones stayed healthy. That left Howie, Carla, and me to help Ma clean up the mess. Zach, too, since I'd finally convinced Jethro and Belle he'd be better off at the farm than at home. No reason to subject him to Mallory's germs more than he already had been.

Ma went into her quiet mode no one dares to interrupt, where she glides around calmly, lips moving in constant prayer, hands in unceasing motion. We worked, our hearts and thoughts with Toby Derstine's family, as well as with our own sick relatives and friends. Soon the ribbons, gift wrap, and paper plates were in the burning barrel, the leftover food was in the fridge, and the lawn chairs and tables were folded up and stashed in the garage. Howie, Zach, Queenie, and I said good-bye to Carla and left Ma to her meditation.

The Derstines' lane was packed with vehicles when we drove by. People stood on the porch and lawn, wanting to show support but obviously hesitant to go into the house. Couldn't blame them. I wouldn't want to take a chance with the virus, either. I glanced at Zach's face and felt a stab of helplessness. I wanted to tell him everything would be okay, but how could it be, with our little neighbor dead?

"I'll go over and pay my respects after milking," I said.

Howie nodded. "Me, too."

Zach glanced at me, but I shook my head. "Not you, bud. We're not chancing it."

He must've agreed, because he didn't protest.

We pulled into our drive and prepared to get back to work. Even with tragedies next door our chores waited, never fully satisfied. I ran upstairs to change, and when I came back out found Howie and Zach in the milking parlor, staring at a couple of very dirty and extremely smelly cows.

"What on earth?" I headed out back. Howie and Zach followed.

"Well, shit," I said. And I meant it. There was shit everywhere. Flooding the lower pasture, clouding up the stream, and making my Holsteins more brown than black and white.

"Them muskrats've sure been busy," Howie said.

"Wow," Zach said.

I crossed my arms and shook my head at my boots, ankle deep in runny muck. The muskrats would chew a hole in the manure pit once or twice a summer, but they'd never been this enthusiastic before.

"Nice birthday present," Howie said.

I grunted, then gave Zach another quick study to make sure he wasn't showing any symptoms of the now-deadly flu. So far, so good. Which meant I could put him to work.

"It's time to milk," I said. "Why don't you guys gather the cows and do your thing while I take care of this?"

Zach looked relieved, but Howie scowled. "I'll do it. You do the cows tonight."

"Nope. I'll feel much better if I take care of it. Besides, I don't think I've had quite enough bodily fluids covering me today. I'll hose off the cows as you bring them by."

Fortunately, the manure had no way to get into the barnyard or the milking parlor, so as the cows made their slow and clumsy way into the barn, I sprayed the crap off their legs and bellies. Some had apparently decided to lie down in it, too, so those got the full-body treatment. Cows may be good livestock, but no one ever said they were smart.

Queenie, ever the vigilant cow-herder, did her best to round them up without getting too poopy, but I ended up having to spray her down, too.

"Oughta get out the camera," Howie said. "Not very often you have a herd that's just stepped out of the shower."

"Good idea. Zach, grab the Polaroid from the office, will ya? Let's immortalize this. And while you're at it, take some pictures of outside before I clean everything off."

Zach was soon snapping away. I wanted to get his mind on something so he wouldn't worry about his sister, himself, or poor Toby, and this seemed a good bet. He was used to the camera, as we have to take two pictures, one of each side, of every female calf in order to register her. Zach had long ago designated himself resident portrait-taker.

I was just ready to check out the manure pit when Howie came out of the barn, a frown creasing his face.

"What?" I said.

"We're short a cow."

"Who's missing?"

"Not sure. I just know we've got an empty stall."

"Great." I sighed and ran a hand through my hair. "I'll go look for her."

"I can—"

"Just let me go, all right?"

He raised his hands in surrender and headed back in.

I walked an uneven circle, searching in the various corners of the barnyard and the long barn where the cows ate lunch. No missing cow. Huh.

The only other thing would be if she'd gotten stuck or injured in the pasture. The cows have the freedom to roam around down there whenever they want, during the day. I crossed the concrete long barn floor and went out the other side toward the pasture that wasn't clogged up with manure. Nobody there at first glance, but there were some places I couldn't see.

Five minutes later I found her. She was lying in the middle of the pasture, on the far side of a little hill, her staring eyes unprotected from a cloud of buzzing flies. I put my hands on my hips and let my head drop. Several hundred dollars had just gone flying out the window.

I squatted down beside Cleopatra—for that's who it was—to see if I could tell what had killed her. There weren't any obvious signs. No cuts, no injuries, no blood. I couldn't imagine what had made her drop dead. If she were pregnant, it could be any number of things, but she just happened to be in-between freshenings.

Out of ideas, I stood. There was no way I could move her myself, so I trudged back up the hill and into the parlor. "Found her. It's Cleopatra."

"Well, damn," Howie said. "Not coming to get milked, is she?"

"'Fraid not."

Shit.

I called Carla to see if she could come figure out what had killed the cow, but got her answering machine, which told me she was out of town and I should dial the on-call number for emergencies. It didn't really classify as an emergency, seeing as how Cleo was a little past reviving, so I just hung up.

Leaving Howie to pump the girls and Zach to play Ansel Adams, I waded back across the cement paddock through an inch of sloshy mess to check out the damage in the lagoon walls. The manure had stopped flowing, so I figured I was looking for a hole above surface level. I made my way around the outside of the pit, trying to avoid the larger puddles of poop.

"Oh, ho," I said.

Right in front of me was a beautiful muskrat hole, six inches wide, edges smooth and shiny. I walked the rest of the exterior, searching for more leaks, and was almost done when I was rewarded with another hole, unfortunately leading right down to the creek.

"Crap-ola," I said under my breath. I bent down and saw that the hole was the twin of the other one.

"Want me to take a picture of that?" Zach asked, pointing at the creek. Its usually clear water was muddied up with manure, and the rocks and plants on the creek bed were covered with brown slime.

"Sure," I said. "Might as well document the entire stinkhole. Watch your step." Zach started to half slide, half walk down the hill toward the creek, keeping the camera up and out of danger.

"Can you get these holes first?" I asked, stopping him. "We can give the muskrats copies for their albums."

Zach laughed and snapped the pictures. "I'll get the creek, then I thought I'd take some pictures of Gus. That okay?"

"More than okay. Have fun."

I watched him as he got closer to the creek and felt my heart climb towards my throat at the thought of losing him to some bizarre illness. Swallowing my unease, I went off to find rocks and mud to plaster up the muskrat holes. With any luck the creek would clear out before it got to someone else's property and I had to dig into my pollution liability insurance.

When I was done filling in the holes I made my way back up to the paddock and started the Bobcat, a tractor-type machine that looks kind of like a forklift, sporting a metal scraper in the front. I use it almost daily to clear the heifer barn and paddock of manure. It would get more of a workout that day.

As I pushed cow crap back toward the lagoon, the Derstines crowded my thoughts. They were good neighbors, always free with smiles and waves, the dad a construction worker and the mom at home with the two kids. Little Toby, ready to start kindergarten in the fall, was a sweet boy. I couldn't imagine how his folks must be feeling.

When my vision started to blur I forced my brain to move on to the issue of Miss Beetle and Abe. I was ticked nobody had told me about her—not that they had a reason to, I guess. It was just if I was going to be the only girl in the "family," I figured I ought to be kept up on important things like Abe's love life.

And Abe, what was with him bringing home a sophisticated city gal? His blue-collar roots weren't enough for him now he was a genuine New Yorker?

I slammed to a stop, banging the scraper bucket onto the ground, and picked up the hose I'd left by the barn. I sprayed off the machine and then the paddock floor, fuming all the while. Shit and shine-Missy-ola all in one day. Not to mention the uterine blood and guts I'd experienced in the morning. After stomping over to check the lock on the paddock gate—all we needed to top off the day was cows running loose—I sprayed off my boots and left them at the office door.

I had just sat down and leaned my head against the wall when the phone rang.

"Yeah," I said. "Royalcrest Farm."

"Stella?"

"In the flesh."

"It's Pam." Her voice sounded heavier than it had just that morning.

"You all right? Hubert didn't do something stupider than usual, did he?"

"No, no, he's fine. I mean, he didn't.… Oh crap, it's just this poor little Derstine kid. It's so awful."

I pinched the bridge of my nose. "Yeah. You realize he's my neighbor?"

"Oh God, really? I'm sorry."

We were both silent for a moment.

"So, what's up?" I said. "Just call to chat?"

She sighed. "I wish. I hated to even bother you, but it's now 'my job.' I got a phone call this afternoon and needed to let you know. Did you have trouble with your manure lagoon today?"

"What? How would anyone know about that? Who called you?"

"So it's true?"

"It was muskrats. You know how it is."

"We never had livestock, but I've heard lots of stories. Anyway, my caller—who asked that I don't reveal any names, and dammit I have to respect that—seemed concerned the creek running behind your farm got polluted."

"Well, you can tell *your caller* it's already been taken care of. For Christ's sake."

"I'm sorry I had to even say anything. I'm sure you have things under control."

"No problem," I said, gritting my teeth. "So what's the council's plan for investigating Toby's death? I'm assuming they have one."

"Sure. It's their highest priority, of course. The State Department of Health is here, and has pretty much taken over the investigation. I think an invitation to the Centers for Disease Control is forthcoming. Their experts should be here within a day or two."

"Good. Meanwhile, tell your anonymous caller to leave me the hell alone."

"You got it."

I slammed down the phone and spun my chair around to look at the wall. Whoever had called Pam would've had to know about the manure leak at the same time, or even before, I did. What did that mean? The creek wasn't moving fast enough for the grungy water to have reached somebody else already.

Queenie started barking, and I heard a vehicle pull into the driveway. I glanced out the side window at a blue Ford Ranger I didn't recognize, and saw Queenie hustling to investigate. Soon there were footsteps outside the office door and then a tentative knock.

"Whoever you are," I said, still facing the wall, "I don't need any, want any, or have the money for it. Go away."

"All I want is a minute of your time."

Rolling my eyes, I spun the chair around and looked at the most beautiful man ever to set foot on my farm. Probably six-two, two hundred, with wavy blond hair highlighting bright blue eyes and a tan that reached down into his collar. Levi's hugged his lean waist, and a dark green T-shirt pulled tight around his broad chest. I was suddenly very aware I had just finished spraying cow shit around for an hour and a half, and was afraid he was, too.

"You can have *two* minutes," I said. "Have a seat."

He sat and stunned me with a smile that was whiter than fresh milk. I couldn't help but smile back.

"So what do you want?" I asked.

"I'm a barn painter. Or handyman, or concrete layer, or fence-builder. Whatever you might need."

What I need, I thought, *is a couple minutes alone with you with my clothes off.*

"I really don't need anything," I said. "And what I said about money was true. I don't have any to spare."

"I come cheap. And I work hard."

Now, the funny thing about these barn painters is that every farmer gets visits from a couple of them during the summer. No one knows who they really are or where they come from, and you're generally thought to be a boob if you fall for their spiel. You also end up paying far more than they're worth—no matter how charming they may be.

I smiled again and tapped a pencil on my desk. "Sorry. No can do."

"Can't blame a guy for trying." He illuminated my office with his teeth. "Sorry I wasted your time."

"No problem. You were a pleasant interruption."

I watched very carefully as he left the room, then stood up and walked to the door just to make sure he got into his truck. No other reason. Honest.

Queenie trotted over to him from her perch under a shade tree, and he knelt down and gave her a good rubbing. *She* seemed to think he was good news. While I studied his profile and demeanor appreciatively, an image of Abe and his new girlfriend's hand slipping around his arm flashed through my mind. *Abie?* My stomach tightened. Why should Abe have all the fun?

"What's your name?" I called from the door.

He stood. "Nick. Nick Hathaway."

"So, Nick Hathaway," I said. "When can you start?"

Chapter Four

The cows were meandering back into the barnyard, udders emptied and stomachs full, and Howie and Zach were cleaning up the parlor. I was watching Nick's truck disappear down the lane, looking forward to seeing him again the next day, when another truck pulled in. Queenie spun around in circles and barked.

Jethro, Belle, Jude, and Marianne spilled out of the Chevy Dually, Jethro's four-door pickup. Queenie ran up to Belle, who graciously, if absently, leaned down to get her face licked.

A shiver of fear raced up my spine.

"What's wrong?" I asked. "Where's Mallory?"

Belle's eyes were swollen and red-rimmed, and she shook her head, like she couldn't speak.

Jethro cleared his throat. "Threw us out on our ears. Said she couldn't stand another minute of fussing."

"So she's okay?"

Jethro glanced at Belle, then said, "If you count not eating anything and having a fever of a hundred and three okay."

"Why isn't she in the hospital?"

"Because they wouldn't know what to do with her. The doc said to treat the symptoms, you know, the bananas/rice/applesauce/toast diet and all that, to help her stomach. Tylenol for her fever. And he said not to take her anywhere. It's all we can do till they figure out what's making her sick."

Belle made a sniffling noise and buried her face in Jethro's shoulder. He put his arm around her for comfort, but looked just as miserable as she.

"So what are you doing here?" I asked. "Zach's okay. I've been watching him."

Jethro forced a smile. "Would you believe we just had to get another look at the birthday girl?"

"No."

"Okay. How 'bout we want to see Zach's new little fella?"

"That's more like it." A good excuse to see Zach, anyway. "Zach's in the barn." I hooked my thumb over my shoulder. "He's almost done, I think."

"Can we go in? I haven't seen the parlor for a while. Anything different?"

"Nothing's changed. But you're welcome to check it out."

The four of them filed into the parlor, Queenie leading and Marianne lagging behind, sulking about something, her lips pushed out in a pout. If I were generous, I would've thought she was worried about her nieces and nephews. In reality, she was probably afraid she'd get poop on her shoes. I followed her in, secretly hoping she'd step in something.

Jethro and Belle stopped just inside the door to watch Zach. From all I could see, he was looking as healthy as he had been half an hour before.

"Can you spare your hired help for a few minutes?" Jethro asked Howie. "We hear he has a new baby."

Howie looked up and sighed dramatically. "I guess he can go. It's not every day a boy has a calf."

Zach grinned and hurried to put up his pitchfork. "C'mon, he's out in the hutch."

"Take his milk," Howie said, gesturing to the bucket of colostrum they'd just gotten.

"Sure." Zach picked up the bucket and scurried out of the barn, everyone hustling to follow. He wasn't wasting any time. He also didn't seem to notice all of the eyes following him and judging whether he seemed sick or not.

"You all set here?" I asked Howie.

"Just about. You can go on out with them. I got the formula bottles ready for the other calves if you want to take them out."

"Maybe I will. When the Grangers are gone, you want to go over to the Derstines'?"

"Once I clean up. Don't want to go in these pants."

"No problem. I should change, too."

I was halfway out the door when I heard Howie ask who the guy in the Ranger had been. I pretended not to hear. I knew he wasn't going to be happy I'd hired Nick the Barn Painter.

Gus was outside of his hutch when I got there, reveling in the pats and strokes of the admiring bunch. Queenie thrust her nose into my hand and I rubbed it.

"Yes, girl, you're still the best," I whispered to her. She rolled her eyes up at me and panted happily.

Marianne stood a little to the side, looking anywhere but at Gus, and I walked up beside her.

"Cute little guy, huh?" I said.

"I guess. If you like that sort of thing."

I looked at her. Who didn't like that sort of thing?

"Seems kind of cruel to take them from their mothers," she said.

"It's the best thing for them. They're bound to get trampled or kicked if they're in with the big cows. And their mothers forget about them real quick once they're out of sight."

"Still seems mean."

I shrugged. "Part of farming. You get some good snapshots of him?" I called to Zach.

He nodded. "One of each side, just like the heifers. He's got great markings, don't you think?"

I smiled. Gus looked like most of the other calves to me, but Zach saw him with a different eye. I was suddenly very glad stupid Wendy had had a bull. Even if it did cost me big bucks for the C-section.

"Jude's fields are looking healthy again this year," I said, trying to find something Marianne would talk about.

She gave me a bored look. "I guess. He thinks he's the ultimate farmer, since everybody else is hurting from the lack of rain."

I was surprised at her sneering tone. "Could be his touch."

"I'm the one who buys the seed."

"Not much to that, is there?"

She turned on me. "What would you know? You haven't planted crops in years."

"What's there to know?"

"Haven't you kept up at all?

I wanted to hit her, but I restrained myself.

"There's all kinds of seed to buy anymore," she said. "They're finding ways to modify it so it will resist bugs, RoundUp, pretty much anything you want to throw at it."

"So you're into that stuff?"

"It's working, isn't it? Our crops look better than anybody else's. I guess no one else thought to buy drought-resistant seed." She snorted. "I've got more brains than any of the dimwit farmers around here. You'd think they never passed the Stone Age."

Now I really wanted to hit her. Instead, I hooked the bottles of formula onto the girl calves' fences. They slurped at them hungrily. Their hutches looked a little messy, so I grabbed a nearby pitchfork and cleaned them up while I ignored Marianne and waited for Gus' love fest to end.

Jude's crops *were* looking healthy. Last year, too, he'd had good luck, while some of the other farmers around had been plagued with drought and bugs. He liked to think it was his tender care, but it sounded like Marianne's choice of genetically modified seed had something to do with it. I wondered how they could afford the seed, but figured it wasn't my place to ask.

Genetically modified crops are quite the rage, but some folks won't touch them. Some places, especially in Europe and California, have banned GM products from being sold in their supermarkets or served in schools for fear of what the altered genes could do to the human body. They quote studies where unsuspecting ladybugs and monarch butterflies have died from eating the crops, and speak in fear about bugs who have been made sterile by ingesting the changed proteins. How they test that exactly, I'm not sure, but not everyone believes these studies, anyway. Since I haven't planted crops for years, as Marianne so kindly pointed out, I've stayed out of the controversy.

When I had finished cleaning the hutches and the others were done oohing and aahing over Gus, Zach gently put him back in his temporary home. He filled the big bottle with colostrum and gave Gus a final pat through the door. Then he stood up and grinned.

"Got another surprise. Come on."

I tagged along, not knowing what he meant. There couldn't have been another new calf I didn't know about—we didn't have any more cows due to calve for a week or so. Zach led us down to the lower part of the big barn, underneath the parlor, to a corner where a few bales of old straw sat, loose from their twine. He got fairly close, then leaned over to look at something.

"There," he said quietly. I waited while the others looked, then got my turn to see the tabby who had been watching the C-section that morning. Her hugely pregnant belly was now flatter, and four little kittens suckled at her nipples.

"When did these come out?" I asked.

"Must've been this afternoon while we were gone," Zach said. "I've been watching for them every day, and when she wasn't around when we got back I searched till I found her."

He was beaming, the proud daddy of a new calf *and* a litter of kittens.

"Now, you gotta admit that's pretty cute," I said to Marianne. She looked at me, then spun around and walked outside. Jude threw a frustrated look at her back, then went after her.

"What's up her butt?" I asked.

Jethro and Belle looked uncomfortable, but didn't answer, so I let it go. None of my business, anyway.

We walked out to Jethro's truck, where Jude stood talking to Marianne, already hidden in the back seat.

"You got room for Zach in there?" I asked.

"Got room for the entire county in there," Belle said. "But actually…."

"What?"

She glanced at Zach, and when her lip trembled she stilled it with her teeth. "We thought we'd take you up on your invitation and have him stay the night here. We don't want him catching Mallory's…whatever it is."

"Aw, Mom—"

"Don't you start, Zachary. We're trying to keep you healthy."

"Fine with me," I said. I tried to sound casual for Zach's benefit. "I've got extra beds. And that way you don't have to drive him over for the morning milking."

"But, Mom—"

"Here." She reached into the truck and pulled out a bag. "I brought you extra clothes."

"This way you can spend more time with Gus," I said. "Or give Queenie a good brushing."

He lit up. "Hadn't thought of that. Okay. Bye, Mom. Bye, Dad." He grabbed the bag from Belle and started for the house.

"Second upstairs bedroom on the right," I yelled after him.

"Thanks, Stella," Jethro said. His eyes were haunted, and he watched Zach until the screen door slapped shut behind him.

"You know he's always welcome here. Especially now."

After a few instructions about bedtime, I shooed them into the truck. "I'll take care of your son. You concentrate on your daughter. Tell her she'd better get well real quick, or I'll have to come over and read aloud from my *Hoard's Dairyman* magazines."

"Now there's something to avoid." Jethro clasped my hand with unusual fervor and climbed into the truck.

Queenie yipped her good-byes while I watched them go, and Howie came out from the parlor. He was about to say something, but I cut him off, figuring he wanted to know about Nick.

"Let's go get our dead cow," I said. "Carla's out of town and won't be coming tonight."

Howie gave me a flat-eyed look, then went to get his truck. Barn painter subject averted. For the moment.

When Howie pulled up beside me, I threw a chain and a tarp into the back of the truck and hopped in. We drove around to the back of the pasture where there was a gate, placed there for emergencies. Howie backed up to Cleopatra and we got out.

"Nope," Howie said. "She's definitely not doing any more milkings."

Between the two of us we got the chain wrapped around her hind legs, and after Howie attached the chain to the truck he pulled her onto the tarp I'd laid on the ground. Luckily the barn basement was on the same level as the pasture on the barn side, so we slowly dragged her as close to the barn door as we could.

I trotted up to the yard and found Zach brushing burrs out of Queenie's fur.

"Get your help for a minute, Zach?" I asked. "You feeling all right?"

"I'm fine. Geez. What do you want me to do?"

When we got back to the pasture, Howie had unfastened the chain from the truck.

"Well, here goes nothing," I said.

Howie and I each grabbed an end of the chain while Zach crouched in between us, pulling on the tarp. Not an easy job, believe me. Ten minutes later, after we had spent about five minutes of actual dragging and five of recovering, Cleopatra lay in an empty stall where she would stay cool and protected from the other cows.

"Get another tarp to put over her, would you, Zach?"

He wiped sweat from his eyes and stood up. "I thought I was here to keep from getting sick, not to get worked into the ground."

I swiped at him as he walked past, but he avoided me. I laid my head down on my knees and tried to even out my breathing.

After about thirty seconds of silence Howie said, "So, who was the guy in the Ranger? And don't pretend you can't hear me this time."

Chapter Five

"You did *what?*" Howie's face turned a mottled red.

"He's only painting the heifer barn," I said. "It needs to be done."

"*I'll* do it! And Zach's around!"

"If he doesn't get sick." Howie glared at me in silence and I looked down to brush some straw off my jeans. "Anyway, Nick said it would take a couple weeks. When are you going to have the time?"

"Well, if *Nick* said it."

"Oh, come on. Don't get your panties in a bunch. Queenie here gave him a thumbs up."

Queenie, hearing her name, wagged her tail enthusiastically.

"And she knows all about barn painters, does she?" He spat on the floor. "And just how little money we have?"

"Give it a rest, Howie." I was starting to be embarrassed by my impulse. "It has to be done, and he'll be here in the morning. It's my farm."

"I guess it is. *Princess.*" He stomped off to his apartment, where I hoped he'd take a shower. That's where I was headed.

I scrubbed down again with my Lever 2000, thinking of the frou-frou soapy stuff Abie and his girl had given me for my birthday. I bet that stuff couldn't cut through the odors of all the bodily fluids I'd been exposed to that day. So what if I ended up smelling more like a man than a woman? At least I didn't smell like afterbirth.

I pulled on a different pair of jean shorts and a Harley T-shirt, grabbed a peanut butter and jelly sandwich, and ate it with a glass of milk, standing at the sink. I looked out at the part of the barn I could see from the window. The heifer barn wasn't the only building that needed paint. We'd see how Pretty Boy did, and if he was playing fair I'd get him to paint the big barn, too. It might cost more than I could really spare, but it would be cheaper than replacing the barn if it wasn't maintained. Besides, as long as Nick was around I'd get viewing entertainment as part of the bargain.

Zach came through the kitchen and I nodded at the bread and jelly. "Make yourself a sandwich, if you want. Sorry I won't have a three-course meal, like your mom."

He held up a Tupperware bowl. "Leftover lasagna. Enough for you, too, if you want it."

I looked sadly at the last bite of sandwich in my hand. "Too late. Maybe for a midnight snack."

He shook his head. "Take it now, or it's gone."

"Fine, you selfish squirt. Eat all that healthy food."

He smiled and dumped the bowl's contents onto a plate. It did look good, but my sandwich had done its work.

I went outside to wait for Howie. Visiting the Derstines wasn't going to be easy, and I had no idea what I'd say to them, but I needed to at least show my face. I tossed Queenie a treat and she scurried away to eat it behind one of the shrubs. Didn't want me to steal it back, I guess.

I heard the door of Howie's apartment close, and I watched as he descended his stairs. By the look on his face, he was still ticked at me. Oh well. Life would go on.

Without exchanging so much as a syllable, we climbed into my truck and drove the quarter mile to the Derstines' house. I parked to the side of the lane so I wouldn't block anybody, then paused to look at the small group on the porch.

"Ready?" I asked.

Howie grunted and opened his door.

The walk up the lane was too short, and I soon found myself giving Claire Derstine, Toby's mother, a hug. She held on for a long time, and I tried not to feel claustrophobic.

"I'm really sorry," I said when she let go.

She gave me the same speechless nod Belle had given an hour earlier, and I hoped she wouldn't start a fresh round of tears. Her husband came over and shook my hand.

"Stella, thanks for coming by."

"Anything I can do, Tom. You holler."

"Thanks."

Howie stepped in to shake hands, and I made a beeline to the front of the porch, where I could see the sky and take a deep breath. I acknowledged a few other neighbors, noting that Toby's baby sister, Greta, was nowhere to be seen.

Another truck pulled into the driveway and Marty and Rochelle Hoffman stepped out of their red Ford F150. Also small-time dairy farmers, I'd known them since I was a tot. They kept busy holding their heads above water, just like me. We'd check in on each other once in a while to make sure we were both still in business, but didn't see each other near as often as we'd have liked.

They headed straight to the Derstines, but after their initial greeting Rochelle stayed with Claire and Marty angled toward my spot at the railing.

"Damn shame," Marty said.

"Yup." I leaned my hip against a porch pillar and shoved my hands in my pockets. "What do you know about this flu, or whatever they're calling it? You're good at keeping up with stuff like this."

He shook his head. "Not much to know yet. The State Department of Health can't even pin it down. Next thing we know our whole town will be quarantined."

"Can they do that?"

He shrugged. "Don't know. We'll see what the CDC has to say. This flu seems limited to about a five-mile radius. Our borough. That's about it."

"And they really think it's the flu?"

"Same symptoms so far. Puking, the runs, fever, aches. It's so new, though, the kids could develop other stuff before it's run its course. And they're just waiting for adults to come down with it. I did hear a couple old folks down at the Home are feeling pretty poorly."

I glanced around to make sure no one was close, then lowered my voice. "So how come Toby died? Other kids have been sick as long as him, but they're holding out."

He clucked his tongue. "Toby had asthma real bad. Docs say it compromised him too much, his body couldn't take the extra stress. He'd been at home till yesterday, when he got lots worse and they found he had pneumonia on top of it all. Poor little guy."

I couldn't think about it. "Greta's not sick?"

Toby's baby sister. Not quite a year old, I thought.

"Nope. But they're not taking any chances. She's been staying with her grandparents. She's still nursing, too, so they're hoping her mom's immunities will keep her safe."

I looked over at Claire Derstine, where she sat with Rochelle on a wicker loveseat. She must've been going crazy the past week, trying to take care of Toby at the same time she was keeping Greta supplied with antibodies. Not a position to be envied.

"You hear about Bergeys?" Marty asked.

"Which ones?"

"Paul and Kristine."

I pictured the older couple. Grew crops when they were younger, now rented out their land to farmers still in production. "They sick?"

"In a way. Got bought out by developers. Signed the papers this afternoon."

My heart sank. "Know who was renting from them?"

"Heard it was Chuckie Moyer."

Shit. Pam's dad.

"Wonder what he'll do," Marty said. "Nothing left around here to rent."

Howie found his way to us and gave me a look. He was ready to go.

"See you soon, Marty?" I said.

"Hope so."

I took another look at Toby's parents, and when I saw they were surrounded by other folks decided they didn't need me interrupting with inadequate platitudes. I was sure they were full up on those.

The trip home was just long enough for me to fill Howie in on the Bergeys, and when I parked the truck in our drive, Howie got out and walked toward his place without a word.

"What'cha doing?" I asked Zach when I got in the house. He was crashed on the sofa, surfing the TV.

"Nothing. You want me to do something?"

Stay healthy. "Nope. Just checking in."

He flipped to another channel, and while I wanted to stay with him, hovering wouldn't keep him safe. It might, however, make him mad.

The phone rang and I stepped into the kitchen to answer it. It was Belle.

"He's all right," I said. "Just lying here watching TV."

"Lying there? You're sure he's okay?"

"He says he's fine. Looks fine, too. How's Mallory?"

"The same. Can't keep anything down. And now she has this awful rash that's driving her crazy."

"Ugh. Give me a call if you need me."

I hung up and walked out to the garage, tired and worried and needing an outlet. Queenie scuttled along beside me, her coat shiny and burr-free from Zach's good brushing.

My Harley sat in the garage, dusty and muddy from the last time I rode it, and I wheeled it out onto the drive. I uncoiled the garden hose from the rack on the house, put a little SU2000 in a bucket, and had all I needed to make the bike shine again.

My bike is a 1988 Low Rider, a Big Twin, for those of you who know your bikes. It's a step up from a Sportster, the smallest Harley-Davidson, and has the guts to make the curving

Pennsylvania roads a pleasure to ride. It's solid black, the only other color the shiny silver chrome I add from time to time. Harley pieces aren't cheap, but they make bikes come alive. I looked forward to putting on the things I'd been given at my birthday party that day. Man, did that seem a long time ago.

I was admiring the shine I'd accomplished so far when Howie came strolling out the drive. If I hadn't known better, I'd say he was nervous about approaching me. His hands were stuffed behind the bib of his overalls and he wouldn't look in my direction.

"What's up?" I said.

He shook his head and stared out across the neighboring field. Since he was giving me the silent treatment, I went back to the bike.

"You okay?" he asked when I had finished the back fender.

"I'm fine. Sad. Worried as hell about the sick kids. *You* okay?"

He shrugged and took a look at the bike. "Looks great."

"Yeah."

He kicked a rock in the driveway, and was such a cliché I had to blink to see if he was real. All he needed was a piece of long grass in his teeth.

"What, Howie?" I said. "Is it the barn painter? Toby? Me snapping at you this morning? What?"

He finally looked at me. "You're twenty-nine now."

"That's how many candles were on the cake."

"You're old enough to run this place on your own. You showed that today."

I looked at him in shock. "Good grief, Howie. You think I want to run this place by myself? Are you nuts? Just because I hired somebody to paint the damned heifer barn?"

Howie sighed. "I don't care about that. I just— You need a different kind of man around here. Someone younger. Someone more your speed."

"Someone who will give me babies? Is that what you're going on about?" I could feel my insides tightening up. "What exactly are you saying, Howie? Are you crapping out on me?"

Howie's head jerked back like I'd slapped him. "No, Stella, I'm not. I just want you to be happy, that's all."

"I am happy." I threw my rag on the seat of the Harley and put my hands on my hips. "Don't I look happy to you? When not worrying about sick or dying children I spent my birthday wading through every bodily fluid known to cows, talking to Hubert Purcell, patching up shit-holes, and practically giving myself a stroke dragging a dead cow. Could a girl ask for anything more?"

I felt my ire rising, but the look on Howie's face stopped me cold. He was trying his best to be the concerned father figure, but the corner of his mouth kept twitching and I saw a sparkle making its way into his eyes.

"Are you laughing at me?" I asked.

"Oh, no."

"Hey, old man. Is my life funny to you? You want me to tell you a few more things that happened today? Want me to tell you about the shower gel I got from Abe's new Barbie doll? You're going to leave me before telling me what to do with *that?*"

"Stop, stop!" His eyes watered with suppressed laughter, and he came over to give me a hug. "You know I'll never leave you, Princess. I'll be here for you till the cows come home."

"That's more like it. I don't want to hear any more of this talk about young guys or marriage or any of that crap. I'll hire the likes of Nick to keep my hormones alive, and that'll be enough."

"But Stella—"

"If my knight in shining armor comes prancing up the lane, I won't let him get away, all right?"

Howie looked at me with concern. The laughter had gone from his eyes and he studied my face. "You sure you'll recognize him?"

"He'll be the one with cow crap on his boots."

Howie gave me another grin and looked back at the Harley. "Missed a spot," he said.

Chapter Six

I woke up suddenly in the middle of the night, sticky and sweaty. I lay there, wondering why my eyes were open, when I noticed it was especially dark. And hot. I turned to look at my clock and there were no red numbers showing. My fan sat silent on my dresser, aimed at me but producing no breeze.

"Oh, great," I said out loud.

I swung my legs over the side of the bed and took a moment to let my head clear before standing up. I used the bathroom in the darkness, then walked back into my bedroom to try to find some clothes. I pulled on whatever was closest and made my way down the dark stairs.

The clock in the living room is the only one in the house that doesn't run on electricity, and I squinted at it. One AM. Good grief.

I went down to the basement to check the fuse box, only bruising my shins twice as I felt my way through the house. Everything looked fine, but I snapped the breakers back and forth to make sure. Still nothing—no flickering lights or reassuring hums. Crap.

Back on the first floor, I glanced out the window at the dusk-to-dawn light, and when I saw it was out figured the breakers in the main barn weren't working either.

I went out to the garage, trotted up Howie's steps, and knocked. He came to the door, bleary-eyed and tousled, in boxer shorts.

"What's wrong?"

"Electric's out."

He sighed. "I'll be there in a minute."

I went back down the steps and over to the tractor barn, where I started the tractor and pulled it around to the front. By that time Howie was outside, moving things out of the way in the garage.

Our generator sits on a trailer in the back corner of the garage, waiting patiently for us to give it some attention. I hoped it still worked—we hadn't hauled it out for about ten years and probably hadn't thought about it more than twice in the time since.

I jumped down from the tractor and helped Howie move things from one place to another. Then, together, we pulled the trailer free from its dark corner and out of the garage. Once it sat close to the tractor, Howie hooked its power take-off shaft to its mate on the tractor, and I got it hooked up to the electrical box in our big barn. I pulled down the main switch and crossed my fingers.

The generator made a few coughing sounds, sputtered, then started to hum, and the dusk-to-dawn light in the barnyard began glowing.

"Thank goodness for that," I said.

Howie grunted. "Zach okay?"

"Far as I know. I'll check on him."

He nodded. "See you in a few hours."

"You got it, old man."

I went back inside, called the electric company to report the outage, and after checking to see that Zach was sleeping soundly, pulled off my clothes and crawled back into bed. Thank God my fan was working again. I re-set my clock and was asleep instantly.

I woke again at five o'clock—well, four fifty-nine. I turned off my alarm and sat up slowly, breathing a silent thanks that the electricity was still on.

I pulled on some jeans, an undershirt, and a flannel shirt— my usual morning milking attire—and made my way to the kitchen, where I downed a bowl of Shredded Wheat and a tall glass of orange juice at the kitchen window. I've never been one for coffee—it's death for a farmer. Get used to your caffeine at five AM, and you'll never be able to get up and do the milking without it.

I had the television on low and was listening to an update on the new flu virus—no more dead children, thank God—when I realized I should wake Zach up so he could get himself together for milking. He had made it clear the night before that I was not to baby him. He'd do his job just like always.

A knock on his door raised no response, so I pushed it open and turned on the light.

"Oh, shit," I said.

I ran to the bed and felt Zach's forehead. Burning up. His face was flushed and his breathing was heavy and ragged.

"Shit, shit, shit."

I hurried to the bathroom and soaked a washcloth in cool water. I wrung it out so it wasn't dripping, then went back to Zach and placed it on his forehead. I left him long enough to grab the cordless phone from my bedroom, then speed-dialed Jethro and Belle from his bedside.

"'Lo," Jethro mumbled.

"He's got it."

The phone slammed down on the other end, and I pushed the flash button and called Howie. He answered, sounding muffled and sleepy.

"Zach's got the flu," I said. "Can you start milking?"

"Oh, no. Of course, Princess. I'll go right over."

I was just pulling the blanket off the bed to wrap up Zach when he started to retch. I grabbed the wastebasket and got it to the bed just in time. When he'd finished, I wiped his mouth with the damp cloth and told him everything was going to be okay. His head lolled and he fell back asleep on my neck.

I carried him downstairs, wrapped in the bed's blanket, and held him on the sofa until I heard a truck speeding up the driveway. I met Jethro at the door, Zach in my arms.

"Oh, my boy," Jethro said. He took Zach and held him against his chest.

I opened the back door of Jethro's truck, and Jethro laid his son gently on a pillow and made sure he was covered by the blanket.

"The doc told me to bring him right over," he said.

"You'll let me know—"

"Sure, sure. Soon as we can."

"I'm sorry, Jethro."

He looked like he wanted a hug, but I was afraid one of us would burst into tears, so I gave him a gentle push toward the driver's door.

He drove away, avoiding the potholes in the lane, going much slower than he had coming in. I watched them for only a moment before turning toward the barn, where I could try to lose myself in my work. Howie gave me a worried glance when I got in the barn, but I shook my head and looked away.

Most of the cows were already in stalls, and the rest sleepily made their way into one as Howie and I prodded them and slapped their huge haunches to get them moving. Queenie did her part to coax them into place, weaving around their legs and giving high, happy barks. There was the occasional oddball cow, who either didn't want to go into a stall or wanted to go into one that was already occupied, but for the most part they behaved, which was good since I wasn't in the mood to deal with delinquents.

We stepped around them, making a quick check for anything unusual, and got them hooked in. Each cow wears a chain around her neck, like a necklace, and we simply attach it to a hook in the milking stall. She still has plenty of room to move around, but we're assured she's not going to start working the room. Once we had them all clipped in, Howie started to feed them while I went to get the milk flow going.

I stood at the head of the row and closed my eyes for a moment, trying to find peace in the quiet rhythm of the morning. I could feel adrenaline making me shaky, and knew I had to stay on task if I was going to do my job. Thank goodness the generator was working well and everything could technically go on as usual. Howie had the radio tuned to Temple University's classical music station, and the sound soothed me, as well as the cows. I had tried every kind of music, but as far as I knew I had the only die-hard classical fans in the dairy field. They liked calming composers like Ravel and Debussy, especially. Mozart and Beethoven were fine, but they tended to get the cows a little more worked up.

I shook myself out of my stupor and started with cow number one, wiping her udder with a wet paper towel to get off manure and straw, then attaching the milking hose to each teat. The hose works in two ways—first it suctions, then pulses, like a calf would do to get the milk going. I got the first four cows pumping, and started cleaning off the next four. I had four sets of hoses working at once, and tried to work ahead so the next four were ready when the first ones were depleted.

I never wear gloves when I'm milking, because I enjoy feeling the leather-like skin on the udders. Before milking, the udder is taut, like a drum, and you can feel the fullness of the milk. Once the udder has been emptied, it is soft, supple, and limp. Until the evening, anyway.

The first four got milked dry, so I unhooked the hoses and got the next ones going. Then I went back to the first ones to spray their teats with antiseptic. Being the first to be done, they would have the longest to relax and eat after their milking.

Howie and I went through the motions, occasionally saying something, but mostly going from chore to chore, patting the cows and doing our best to avoid urine streams which shot out at random. We were on the last set of cows when we heard Queenie start to bark at a truck pulling in the drive.

"Probably your new boyfriend," Howie said. He stretched his back as he looked out the window. "Looks like a healthy one."

I threw a bunched-up paper towel at him and stood to look out the window. He was right. Nick's Ranger was parked next to the heifer barn, and Nick himself was climbing out of it. The events of the morning had pushed his existence from my mind, which was hard to believe. Today he had on a blue T-shirt and another pair of those well-fitting jeans. Queenie was already getting her head rubbed, and her tail was wagging so hard her rump was moving from side to side. I had to make sure to keep my butt in line when I talked to him.

"Gonna go out and greet him?" Howie said. "Don't want to miss a chance to see him up close."

"Oh, can it, Howie. I'll go out, but just to make sure he knows what I want done."

"Sure," Howie said. "You do that."

I left Howie grinning to himself and went out to talk to Nick. He had his gear with him, so I assumed he was there to get started.

"Morning," I said.

"Morning."

"You always start work at six-thirty?"

"Actually, I'm a little late. I try to start as early as I can, to avoid the hotter hours of the day. If it's okay with you, I'll work till noon or so, then come back later in the afternoon and work through the evening."

I shrugged. "Whatever. I'm up by five, so you won't be waking me." I nodded at the heifer barn. "Anything you need from me?"

Nick shook his head. "I think I've got everything. I may have to make a run or two to the paint store, but other than that I'm good to go."

Good to go. Seeing him, I was good to go, too, but he didn't need to know that.

"Well," I said. "You need anything, you just come find me. I'll be around. Or you could ask Howie, my farmhand. He knows this place almost better than I do."

"Will do." He gave me his hundred-watt smile, and my stomach contracted. I did my best to look unaffected as I turned and walked back into the barn.

"You did real good, Princess," Howie said. "I couldn't see you sweating or anything."

I ignored him and switched the hoses to the last set of cows.

"I'm going to call Carla about Cleopatra," I said. "Be back in a minute."

Carla answered on the first ring and said she'd come out after her first appointment. It was too hot to let the dead cow go any longer, even if it was in the cool barn.

I hung up and punched in Jethro and Belle's number.

"What did he say?" Belle sounded out of breath.

"Oh, sorry, Belle. It's Stella. I wanted to know what you found out about Zach."

I heard a muffled sob. "I'm still waiting. I wanted to go, too, but...."

"Sure. Someone had to stay with Mallory. Call when you hear, okay?"

I went back to the parlor, nerves strung even tighter, where Howie and I milked for another hour, till all the cows were done. I had to take occasional breaks to check out Nick's work, of course, but other than that, things went as usual.

"Only have three that need separate milking," Howie said. "Pansy went off her antibiotics. You want to do them while I get the others out?"

I nodded and headed to the back stalls, where we had clipped in the ones who needed special attention.

There are a couple of reasons you milk cows apart from the rest of the herd, sending their milk into a separate storage tank. New mothers give the precious colostrum calves need and people don't want, and any cow on antibiotics gives milk that is tainted and can't be sold.

When Wayne, or whoever hauls our milk, does his rounds, he takes a sample of each farm's milk, and if the tank tests positive for antibiotics when he gets to the plant, the farmer who tried to cheat gets to pay for the entire load, plus receives a heavy fine and a blast to their reputation. Definitely not worth trying to get bad milk past the tests. And the restrictions get tougher every year.

"Any preference as to which water source I use?"

I finished putting the milker on Wendy, the mom of Zach's new calf, and looked up at Nick, who stood leaning against the doorjamb of the milking parlor.

"What do you need it for?" I asked.

Nick smiled and raised his eyebrows, like I didn't trust him.

"I don't *care* what you're using it for," I said. "I just need to know so I can tell you which spigot to use." *Geez.*

"I'm going to start powerwashing the heifer barn. I want to get all the gunk off before I start any repairs or painting."

"Gunk," I said. "Is that the technical term?"

"It was at Barn Painter University. Or I could be more specific and say peeling paint, wayward ivy, and pigeon poop. Would that make you feel better?"

"Lots. There's a spigot inside the heifer barn we use to fill up their water tank. You can use that. Go through the door to the right."

"Yes, ma'am." Nick gave me a small salute and went back to work. I knew he did—I watched him go. I smiled and even gave stupid Wendy a pat on the rump. Hard-liners like Howie might laugh at me for hiring a barn painter, but so far it was worth every penny.

And he hadn't even done anything yet.

Chapter Seven

"Excuse me," I said.

The cow stared at me and slowly blinked her long eyelashes.

"Cindy," I said. "I will get out of your way if you will kindly move a few inches to the left."

Cindy, a third-generation Royalcrest cow, gave no indication that she understood, so I sucked in my stomach and squeezed between her and the wall. She was almost eighteen, after all, and deserved some respect. As soon as I was past, of course, she decided to move her big rear and go outside.

Howie had unclipped the cows and they were meandering out of the barn, into the pasture, back into the barn, and into stalls to finish up leftover food or to take a nap in the shredded newspapers we use as bedding. They were free to roam where they pleased, within the confines of the electric fences we had set up in the farmyard to keep them out of the yard, the feed barn, and what garden we had. They mostly chose to do whatever took the least effort.

I changed the radio to WMMR, Philly's classic rock station, and Queenie was keeping me company (getting in the way) as I scraped the floor, cleaned out any stalls that needed it, and put lime on the concrete walkways to make them look clean. Well, maybe not clean. A little whiter, anyway. Some farm cats were watching me do a half-hearted dance with the pitchfork to ZZ Top's "She's Got Legs" when Howie came in, chuckling.

"I never said I could dance," I said.

"I'm not laughing at you, Princess. Have you taken a look at your new boyfriend lately?"

Surprisingly, it had been about a half-hour since I'd taken a break to check out my new hire. A little leery since Howie was so amused, I put down my dance partner and walked outside.

Nick was hard at work, powerwashing the heifer barn, water going everywhere, taking old paint and probably a little bit of the barn with it. I glanced at Howie, unsure what the punch line was.

"Take a closer look," Howie said.

I walked a little farther toward the heifer barn and finally got the joke. Nick saw me out of the corner of his eye and stopped spraying.

"Need something?" he asked.

I burst out laughing.

"It's the shoes, right?" he said. "I knew I shouldn't have worn these."

I kept laughing and shook my head. No one would know that Adonis lurked under all the paraphernalia he wore. He was completely covered, from head to foot, in coveralls, boots, and gloves, accented by paint specks, dirt, and who-knows-what-else. His hair was covered with a painting cap, and he wore big, bug-like goggles.

"I know," he said. "I'm the most anal retentive painter you've ever met."

I nodded.

"You need something?" he asked again, I thought a little testily.

I shook my head and tried to get rid of my smile. "Don't stop working on my account."

He turned away, and water resumed pounding the barn.

"Lovely," I said, walking back to Howie.

"Gotta give him points for knowing his job, if not fashion," Howie said, smirking.

"I suppose your overalls are on the runway in Paris."

"I wear only the best, b'gosh."

I groaned and made my way back into the barn. Howie followed.

"At least I know the ugly ducking out there really is a swan," I said. "Unlike some other guys I know."

Howie threw a wad of newspaper at me and Queenie ran after it and took it back to him.

"So what are your plans for the day?" I asked.

Howie threw the paper for Queenie again. "I need to fix the conveyor belt on the heifer feeder, then I'm going to scrape the lots that didn't get cleaned yesterday during the poop fiasco. If I have time before lunch I'm going to haul some hay over for the heifers. You?"

"I think I'll mow the yard. The way it's looking we may as well let the cows out on it. Zach was going to do it, but...."

"Poor little Zach. Any word from Jethro yet?"

I shook my head, trying to ignore the fear creeping back up my throat. "God, he looked awful, Howie. I've never felt anyone so hot before. And he practically puked his guts out."

"I know, Princess. But he's in good hands. His doc'll take care of him."

"Yeah, sure." I kicked Queenie's wadded-up paper and she scuttled after it. "I hope we don't get sick, too. What would we do?"

"You won't," Howie said. "Your immune system is made up of warrior blood cells."

"Regular Klingons. Okay, I get your point. Why worry? See ya later."

Howie headed out to the barnyard, Queenie trotting after him, and I finished up the stalls in a few minutes. I grabbed a bucket, dumped in some of the milk from the mama cows, and mixed two bottles of formula for the little heifers. I was just getting ready to go when Carla walked into the barn.

I had to laugh. She was wearing an outfit that was surprisingly similar to Nick's—coveralls, a large rubber apron, and goggles perched on the top of her head. I knew those huge gloves would go on, too, effectively hiding the last bit of her I could see.

"Sorry I couldn't come out last night," she said. "I was out of town for a seminar. A special program on mad cow disease. Kind of fitting with what's going on around here, unknown virus and all."

I set my bucket on the ground. "You hear about Zach?"

Her eyes widened. "What?"

"Got sick just this morning." I explained how I'd come to find him. "So I'm waiting for a phone call."

"Oh, Stella."

I bent over to pick up the bucket.

"Anyway," Carla said, "I'm sorry I wasn't around to help with your cow yesterday."

"No problem. I figured Cleo wasn't going anywhere, so I didn't want to bring your on-call guy from wherever."

"He couldn't've come anyway. He had a horse who'd sliced himself up real good on a fence. Not pretty. So where is she?"

"Basement. In the empty stall."

She sneezed, then coughed.

"What's up with you?" I asked.

"Just a cold. Too many late nights and early mornings pandering to my elite dairy clientele."

"You sure it's not that flu?" I stepped closer to look in her eyes, and she batted me away.

"Of course it's not. Only kids are getting that."

"Maybe you should see your doctor just to—"

"Look, I came here to cut up a cow, not find a mother."

"Sorry. You know your way downstairs."

She went back out to her truck, grabbed a huge toolbox which I knew would contain an axe and a large knife, and lugged it out of sight. I went back to work.

Gus and the other two calves were waiting for me, pushing their soft, whiskery noses against the metal grating on the front of their hutches. We only had the three right then, including Zach's new fella. We keep calves in the hutches for six weeks or so, feeding them colostrum the first few days, then formula after that, then sell bull calves to my neighbor and send female calves to the yearling paddock. The two females were waiting to be moved the next day. Gus would go to his own private stall soon after that.

Gus stood on legs that were surprisingly strong and slurped up the milk I poured into his bottle. He looked like he'd be a good bull for Zach. I reached my hand through the wires on the door and scratched his ears. He gazed at me with his liquid eyes and I could swear he smiled. After a final pat I decided it was time to face my overgrown yard.

First, I went into my office to make sure there weren't any messages from Jethro or Belle. No flashing light. I considered calling them, but forced myself to leave the phone on its cradle. They'd call when they could.

The lawnmower was housed in the garage, and I tried to keep a straight face as I passed Nick. He probably didn't notice me, anyway, with all his camouflage.

I yanked open the garage door and let my eyes adjust to the darkness. The only light was on a pull chain in the center of the room, and as everything was still in disarray from pulling out the generator, I didn't feel like wading through machinery to get to it. I gave my Harley a pat as I passed it, noticing it already had a fine layer of dust on it. These dry summer days were terrible for keeping things clean.

I pushed the lawnmower into the driveway to check the oil and gas, and it was only when I was screwing the gas cap back on that I noticed the crack running through the deck almost the whole way across.

Well, crud, I thought. I stood and put my hands on my hips, checking out the yard. I had been saying for the past few days that it could wait another day, and if I said it once more I might as well have just planted wildflowers, set up a booth, and rented out campsites. Besides, the mower wouldn't fix itself if I stuck it back in the garage.

I got my truck and heaved the mower into the back, muttering under my breath about fourteen-year-old boys who don't tell when they break things. I probably should have asked for help getting the mower into the truck, but impressing Nick was more important at the time. Whether or not he noticed was a mystery.

I was ready to leave when an electric company truck pulled in. The company was usually very good about quick service when a farmer needed it, and I was pleased to see someone already this morning. A young, chubby guy in a uniform hopped out of the cab.

"There an accident or something?" I asked. Usually when we lost electricity it was from some drunk hitting a pole.

"Actually, you're the only one with a problem."

"Really? How could that be?"

"Dunno. I'll take a look, though."

I wondered if I should stay to get the news myself, but figured it would take him a while before he knew anything.

"I'm just headed out," I said. "You need anything, Howie's around. My farmhand. He can help you with whatever."

"Okey-dokey."

I whistled for Queenie and she came running, her nose full of cobwebs. "Where you been, girl?" I wiped off her nose. "Want to go for a ride?" She jumped into the truck and had the side window full of smears before I had a chance to open it. I rolled it down, and we were off.

Granger's Welding sits off of a dirt road about two miles from my farm. Jethro runs the place, and two of his brothers make up his employee list. I could hear the welding compressor when I opened my door, and hoped I wouldn't have to wait too far back in line.

The shop looked like an over-sized service garage, with two huge roll-up doors and a little office at the side, shut off from the noise by a flimsy wooden door. They hadn't bothered to paint the concrete, so the building ended up looking a lot like one of those big cinder blocks mice like to make nests in.

"I'll be right back," I told Queenie.

She whined when I slid out by myself.

"I can't let you out, girl. There's all kinds of little metal pieces, screws, and other dog hazards. I'll be back in a minute." I made sure the cab was in the shade and the windows were cracked, then got out and walked toward the open garage door.

"Anybody home?" I said loudly. I could see somebody at the welding machine, but didn't recognize him until he stood up straight and took his safety mask off.

"Hey there, Stella," Jermaine said.

Now, I know you're thinking Jermaine doesn't sound like a Bible name one of Ma Granger's kids might have. If you saw Jermaine, you wouldn't think he looked like one of her sons, either.

Jethro, as I've said before, is a big guy, but Jermaine is probably the biggest man I've ever known, his shoulders easily measuring three feet across and his chest so big I couldn't get my arms all the way around him if I tried. The best way to describe him is to say he resembles one of those NFL linebackers who look like they couldn't move, they're so big and kind of fat looking. But when you get a close-up look at Jermaine you see that underneath the fatty exterior is a mass of pure, hard muscle. Making Jermaine all the more amazing is the rich, black skin that lies tight and shiny over all his body, including his shaved head.

Ma didn't have an affair to get this son—don't even think it. Jermaine came from New York City to the Grangers as a Fresh Air kid, and he never left. Ma said he fit right in with her boys, plus his name started with a J—God must have meant it to be. Jermaine's mother—uncomfortably quickly—agreed. No one ever looked back, and if anyone ever questioned Jermaine's rightful place in the Granger flock, they had Ma to answer to.

"How's the family?" I asked.

In a flash Jermaine's face turned from serious to lighthearted and back to serious.

"They're great. No sign of the flu yet. Vernice is back at work and Lavina is the cutest little thing you ever saw."

Jermaine's wife, Vernice, runs a day care for single mothers only. Her mom had taken it over for the past three months while

Vernice got to take care of her own new baby. Now that Vernice was back at work, Lavina would be the only child at the day care with the benefit of a mother and a father.

"Lavina going to the day care with Vernice?" I asked.

"Huh-uh. Too worried about this flu thing. Seems like you can't tell who's got it till it's too late. My mother-in-law's watching the baby."

"Vernice still nursing her? Getting her those antibodies?"

"Sure is. Anything we can do to fight off this nasty bug."

A good plan. "Any word on Zach?"

"Just that he's back home. Jethro showed up not long ago, but he wasn't in a talking mood and I didn't want to push. I guess Belle kicked him out of the house. He was being a mother hen and driving them all crazy. He and Jordan are out back. Jude's got some combine trouble and they're all standing there scratching their heads. Now, what's up? I mean, why are you here?"

"My mower." I jerked my thumb toward my truck. "Got a cracked deck."

Jermaine walked to my truck and lifted the mower out of the bed with one arm. He set it on the ground and squatted to get a look at it. Queenie yipped at us, and I stuck my hand in the window to make sure she wasn't getting too hot.

"I need to get my lawn mowed today," I said.

Jermaine grunted and stood up. "I could fix you up if you want to wait, although it won't be as pretty as if you'd left it here for a day or two."

"I don't want to enter it in a contest. I just want to cut my grass."

Jermaine picked up the mower like it was nothing. "I'll be back in a few minutes."

"Thanks. I'll be back with the guys if you need help."

Jermaine smiled. Like he would need help from me with this eensy-weensy machine.

I found the three Granger brothers out behind the garage. Jethro and Jordan were hunkered down beside the red Case

International combine, their heads hidden underneath it, while Jude sat on a stack of tires, looking like his dog had died.

"Hey," I said.

They all ignored me, but I decided to be gracious and put it down to extreme concentration. I moved behind Jethro and spoke into his ear. "Hey."

Jethro jerked up and hit his head on a piece of metal that stuck out from the body of the combine. "Geez, Stella, nothing like sneaking up on folks."

"Sorry. What's going on?"

"Jude's combine decided it was time to go out to pasture," Jordan said, standing up and rubbing dirt off his knees.

Jordan is the third of the Granger eight, and the only brother—other than Abe—who's not married. I'm sure there's speculation about this, since Jordan is thirty-seven, but seeing who his brothers are, no one ever says anything so the Grangers would hear it.

"What'd it do?" I asked, eyeing the combine.

"Not sure," Jethro said. "But from what Jude says, it sounds like the motor's messed up bad. It was doing all this jerking and stalling yesterday, and he seemed to think if he ignored it, it would go away." He looked like this was paramount to pushing the red button and launching a nuclear missile at Canada, but Jude was his brother, so he would never actually say how stupid he thought he was.

"Finally bit it today?" I asked.

"In a big show of dust and smoke. He was cutting hay on that big incline on the back corner of your west field, and the engine cut, the steering wheel locked, and he ran right into a tree. We had to pull him out with a front end loader."

"How come nobody called me?"

"Why would we? Nothing you could do with your little baby Ford."

I punched his shoulder. "So Jude's pretty shook up, huh? Looks shell-shocked."

"Fixing this is going to about put him under. Insurance won't cover this kind of stuff."

My stomach did a flip-flop. Jude's whole life was farming—if he lost that, I didn't know what he'd do. He didn't have training for anything else. Besides, he loved his life as it was. Marianne would probably be overjoyed to move on to something different, but she'd have to endure some tight times first.

"Marianne know?" I asked.

Jethro looked away, seemingly embarrassed, but Jordan shrugged. "She's off at some fertility clinic in Philly since early this morning. She won't be home till this afternoon."

"Fertility clinic?" Suddenly Marianne's bad attitude about the calf and kittens made sense.

Jethro gave Jordan a look which I could only interpret as "shut up." "She didn't want anybody knowing about it," Jethro said. "I only know 'cause Belle had to drive her a coupl'a times."

"And Jordan?"

Jethro hemmed and hawed a bit before Jordan grinned. "Jethro needed to share."

"Sure," I said. "Now I know who to tell my secrets to if I want everyone to know them."

"Naw," Jordan said. "Jethro's just tired of Marianne's snottiness and doesn't care who knows what about her."

"Snottiness?"

"Anyhow," Jethro said gruffly, "this combine is dead as a doornail, you ask me."

"You want I should throw it in the Dumpster?" Jermaine said from the garage. We all looked at him, thinking he probably could if he put his mind to it.

"Your mower's done, Stella," he said.

I acknowledged him with a wave.

"What'd the doctor have to say about Zach?" I asked Jethro. I wanted to scold him for not calling me, but didn't have the heart.

His face dropped. "Not enough. They don't have no idea what's going on. You'd think with all we pay 'em...." He stopped talking and picked at a fingernail.

"So what's the plan now?" I asked.

He shrugged. "Same as Mallory. Treat the symptoms. Call if it gets worse. Bunch of bullshit."

I agreed, but didn't want to fan the flame. "Well, tell Zach I fed Gus this morning and he's doing great, but I'm sure he'll be glad to see Zach when he can get there. And tell him I'll check on the kittens, too."

"Sure."

I wanted to say something more, but wasn't sure what it should be. In the end I let it go. Nothing I could say would help Zach get better any quicker.

"Good luck with this thing." I gave the combine a thump and walked back toward the garage, stopping by Jude on my way. "You can use my tractor till you get this taken care of, if you want. I've got my dad's old pull-type combine stashed away in the barn. It's not what you're used to, but I'm sure not using it."

He looked up at me, glassy-eyed. I didn't think what I said registered, so I just squeezed his shoulder and started to walk away.

"Thanks," Jude said.

I turned, but he had already gone back into his own little coma.

Chapter Eight

The mower worked as good as new, even with the ugly scar across the top of it. You'd never have known it just got out of surgery. I was on the last section of lawn, having taken only one short break to check out Nick's progress on the heifer barn, when Carla came walking up, looking serious.

"So what was it?" I asked.

She shook her head.

"What? You can't tell?"

"Oh, I can tell. I just don't believe it."

"Believe what?"

She bit her lips together, then said, "Cleopatra was electrocuted."

"*Electrocuted?*"

"I saw a burn mark right away, traveled down her leg to the ground, skin and hair burned along the way."

"But she was in the middle of the pasture."

She raised her eyebrows. "Exactly. So I did the whole business, cut her open, checked her out. Her lungs are edematous—filled with fluid—and she's got hemorrhages on her heart. It all fits."

"But that means...."

"Yes," Carla said. "That means Cleopatra was murdered."

"*Electrocuted?*" Howie said.

My head pounded. I shook it and took a few steps back and forth, flexing my fingers. "Zapped in the middle of a dry pasture. And we haven't had any storms."

Howie leaned on the scraper and peered at me over the top of it. "But, why?"

"Who the hell knows? Why would someone drain our manure lagoon? What have we ever done to anybody?" I smacked the scraper and my hand stung.

Howie pushed himself straight and scratched his head. "Electric guy said there were squirrels in the box. Think that was somebody's doing, too?"

I stared at the ground, rage making my vision spotty. "But why? Why would someone be doing this?" I spun around and started for the house.

"Where you goin'?" Howie said.

"Where do you think? I'm going to tell the police to nail this creep's scrawny ass to the barn wall."

I was headed out the door, keys in hand, when the phone rang.

"Yeah?"

"One of these days you're going to have to be a little more civil," Abe said.

My mouth went dry, and an irrational spasm of guilt hit me as I remembered ogling Nick's behind.

"What do you want?" I asked. "Is that civil enough?"

"Never mind. I, uh, have a favor to ask."

"What?"

"Well...."

"Spit it out, Abie, I'm in a hurry."

He cleared his throat. "It's, uh, actually a favor for Missy."

"Oh, great. Little Miss White Collar needs some help from the stinky farmer?"

"Cut it out, Stella."

"She did give me all the good-smelling stuff. Oh, sorry, you *both* gave me the good-smelling stuff."

"Forget it. See you later."

"Sorry," I said. "Sorry. I just found out someone killed one of my cows. I'm on my way to the police station."

"*What?*"

"I know, it's crazy. So what's the favor?"

"Never mind. I don't want to bother you."

"Come on Abe, what?"

"Well, Missy wondered…she wants to come help milk the cows."

I rubbed my eyes.

"Stella?"

"When? When does she want to come?"

"I was going to ask about tonight, but it sounds like—"

"Fine. Tell her to come at five-thirty."

"Really?"

"The cows have to be milked." And Howie does the evenings.

"Great. Thanks, Stella."

"You owe me." Big.

On my way out to the truck I noticed Queenie's food bowl was empty, so I made a quick detour to get a scoop of her dry food. I dumped it in and waited for her to come running. The sound of the food hitting the plastic is usually just as good as a whistle, but that time it didn't work.

"Queenie!" I called. "Lunchtime!" I put two fingers in my mouth and whistled.

"Dog missing?" Nick strolled up to me, now in only one layer of normal work clothes.

I lifted a shoulder, trying not to show my anxiety. "Probably found something else for lunch."

"Something like…?"

"I try not to think about it."

He made a face. "Is everything else okay?"

"No, it's not. I've got a dead cow."

"Dead? From what?"

"She was electrocuted."

Nick looked like he had more questions, but Howie was watching from across the barnyard. I waved at him and yelled, "I'm going, I'm going." I started toward my truck.

"I'm heading out for the afternoon," Nick called after me. "I'll be back this evening."

"Fine. See you then."

I broke too many traffic laws on the way to the police station, but our town has about one cop on patrol at any given time, so I made it no problem. I stepped into the foyer and rang the bell.

A uniformed officer came barreling through a door to my left and ran smack into me, knocking me sideways. I caught my balance and rubbed my hip where his gun had whacked me. He squinted at me angrily, and I stared right back. It certainly wasn't *my* fault the jerk wasn't looking where he was going.

The receptionist came to the barred window and the rude guy slammed out the front door. After directing a frown toward the departing officer's back, the woman smiled at me. "Can I help you?"

"Name's Stella Crown. I need to report some sabotage on my farm."

"No problem. The detective's running late, so he's still here. You'll hear a buzz, and that door will unlock."

I went and stood where she pointed, swinging the door open when I heard the sound. A man met me inside.

"Detective Willard," he said, holding out his hand. "Please follow me." I studied his back as we walked. He was in his forties, probably, taller than me, and stocky. A lumbering walk, like you expect from a cop. Or a biker.

In his office, he waved me to a chair and sat down behind a cluttered desk. I looked around at all of his books, papers, and certificates, and was glad my office had a little more order. And space.

"So what can I do for you, Ms. Crown?" he asked. He pulled out a notebook and held a pen over it.

Now we were face to face I saw that his skin was pale and blotchy, and dark circles underscored his eyes. I hoped he wasn't coming down with the flu. Just what I needed.

"Someone murdered one of my cows."

"Excuse me?" He stared at me, mouth hanging.

"I've got a murdered cow, a sabotaged manure lagoon, and someone messed with my electric. It's got to stop."

"I'd say so." He recovered his composure and snapped his mouth shut. "Give me details."

I told him everything I knew. It wasn't much.

He brought up a new screen on his computer. "Tell me where you live and I'll come out and take a look this afternoon."

"Not much to look at. No fingerprints on the manure lagoon."

"I'll come all the same."

I gave him my address. "Anything I can do to help get things ready?"

"No. Please. Just leave everything as it is."

"You got it."

"Now," he said. "Any ideas who would do this to you? And why?"

I shook my head. "My first reaction was kids I'd turned down for jobs." I stood and reached into my pocket to pull out a list of all the applicants' names and addresses. "But this seems too mean for them."

He took the paper. "You never know. Anybody else? Business enemies? Competitors?"

I thought about Marty Hoffman sneaking onto my farm to kill a cow and almost laughed at the outrageous idea. "Nobody like that." Something flitted across my mind, and I caught it. "Of course. Hubert Purcell, that bastard." I smacked my fist on the back of the chair.

Willard raised his eyebrows. "The developer?"

"The one and only. Goddammit. It has to be him. I'm gonna rip his lungs out."

"Whoa, whoa," Willard said. "Why don't you have a seat and tell me why he'd do this."

I considered the chair, but knew I couldn't sit still. "He's been after my farm forever. Probably thinks if I have enough troubles I'll up and sell."

"And would you?"

"Never. But Hubert would, so he figures I'll break, too. Now, if that's enough, I have a developer to lynch."

Willard quickly stood. "Hold that thought and consider what I'm going to say."

"But—"

"*Consider it.*"

I put my hands on my hips and stared at the floor. "Fine. What?"

"If you're wrong—" I jerked my head up and he held out his hand to stop me from talking. "If you're wrong, he'll sue you to your last particle of grain. You know he will. And then he'll win for sure."

I gritted my teeth. "I can't do *anything?*"

"Not if you're smart. Which I know you are."

I sighed. "So what are you going to do?"

"Check him out. Discreetly. Along with all the kids on your list." He pinned me with his eyes. "You understand what could happen if you take this on yourself?"

I met his gaze. "I understand."

"Good." He came around the desk, gesturing to the door. "I'll be out to your place as soon as I can. I've got some patrolling to do, then, with luck, I'll be free."

He led me out of his office, but I stopped at the front door, wondering at his pasty complexion, ready to be pissed if he was knowingly subjecting others to the virus. "You know any more about this flu than what we're hearing on the news?"

He dipped his chin to his chest, then looked up, his forehead wrinkling. "My son, Brady, has it. Pretty bad. He's been at Grand View Hospital since Thursday."

"Oh, crap. I'm sorry." Should've kept my mouth shut.

He leaned across me and opened the door. "Thanks. I know I'm not the only one with worries. But it sure eats away at your insides."

I didn't know what else to say. So I left.

I was way too deep in thought when I got stopped at a green traffic light. A cop stood in the middle of the intersection, barring my way, and I luckily came out of my fog before smashing her flat. I looked around, wondering at the hold-up, and realized there were people lining the sidewalks on the crossroad. A parade. The usual mid-summer, county-fair's-a-coming-soon parade.

Shit.

I put the truck in neutral and sat back, stepping on the emergency brake. So this was the patrolling the detective was late for. I rolled down both side windows to fend off heat suffocation, and let my eyes wander over the floats that came by. So help me God, if Hubert had a spot in the parade I couldn't be held responsible for my actions.

There were only half the amount of by-standers as usual. Either the kids were sick, or the parents were afraid to bring them to such a child-attended event. I knew several kids in my own world who wouldn't be attending. A fresh wave of worry washed over me and I tried to focus on the passing entertainment.

First came a marching band from the local high school. Most of the musicians were in step. Following them were a few cars with state representatives, a float with Girl Scouts, and a fire truck. I was really starting to get antsy when I saw a familiar face.

Pam Moyer sat in the back of an old yellow Mustang convertible, waving stiffly to the crowd. The Town Council President, Sonny Turner, sat beside her smiling and throwing charisma everywhere. I was surprised he wasn't throwing actual cash, he had so much of it. Little future politicians ran alongside, tossing candy to outstretched hands. Pam soon turned toward my side of the street, and when her glance reached my truck, our eyes locked. She froze for a moment, then gave me my own special wave. I lifted my fingers off the steering wheel, too lazy to raise my hand for—in Hubert the Bastard's words—our "very own Ivy Leaguer." At least I supposed that's why she was sitting there beside the prez. They probably wanted her to take over when Sonny retired. She'd do a good job.

I couldn't help but wonder how her dad was faring since he found out the Bergeys sold the land he'd been farming. Or if he and Pam had gotten any sleep the night before.

Once Pam was gone I had to sit through a very un-synchronized baton troupe before a break became obvious and the police officer started moving to the middle of the intersection. I let off my emergency brake and put the truck in gear. The police officer frantically waved me on, and I got out of the town proper.

God, I needed a break. And I knew where I needed to take it.

The Biker Barn is a Harley-Davidson motorcycle repair and retail shop about ten miles from my place. It's the official sponsor of my Harley Owners' Group chapter, and it's a home away from home. A haven of chrome and leather, Harley parts claim every available space, alongside gift items like mugs, playing cards, and watches. But even more than just for buying stuff, I go to see people who occupy a special corner of my life. I needed to see them now.

I pulled into the parking lot and checked out the lot. Early Sunday afternoons mustn't be too busy, because the only bike there was an old Shovelhead that looked like it had been through both World Wars. I wished I was on my bike, too, but hadn't wanted to take the time to get gussied up before going to the police.

I went into the store and the bell on the door chimed, surprising me, as always. I never expect a little ringing sound when entering a small, smoky building filled with metal and leather.

"Hey, Bart," I said.

Bart Watts laid down his cigarette and leaned on the glass counter. "Well, well, if it ain't the princess. Where you been?"

"Same as always—knee deep in cow crap."

I sat on a tall stool in front of the cash register and glanced around the shop. Bart looked as usual—his hair in a single braid down his back, his beard trimmed short and even. The serpent tattoo that began on his right wrist disappeared into his T-shirt, only to escape again on his left arm, slithering down to his hand. He wore black jeans tight on his skinny legs, cowboy boots, and a thick gold chain around his neck.

"You look like hell," he said.

"Gee, thanks."

"I mean that only in the nicest way."

I shifted on the seat. "Someone killed one of my cows."

"No shit?"

"And Zach Granger is sick with the same illness that killed my neighbor boy."

"Oh, man." He straightened up and ran a hand down his beard. "I got two nieces with this flu. They're holding their own, but who knows for how long?"

I picked at a spot on the countertop. "Whose Shovel?"

"My brother-in-law's. Needs some top-end work."

"Ugh." I knew what was involved with that, having done it to my own bike the previous summer. "Any new stuff?"

"Got some of those Samson drag pipes you were asking about before. But anybody asks you, you got 'em from somebody as a gift, and can't remember who."

I grinned. The drag pipes I'd been lusting after sounded so throaty, rumbling around the countryside, but they weren't exactly legal. On the other hand, I've never heard of anybody actually getting busted for them.

"How much?"

"Three hundred."

"Geez, Bart, you trying to break me?"

The door to the garage creaked and Lenny, Bart's business partner, came in, wiping his blackened hands on a rag.

"Who's breaking who? Or would that be whom?"

"Whom cares," Bart said.

Lenny was the motorhead of the H-D Biker Barn, and Bart was the brains—or so Bart wanted you to think. I liked to imagine that Lenny had a doctoral degree secretly stashed away, while Bart was still up late at night working on his GED. What everyone knew for sure was that Lenny was the wallet of the operation and Bart did his best to keep the money in-house while Lenny liked to spend it.

Lenny is the complete opposite of Bart physically, as well, his belly spilling over his grease-stained blue jeans, his red hair and beard wild and untethered. He looks more like the stereotype of a biker, but he's actually the tamer of the two. He had what he calls his "former life," which he never wants to talk about, but he tries to forget those days. His nickname, Hammer, still holds on, but those of us who see him often know he prefers his given name. He's never told me exactly what Hammer stands for, but I get the impression it's for something a bit more illegal than his tendency to ride fast.

"Bart's trying to sell me drag pipes for a fortune," I said. "I can't afford one, let alone an actual pair."

"I'm quoting you a great price," Bart said. "You get 'em at cost, it's still gonna run you two-fifty, two-seventy-five."

"What's the occasion?" Lenny asked me. "You haven't been here in a while."

"Not my choice," I said. "The bank account's the boss. But yesterday was my birthday and I got a few bucks to throw at you. *Few* being the important word."

"You hear that, Bart? We got us a birthday girl, and you mean to take every dime."

"Yeah, yeah, make me the bad guy," Bart said. "You want to stay in business or not?"

My shoulders began to relax as I listened to their good-natured bantering.

"Before we're too far gone on the pipes," I said, "what else you got?" I slid off the stool and walked around, checking out the various chrome pieces mounted on the Peg-Board.

Bart came out from behind the counter, and Lenny disappeared into the recesses of the back.

"Check this out," Bart said. He pulled something off the wall and handed it to me.

"I already have a timing cover," I said, not looking at it.

"Yeah, but you don't have this one."

I looked down at the package. In prominent relief on the otherwise smooth chrome was a chilling skull, its teeth bared in a grin, its eye sockets dark and deep.

"Too cool," I said.

Bart rocked on the balls of his feet and looked smug. "Thought of you as soon as it came in last week. Told Lenny you'd have to get it. It'll match that pretty little tattoo of yours." He pointed to the eyes. "And look at those."

I laughed. "You mean the eyes actually light up?"

"Wire 'em right in, and those eyes'll glow real eerie-like."

I looked at the price and shook my head. Forty was still too much, seeing as how groceries were going on a credit card that month.

"What about blue lights?" I asked. "Got any of those around?"

"It would be the same deal as the pipes," Bart said. "They just showed up on your scooter and you didn't know where you got 'em."

"How much?"

Bart shrugged. "Fifteen."

I let out the breath I was holding. The lights wouldn't run me into the red like the other stuff, and they were something I'd been wanting. You mount them on the underside of your bike, and when you ride at night, they glow off the chrome, looking spookily supernatural.

"Okay," I said. "Ring 'em up."

Bart dug some out from under the counter and punched the cash register. When he leaned down again to get a bag, Lenny came up behind me, lifted the back of my shirt, and stuck something in the waistband of my jeans. I looked at him, and he winked.

"Jude working the fields at night now?" Bart asked.

"Not that I know of. Why?"

"I was headed toward Quakertown the other night and drove past that field of yours that fronts Telford Pike. Saw lights way back in, toward your place. Thought maybe Jude was doing some catch-up."

The hair on my neck prickled. "I doubt it. Working in the dark makes him nervous. What night was it?"

He thought for a bit. "Let's see, I was coming home from the grocery store...I guess it was Friday. Friday night."

And the next day I had a dead cow and a punctured manure lagoon. I couldn't picture Hubert stomping around a field at night, but I wouldn't put it past him, either.

Bart handed me the bag with my birthday purchase. "Receipt's in the bag. You know the return drill."

"Got it."

"Come back and get those pipes or that timing cover. Your ride would look and sound like a different beast. Gotta have 'em."

"I'll save up."

"And let us know what happens about that cow. That's some nasty shit."

Lenny walked me to the door, I think so Bart wouldn't see how lumpy my butt looked with whatever was jammed in my jeans.

"You come back soon now, Stella," Lenny said.

"As soon as I can."

Lenny gave me another wink and went back inside, the bell ringing daintily.

I walked over to my truck, tossed my new lights on the seat, and pulled the thing out of my pants.

It was the timing cover with the skull, smiling at me.

Chapter Nine

As soon as I got home I tried calling Jude. There was no answer, so I left a message on his machine to call me as soon as he got in. If he wasn't the one in my field the other night, I wanted to know who was.

Feeling at loose ends, I went out to the barn and checked on the kittens. I knew Zach would be asking about them, and wanted to be able to give a report. I found them, snoozing comfortably, almost hidden under their mama's fur.

Queenie, however, was not in her spot, and she hadn't met my truck when I'd come home. I felt a fresh stab of worry. It wasn't the first time she'd ever been gone this long, but it was unusual, and someone had taken it upon themselves to give me one less cow. I spent about fifteen minutes calling her, but had to stop when Detective Willard drove in. He stepped out of his unmarked Caprice Classic and walked over to me.

"Came out as soon as I could. I wanted to start on your list of names before heading here."

I opened my mouth, but he beat me to it. "Haven't found out anything yet. About anybody."

"Well, I already know Hubert did it," I said. "We just have to nail him. And I have a new time slot for you to check out." I told him about Bart seeing lights in my field on Friday night. "As far as stuff here, I'm really not sure what you're going to do."

"Why don't you just show me what you got?"

I took him on the tour of crime, pointing out the spot where I'd found Cleopatra, the now-patched-up manure lagoon, and the electrical box. Last was the corpse in the lower floor of the barn. Willard didn't bat an eye. I guess when you're used to seeing human remains during the course of your job, seeing the body of a cow doesn't really bother you. Even if said body is spread out in piles on a tarp.

"The vet record her findings?" he asked.

"Even took pictures."

He nodded and turned to me. "Gonna be straight with you. From what I see, there's not a whole lot I can do. I'll do a search around where the cow was found in the pasture, just in case the perpetrator left something behind, and check for fingerprints on the electrical box, but I don't hold high hopes."

I shrugged. "What I figured."

"As far as the manure lagoon goes, it looks like any evidence would probably have been washed away."

"Yup."

"But it's good you came by the station. I'll make out a report, and I hope you'll call at the first sign of anyone tampering with anything else."

"You got it. Thanks a lot."

"No problem. What I'm here for."

He loped to his car for his tools and disappeared around the back of the barn. I checked Queenie's food bowl, and when I saw it was still full, went to find Howie.

"Cop's here looking around, so don't be surprised if you see him."

Howie glanced up from the conveyor belt he was fixing. "Think he'll find anything?"

"No. But I think I know who did it."

He waited.

"Hubert."

His face cleared. "Would make sense. Damn. What you gonna do?"

I frowned. "Nothing. At least not till the detective checks him out."

"Unbelievable. Him, I mean."

I looked around the barnyard. "You seen Queenie?"

"Not lately. She missing?"

"Didn't come out for her lunch."

He shook his head. "Haven't seen her since morning."

We stared at each other.

"Let's go," I said.

Howie dropped what he was doing and we split up, searching the buildings and pastures. When that was unsuccessful, Howie reluctantly went back to work and I drove around the neighborhood, hoping I wouldn't find my beloved collie lying in a heap by the side of the road.

No sign of her anywhere. I wondered if I should tell Willard, but decided I might be jumping the gun. It's not unheard of for farm dogs to go off on a day's journey. I hoped that was all it was.

When I got home I checked the answering machine for any news on Zach, but there weren't any messages. I tried to push away my worries by finishing up the lawn and shredding newspapers. I was in the middle of that job when Howie came in, holding a rag over his hand, red soaking through the fabric. I shut off my machine.

"What'd ya do?"

"Sliced myself. Not too bad, but I guess I oughta get stitches."

"Need me to drive you?"

"Nah. If you could just help me get this tied on so's it won't come off."

"You wash it?"

"Yeah. It's ready to go."

I got some duct tape and wrapped it around the makeshift bandage, making Howie wince. I walked him out to his truck, and when I was assured he wasn't going to faint at the wheel, closed the door behind him.

"I guess you'll have to do the milking," he said. "This'll probably take a while."

"No problem."

"And I didn't quite get that belt done."

"I'll finish it."

I tapped the door and he drove off. The dust hadn't even settled when I remembered Missy would be coming for the evening milking. As if I hadn't already had enough trials for the day.

Detective Willard soon found me trying to loosen a stuck bolt on the conveyor belt, and leaned on the fence outside of the paddock. I walked over to him. "Find anything?"

"Nothing to find. But, like I said, I'll write up a report. Call me at the first sign of anything else out of order."

"Will do."

"And I'll let you know as soon as I hear anything about your list of suspects."

I tapped the wrench on my palm. "Can you give me a time frame before I can begin making Hubert's life hell?"

He shook his head. "The time frame is never. You'll just get yourself in trouble. Not that you probably care much."

"Oh, I care a little. Thanks for coming out." I noticed again the bags under his eyes. "Hope your son can come home soon."

"Me, too." He looked liked he was going to say more, but gave a little wave and headed toward his car.

When I finished the conveyor belt I had about a half-hour till milking, so I went to the office and dialed Jethro and Belle's number. Belle answered.

"How's my farmhand?" I asked.

"Same. Stubborn, like his sister."

"Well, that's good. They start letting you coddle them, you'll know it's serious."

She chuckled half-heartedly. "Mallory seems to be perking up a bit. Actually kept down half a piece of dry toast."

"Yum. You'll call me if I can do anything?"

"We'll call."

I had just booted up the computer and opened a spreadsheet of my milking records when someone pulled into the drive. I leaned over, hoping to get a glimpse of Nick, and spilled an entire container of paper clips onto the floor. Great. I was kneeling under the desk, picking them up, when someone tapped on the door.

"Yeah."

The door squeaked open and instead of Nick's work boots I saw a pair of New Balance tennis shoes at my eye level. Scooting out from under the desk I glanced at my watch, trying not to sigh so Missy would notice.

"You're early." It was only five-ten.

"Sorry. I didn't want to keep you waiting."

"That what you're wearing?" Besides the fancy tennies, she had on a lemon yellow short-sleeve shirt and jeans with a pleat, for God's sake.

"Will I be too hot? I thought jeans would be better than shorts."

I looked at her, trying to read exactly what her city mind would tell her. "Jeans are fine. Don't mind me." I stood up and brushed the dust from my knees.

"You okay?" Missy asked.

"What?"

She pointed at my shirt, which had a good amount of Howie's blood on it. Oh well. I needed to change my grease-stained jeans, anyway. "I'm gonna go change quick. You can come in if you want."

I didn't really think she'd take me up on that, since there were other more interesting things to inspect, but she followed as close as Queenie does when she's feeling needy.

Queenie.

I dropped Missy off in the kitchen.

"I'll be right down." I suppose I should have said "Make yourself at home," but it would have been insincere.

Five minutes later, dressed in a different pair of old jeans, my usual tank minus the flannel shirt since it was so hot, and rubber boots, I led her across the yard to the milking parlor.

I was astounded to see the cows almost all in their stalls and clipped in.

"What the hell do you think you're doing, Howie?" I couldn't see him, but I knew he was there. He popped up from behind a cow.

"Just getting the girls ready for you, Princess. Stitches didn't take as long as I expected. Oh, hi Missy."

"Hi, Howie," she said, sparkling. I know that sounds stupid, but she really did sparkle.

"Well, get your ass out of here," I said. "How am I going to get enough sleep if I have to take you to the hospital tonight after your stitches open and you bleed to death?"

"Yeah, yeah."

Missy looked at him, concerned. "Are you injured?"

"Nothing he won't live through," I said. "I'm just giving him shit."

"Oh," she said, beaming again. "I'm very glad to hear that."

I closed my eyes and took a deep breath. When I opened them, Howie was sneaking out the door, trying not to laugh. He really was going to take off and leave me with the prom queen. I'd get him back later.

"Okay," I said. "Might as well get started. Come on."

"I'm so glad you agreed to let me help," Missy said. "Abe's always talking about you and your farm, and I thought it would be nice to see what you do. We may be friends for a long time."

I grunted, trying to ignore the sudden ache in my chest. "Here." I handed her some paper towels and a bucket of water. "Wipe the cows' teats off. You want to have them clean for the milkers to go on."

Missy eagerly took the towels and hunkered down by the first cow.

"Watch out for the hind feet," I said.

"All right." She looked wary.

"They don't usually kick, but you don't want to be caught off guard."

She nodded and set to work. Thirty seconds later I came back with the milker hose, and Missy was still by the first cow.

I stopped behind her. "I said clean it off, not detail it."

"Sorry."

"This one next." I pointed across the aisle.

She scurried over.

I stuck the milker on the first cow and went to get the grain so the cows could start eating.

We had a few minutes of pleasant non-verbalizing—listening to Rachmaninoff, I believe—Missy trying to avoid the poop in the stalls, and me dumping food into the trays in between switching the milkers. I wondered if she knew more about Zach's health than I did, and felt a stab of jealousy that she'd infiltrated the family.

"So how'd you get started milking?" she asked, stopping my pity-fest.

"Abe didn't tell you that part?"

She shook her head.

"My folks owned this farm. Dad died when I was three, Mom when I was sixteen. Howie stayed on, kept the developers from running me over. So I never really started milking—it's been my life since day one."

Missy was looking at me, shocked. "I'm sorry about your parents."

"Old news, now. Clean that cow will ya?"

Shaken, she bent down by the cow and cleaned the udder. I thought we were going back to the pleasant quiet, but I was mistaken.

"How old do cows get?" Missy asked.

"Oldest right now's eighteen."

"Wow. What do I do with this one? She won't get up."

The cow was lying down, chewing her cud and looking completely immobile.

"Kick her in the butt."

"*Kick* her?"

"Not like you're punting a football. Just bother her."

Missy gave me a concerned look, but stuck her foot on the cow's haunch and starting wiggling it. Eventually, the cow lumbered to her feet.

"Eighteen years old," she said. "How long will she live yet?"

"This is probably her last season. Her milk production has gone way down, so this fall she'll probably retire."

"She'll be the queen of the herd, then?"

"Actually, she'll go to the meat packer's."

Missy shot up, stricken. "You're going to *kill* her?"

I sighed, having forgotten the world Missy was coming from.

"She's not a pet, Missy. She's a business commodity. Every retired cow I keep is just another mouth to feed. Winter's coming up and the pastures won't be any help."

"I can't believe you *do* that!"

I clipped the milker on the next cow and turned on Missy. "Who's going to pay me to feed her? I don't see the Humane Society banging down my door. You going to sponsor my retired cows so they can live in luxury?"

Missy glared at me, but had nothing to say. She faced the wall for a few minutes before speaking again.

"What about Queenie?"

I glanced at the spot where Queenie usually sits and felt a small pain behind my eye. "Queenie's a dog."

"So?"

"She's my friend."

"What about your truck?"

I shook my head, confused. "What about it?"

"It's not a cheap truck."

"It's more than ten years old, and a farm truck, for Christ's sake."

"Well, then, what about your Harley? Those aren't cheap, no matter how old they are."

I looked at Missy, a stranger until yesterday, and now she was picking apart my life and placing me in the role of villain, attacking me even as she made herself a part—however small—of my farm. I choked back the words I *really* wanted to say and settled for a tamer spiel.

"Not that it's any of your business, but I basically picked that bike out of a Dumpster and put it back together piece by piece, with my own two hands. It's not a show bike. Now, any more questions, or can we get some milking done?"

We stared at each other, each daring the other to say more. I finally won the contest, and Missy went back to work. We stayed in stony silence for about ten minutes. Finally, I felt it was time to mend the fence, or Abie-baby would have my hide for scaring his little Snow White.

"Want to try sticking the hose on?" I held up the milker.

She turned to me, her face solemn, and after a moment she came over, setting the paper towels on the ground. I showed her how to apply the milker. Her enthusiasm returned and she actually clapped when she got it on.

"Look at the milk in the tube!" she said, pointing. I looked, and it was the same as always.

"Take the milker off the next one and put it on the one beside her," I said.

She figured out how to take it off and it only took her two tries to attach it to the next cow. She caught on quickly—I had to give her that.

I finished giving out the grain and was in the feed room getting the hay when I heard a screech. I walked back into the parlor and found Missy sitting in a cow pie.

"Whoops," I said.

She looked at me, dismayed.

"There's a sink over there," I said. "Wash your hands."

She gingerly picked herself off the floor and brushed off what she could. Her fancy white sneakers would never be the same.

"Want to take over feeding them?" I asked, giving her an out.

She shook her head, washed her hands, and switched the next milker. We went on like before, and I turned to tell her to start on the next row when I saw the cow right behind her lifting her tail. I'd like to think I didn't have time to say anything, but in reality, how long does it take to shout out that piss is going to fly?

About a gallon of urine came spurting out of the cow, drenching Missy's shirt, jeans, and sneakers. She stood, dripping, and looked at me with horror.

"Sorry," I said.

Without saying a word, she shook herself off, went to the next cow, squatted down, and switched the milker.

"That was deliberate, mean, and nasty—and I wouldn't have missed it for the world."

Nick stood in the doorway, close to where I was filling troughs. My hormones began a hundred-meter sprint, even though he was wearing his cover-up outfit again. At least the goggles were hanging around his neck and not giving him bug eyes.

"Glad to provide some entertainment," I said.

"Oh, you provide plenty."

I squinted, unsure how to take his comment, until he gave me his slow smile and leisurely made his way back the direction he'd come. When he was out of sight I leaned my head on the closest cow's back.

"You okay, Stella?" Missy asked.

I straightened up and gave her a scowl for good measure. "I'm fine."

"Fine."

The main herd was finally done. We got the new mamas on their separate milking, unclipped the rest of the cows, and soon the milking tubes were going through their cleaning routine. Before letting the mamas go I got out the can of antibiotic spray Carla had given me and gave Wendy's incision a good going over.

Missy sat on a bale of hay and leaned her face into her hands. I felt a twinge of guilt about the wet and smelly state of her clothes. But *just* a twinge.

She sat up. "God, that's tiring—and, unfortunately for me, somewhat disgusting."

I gave her a small, hopefully not *too* nasty smile. "Sorry you're so bushed," I said. "'Cause we ain't finished yet."

Chapter Ten

"*Now* are we done?"

Missy and I stood looking at the milking parlor, which had clean stalls, fresh bedding, and limed walkways. As much as I hated to admit it, Missy worked hard—even with her putrid clothes.

"We're done. Now I take the milk from the new mothers out to Gus and formula to the other two."

"Oh, can I help?"

I was afraid she was going to start clapping again, so I grabbed a bucket of colostrum and handed it to her. She strained under the weight as we walked toward the hutches, but clamped her jaw and bumped along beside me.

"It's so wonderful that you gave Zach this calf," Missy said with effort. "It's given him something to think about while he's...laid up."

I grunted.

"It's something how the Grangers support each other," she went on. "Everybody has been by Ma's to keep her up-to-date. Well, not Marianne, I guess. Jude's been around, but without her. Not surprising, I guess, with the way she hates farming and all. Abe says she's never really made herself part of the family."

We were about a hundred feet from the hutches, me trying to shut out Missy's voice, when I knew something was wrong. I dropped the formula bottles I was carrying and started running.

Missy's bucket sloshed down and her footsteps raced along behind me.

Gus' hutch was turned on its side, and Gus' face stuck out in between the wire door and the hutch, distorted and grotesque, his tongue swollen out the side of his mouth.

Missy gagged and ran behind the nearest barn, where I'm pretty sure she emptied her stomach. I squatted down in front of the hutch, sick and angry, unsure where to look. I stood and turned away, taking a deep breath. Missy came back from the barn, wiping her mouth on her sleeve.

"What happened?" she asked, tears in her eyes. "That's Zach's calf, isn't it?"

I didn't want to tell her what I was really thinking, so I said, "It happens sometimes. He must've gotten overly excited about something, or something scared him, and he got caught in the door." I tried not to let rage and fear slip into my voice.

"Why don't you use something different if this happens a lot?"

"I didn't say it happens a lot. I only remember two other times in my whole life."

"I hope you're not so hardened *this* doesn't bother you."

"Shut up, Missy."

She hiccupped and wiped her face again. "I'm sorry."

"The other calves need to be fed. Why don't you go ahead and give them their bottles."

Missy got herself together enough to figure out how to clip the bottles on the cages. Detective Willard wouldn't want me to move anything, but I just couldn't leave Gus hanging there. I did what I could to extricate Gus from the hutch, being careful not to touch much, and laid him down beside it.

"How long ago did he die?" Missy asked.

"Don't know. Had to be this afternoon, though. I fed the calves this morning and then was mowing the yard—I can see the hutches from there and would've noticed. Damn."

"You going to call him?" Missy asked. We both knew I had to tell Zach.

"No. He needs to hear this in person."

"Want me to come along?"

"Thanks, but no."

"Can I do anything else?"

I shook my head.

"I'm sorry, Stella." I knew she was talking about more than Gus.

"Forget it. Thanks for helping with the milking."

"Sure." She looked like she wanted to say something more, but turned and walked to her car. She pulled a blanket out of the trunk and draped it over the driver's seat before sitting down. Smart move.

I walked to the garage and rang Howie's bell. He appeared at the top of his stairs. "What now?"

"Gus got hung in his hutch."

"Oh, shit." He shut his door and came down. "Is it Them again?"

I looked out over the cornfield behind the garage, beautiful with Jude's crop. "Probably. Could be a nasty coincidence. There's no way to know."

"Still think it's Hubert?"

I shrugged. "Don't know. I would never have thought he had it in him. He's slimy, but this? He'd be petrified of Queenie seeing him and ripping his throat out."

"Yeah, unless he knew she was gone."

Oh, hell.

"You gonna call the cops?" Howie asked.

I sighed. "Next on my list. Damn."

Howie closed his eyes for a moment, then opened them. "What can I do?"

"I'm gonna go over and tell Zach after I call Willard. Can you get Gus covered up and maybe start on a hole? I want Zach to help bury him if he's not too sick."

"You bet, Princess. I'll get right on it."

Detective Willard was gone, as was the receptionist. A recording told me to call 911 for emergencies. I punched in the number and was soon telling the dispatcher what had happened. He contacted the borough police as we spoke.

"A patrol car should be coming by," I told Howie, when I found him. "Don't know if Willard will show or not."

He nodded and shoveled another clump of dirt in the field behind the feed barn.

I got in my truck and drove as slowly as traffic would allow over to Zach's house. It took fifteen minutes and I still had no idea how to tell a boy his new pet was dead.

Belle met me at the door and, just like with Howie, my face was an open book.

"It's Zach's calf, isn't it?" she said.

I nodded, amazed at what mothers can know.

"Come on in. Mallory's taking a nap upstairs and Zach's sacked out on the couch, watching old Disney movies."

"Yikes," I said. "How is he?"

She concentrated on shutting the door, then said, "About the same. He's on a diet of penicillin and clear liquids. Mallory, too. Nothing else we can do till they know more." She took a sob-like breath. "At least no one else has died yet."

Small consolation for Toby Derstine's parents.

"Will you be going to the funeral tomorrow?" Belle asked.

"Toby's? It's tomorrow already?"

"The cops, or whoever, are done with his…autopsy. Claire and Tom want to put him to rest right away."

"Sure, I'll go." Didn't want to. Never had been to a kid's funeral before.

Belle turned to walk toward the living room, then stopped, not looking at me. "Betsy's got the illness." Jacob's wife. "And Penny." Joshua's. "And Josh said he's not feeling too good, either."

So it had started. Adults were now fair game.

Belle and I walked into the living room and my first impression of Zach was that he'd paled a few shades. His face looked gaunt after just the one day since I'd seen him. I was afraid to tell him about Gus, for fear it would make him even sicker.

"Hey, Stella," Zach said.

"Hey."

Belle turned off the TV.

"What's going on?" Zach asked.

I looked at my shoes, then at Belle, and finally at Zach. "Gus…is dead, Zach."

He looked at me blankly.

"He hung himself in his hutch. I'm sorry."

Zach's lower lip began to tremble, and he sat up abruptly. Belle made a little move like she would go to him, but stayed where she was. Zach turned his head so I couldn't see his face.

"I *told* you he should've been in the barn."

"I'm sorry," I said again. "I thought it was the best thing for him to be in the hutch. Calves are normally safest there." When a maniac isn't running loose.

"Lot of good that did Gus." He sat completely still, keeping his head turned away. "Why don't you go now, Stella."

"Zach—" Belle said.

I put a hand on her arm. "It's okay." To Zach, I said, "Howie's digging a hole. You feel well enough to come and help bury Gus?"

His back stiffened, then twitched. "Will you take me, Mom?"

She looked at him, then at me, I suppose thinking I might be offended he didn't want to ride with me.

I nodded at her. "If you think it's okay."

"Sure, honey," she said to Zach. "We'll go right over."

I left. There was nothing else to say.

When I got home Howie was showing a police officer the hutch. The same police officer who'd practically run me over at the police station. Great.

They turned toward me as I approached, and recognition sparked in the policeman's eyes. I think we both wished Willard had gotten the call. I know I did.

"So what's the plan?" I asked. "Officer…."

"Meadows." He crossed his arms and tapped his fingers against his side. "I can't really do anything. The detective is at the hospital with his son, and the only other officer in the department who does fingerprints just came down sick, herself. It's not supposed to rain tonight, so the detective can come by in the morning to check things out. Not that it will help, seeing as how you already messed with the crime scene. If it really is one."

Oh, that was just dandy. "I have no doubt a crime was committed, *Officer*," I said. "And that means we've got to protect the rest of my livestock. What are you going to do about that?"

He snorted. "We've got two people on a shift these days. Can't afford any more because of the town council's budget cuts. I guess we could drive by your place a few more times than usual, make our presence known, but there's not much more I can offer."

I fought down anger, knowing he was right, but ticked all the same. Ticked at him, at the borough. Enraged with whoever was pulling this crap.

Meadows shrugged. "You could hire private security."

I glared at him. "You tell me where I can get money for that, I'll look into it."

He shrugged again. "I'll let Detective Willard know what happened. I'll write up a report, too, but there's really nothing else I can do."

I looked at Howie, and I knew by his blank expression he was as annoyed as I was by the cop's lazy responses.

"You can help us dig the grave," I said.

Meadows stared at me like I'd suddenly grown a second head—a *cow's* head—till I spun around and walked toward the hole Howie had started. When I got there, I looked back and saw Meadows getting into his car. Howie was trudging toward me, holding his bandaged hand up by the wrist.

"Oh, shit, Howie," I said. "I forgot about your hand. I'll dig the rest."

"Won't argue with you on that." He planted himself on a patch of weeds—hopefully not poison ivy—and watched, keeping his stitches above his heart.

I was finishing up ten minutes later when Belle and Zach pulled into the lane. I gave Howie a hand up and we walked over to meet Zach at the still, tarp-covered figure.

Zach didn't look at us, but knelt down by Gus and pulled back the plastic sheeting. He stroked his calf's head, lingering on the soft nose and ears, flattening the short whiskers around his mouth. His fingers traced the markings on Gus' back and side, then he laid his palm where there should have been a heart beating, and stood up.

"Okay, Mom. Let's get out of here." He turned and walked to the car without looking back.

Chapter Eleven

"Sorry about the calf," Nick said.

"Yeah." I was sitting on the side steps of the house, my boots on the ground in front of me, wondering where on earth Queenie had gotten to, and how in hell I was going to protect my farm. Would someone who kills cows go after collies, too?

It was good to have an excuse to sit, because I couldn't summon up the energy to go inside, change, and get supper. I kept envisioning Zach's face, burning with accusation, as well as fever. Thinking of fever made me remember that adults were now getting sick, and I put a hand on my forehead to check if I was above the usual ninety-eight point six. Couldn't tell, of course.

If I did have a fever, it could just as easily have been from rage as the flu. Whoever was attacking my farm—Hubert or not—I was impotent. Willard had ordered me to stay away from Hubert, and if it wasn't him I had no idea where to look. The teen-agers just didn't seem like realistic suspects anymore.

Willard hadn't called back, and I assumed it would be morning till I heard from him. I didn't know how to arrange security for my farm without any money, and I knew Howie and I couldn't do it twenty-four/seven and still run the place. Normally I'd ask the Grangers, but they were all busy caring for sick children or getting sick themselves. I tried calling Bart and Lenny, but the Biker Barn was closed and neither one was home.

Hell.

Seeing Nick standing in front of me didn't even arouse any enthusiasm, so I knew I was really in a funk. I looked him up and down, which was a pleasure, if not invigorating. "You're looking awfully clean."

"Changed out of my painting clothes, even though I know you liked them."

I managed a grin.

"Dog still gone?" he asked.

"Yeah." I tried to sound in control. "Probably checking out a dead raccoon somewhere."

"Mm-hmm." He held up a bag. "Got a big Italian hoagie. Want to split it?"

"Hot peppers?"

"And sweet."

Even in my aggravated state I couldn't resist. Besides, I had to eat. "Sounds great. Let me grab some drinks." I stood and paused in the doorway, wondering if I should do what I was about to, then gave in to my impulse. "Come on in. You might as well make yourself at home."

Nick followed me into the kitchen, where I grabbed paper plates, a couple of sodas, and a bag of chips that was gathering dust on top of the fridge. Nick eyed the chips warily.

"They're not *that* old," I said. And they weren't. They crunched just fine if you stuck them in your mouth whole and tried not to chew much.

"So how's your little farmhand doing?" Nick asked after we'd both taken bites and done the appropriate lip smacking. I glanced up at him, not sure if he was talking about the flu or Gus' death, then realized Nick probably wouldn't even know Gus had been Zach's.

I raised a shoulder, not wanting to think about it. Zach's anger—let alone his illness—was enough to make the hoagie unappetizing.

"Okay," Nick said. "Tell me about the helper you had for milking tonight."

"Helper?" I waved my sandwich at him. "You mean Miss Nosy Britches?"

He grinned and talked around a big mouthful. "How come you're so down on her? What'd she do to you?"

I shoved my hoagie into my mouth to give me time to think. What *had* she done, other than come home on Abe's arm? I swallowed. "She's just such a white bread, white collar, Miss America-type. Gets on my nerves."

"Seemed to me she held up pretty well to all the crap today. Literally."

I glared at him, because he was right. "Okay, she did. But you must admit it *was* funny when she got pissed on."

"I'm not denying that." He smiled and took another bite.

I watched the oil dripping from the end of his sandwich and realized this was the first time I'd shared a meal with a guy at my table that I could remember. Well, Howie or Abe might have been there, but they didn't count.

"You go to agricultural school?" Nick asked.

I shook my head. "High school. Never really thought about college. What about you? You look like a frat boy."

He laughed. "Especially when power washing, right? I went to a year of college, couldn't stand the schedule or the confinement, blew off the frats, and quit after the first year, making my folks crazy." He shrugged. "Who knows. I may go back once I figure out what for." He stopped to put back toppings that had fallen off of his sandwich, and I wondered at the suddenly serious expression on his face.

"You going to hand this place down to your kids?" he asked.

"What kids?" I finished off my sandwich and got up to get some napkins. "If there *were* any kids, I'd want them to take it over, but it's pretty unlikely."

"Kids or kids farming?"

"Either, really, but what I meant was kids taking over the farm. Not a whole lot doing that anymore."

"I was wondering. I was running out of farms to hit up for work when I came across you. Once I saw you, I figured I'd see the bottom of your boot before you even said hello." He grinned, taking the sting out of his words.

"You weren't far off." I leaned against the counter and crossed my arms. Enough about me. "Where are you from, anyway?"

He took a final bite of hoagie, then wiped his mouth. "Not PA."

He didn't seem like he was going to offer any more. Not liking nosy parkers, myself, I let it go. I started cleaning up the table and threw everything—including the chips—into the trash.

"Come on." He stood and held out his hand.

"What?"

"Come *on*. There's something I want to do."

"What?"

"Trust me."

I looked at him and decided to ignore the nagging feeling of apprehension knocking at my gut. Howie was around, so I wouldn't be leaving the farm unguarded if I took off for a little.

"Okay," I said. And for the first time since fifth grade, I let a guy take me by the hand and tell me where to go.

The sky was brilliant with stars, and it looked even better than usual since I was lying on a blanket beside Nick in the bed of my pickup. The cicadas and crickets were having a riot of a time singing around us, and we could hear an occasional car or truck in the distance, but other than that, there was no noise.

Nick had taken me outside and ordered me to give him the grand tour of the farm, from the tractor barn to the milk storage tank, then wanted to ride around in my truck—since his was full of painting gear—to see my land. I tried not to feel nervous when I pointed out the manure lagoon and the spot where Cleopatra had died, but I had to wonder what would be next.

Now I had a blanket under my head, a gorgeous man beside me, and endless space above me. If only I hadn't had dead cows, a missing dog, greedy developers, and a fatal illness to think about, it couldn't have gotten any better.

"So what are you gonna do?" Nick said, interrupting the quiet.

"About what?"

"The farm. Zach. Kids."

"Oh. Everything."

"I guess."

"Zach's a tough one. He wanted Gus to be in the barn and I said no. He'll blame me forever."

"Was it your fault?"

I thought about the scumbag killing my cows, and wondered if I could've prevented Gus' death. "I don't think so."

"Will you give him another calf?"

"As soon as he wants one. Which, if he's as upset as he seemed, could be a while."

I took a deep breath and closed my eyes. It hurt to think about the calf. Well, not the calf so much as what it meant to my relationship with Zach. I was used to animals dying. What I wasn't used to—besides animal cruelty—was having friendships threatened because of it.

"Kids?"

I opened my eyes and turned my head toward Nick. "Why should I tell you my life plans?"

He rolled onto his elbow and looked down at me. "Why not?"

My breathing grew shallower as I looked into his eyes, and a flash of heat made my body sticky with sweat. He smiled at me, looking at my mouth, and when I thought it was inevitable that he was going to kiss me, I got an attack of shyness and sat up, wrapping my arms around my knees.

Nick pushed himself up beside me and let his feet dangle off the tailgate. "Won't you regret it if you don't have kids?"

I looked around at the field where we sat. We were right in the middle of my eighty acres, having followed the irrigation path through the rows of corn. I thought about little kids running through the fields, Jude and Marianne going to a fertility clinic, and the sight of all the Granger children playing and squealing at my birthday party the day before. I also thought about the handsome and, apparently, available man sitting next to me.

"I can't abandon this," I finally said. "If I had kids, my priorities would change. Who's to say I wouldn't get scared and sell my farm, only to see it raped into submission by somebody like Hubert Purcell?"

Nick had no reply, and the silence stretched into minutes before he spoke again.

"Who will be with you when you're old? When you can't farm anymore? Not Howie."

I jumped off the end of the truck and walked a few steps away, sticking my hands in my back pockets. Just who was this guy, and why was he pushing all my buttons? Did he know I sometimes lay awake at night wondering the same thing, sometimes so fiercely I had to get up and turn on the TV just to scare away the thoughts?

"The Grangers will be around," I said. "There are too many of them to all die before me." I bit off my words, terrified some of them just might die, and soon.

Nick was oblivious to my worry. "They're not family."

I gave a harsh laugh. "Don't tell Ma that."

"You know what I mean. Don't you sometimes wish for someone to be a permanent part of your life? Someone you go to sleep with and wake up with?"

I turned to him. "Just who are we talking about here? Me or you? You're the one traveling around without a permanent residence. Or do you have someone waiting at home, wherever home is?"

He shook his head slowly and lay back down on the truck bed, his hands behind his head. "I'm not making a life out of barn painting. It's just something to do till I figure out what's next. Come on." He patted the blanket beside him. "Relax. I didn't mean to spoil the mood."

I walked back to the truck, shoved his feet up onto the tailgate and slammed it shut, surprising him onto his elbows. "There was no mood. There was just me being depressed and you trying to pick my brain."

He smiled at me with such tenderness I almost changed my mind and jumped back up beside him. But I didn't. I got into the cab, and he lay down in the bed to watch the stars as I drove us home.

Chapter Twelve

Nick's taillights disappeared down the drive, and I went into the house to flip a switch by the side door. The yard and outbuildings flooded with light, almost as bright as day. I picked up the phone, noticing the answering machine was blinking. I punched Howie's number.

"Good idea, Princess," he said.

"Won't keep you awake, will it?"

"Naw. My bedroom's on the far side. Besides, it's better to be careful."

"All right. Just wanted to make sure."

"You want I should sit up and watch?"

"I'll take the first shift and get you when I'm ready to keel over. How's the hand?"

"Ibuprofen's keeping the throbbing down pretty good."

"Great. See you in the morning."

I hung up and hit the play button on the answering machine. The first message was Jethro, telling me to call ASAP. I hit speed dial, my heart pounding. He answered on the first ring.

"You hear, Stella? They made a breakthrough. I guess when they did little Toby's autopsy they found something unusual." I heard a paper crackling, like he was smoothing it out. "Something called aflatoxin." He said it slowly, pronouncing each syllable carefully. "It's some fungus they find on plants. Somehow people around here are eating stuff that's laced with it."

A chill crept up my back. "Laced on purpose? Like terrorists?"

"They ain't saying that. They're checking local produce. Corn, tomatoes, green beans. Everything. This'll kill the farmers' market."

"Better than killing kids."

"You said it."

"So what do we do? Stop eating anything that's not canned or boxed?"

"I suppose. Nothing fresh, that's what I'm hearing. Unless you've grown it yourself."

No more veggies for me.

"So what about Zach? And Mallory? What do you do for them?"

"Get them off any of that stuff. And they're taking something called, oh good grief, I don't know what it's called, but Doc says they should be better within a day or two."

"Super." I tried to sound enthusiastic, but hadn't the kids already been on the BRAT diet? They weren't any better yet.

We said our good-byes, promising soberly to see each other at Toby's funeral the next day.

The second message was from Detective Willard.

"Sorry to hear about that calf of yours," he said. "I'll be out tomorrow to check it out. I did get lucky on a couple alibis. One being Hubert Purcell. Looks like he's not your man."

My head started to hurt. If it wasn't Hubert, I was back to square one.

"His alibi's tight," Willard continued. "And I didn't even get it from him. Saturday, when your cow was electrocuted, he was with Pam Moyer most of the day." Dammit, I'd forgotten that. "She says they even visited you in the morning. She was with him from breakfast on till after lunch. The night before, his neighbor says he was home all evening, grilling supper out on his patio. Didn't go out any time that night, and believe me, this lady would know.

"Today he was in a meeting with county supervisors all afternoon till dinner. It sounds like he's in the clear." He paused.

"That might be a relief to you, but it might also be frightening. All I can say is we'll do our best to find the culprit. See you tomorrow."

I breathed carefully through my nose, trying to squelch the fear tightening my chest. I had been banking on Hubert. The devil I knew.

I forced myself outside to fetch a lawn chair from the garage, then planted it in the side yard, where I'd be in full view of anyone coming to call. If I'd been a different kind of woman I could've used the time to knit a sweater or snap green beans. Instead, I found myself fidgeting, yearning for Queenie's company, worrying over just who was messing with my farm. No one but Hubert had any motive. I wasn't political. I wasn't religious. Hell, I wasn't much of anything except a farmer who made sure milk found its way to people's refrigerators.

The news that they'd found the "flu" culprit should've been a huge relief, too, but a niggling doubt inside me said they were missing something. It seemed too easy. I'd have to ask Pam about it, seeing as how she was our new resident agricultural expert. Maybe I'd call her in the morning.

My chin dipped toward my chest, and I snapped back awake. Not even ten o'clock and I was drifting off. Some guard. I needed action.

I walked over to the garage and let the door up slowly, hoping I wouldn't wake Howie, then wheeled my Harley over to the barn where I do my mechanical work. If I couldn't sleep, I might as well use the time to do something productive. And fun.

I gathered up the new bike parts from my birthday party and the Biker Barn and spent the next couple of hours trying to lose myself in chrome. I couldn't wait till the next time I went riding at night and saw those blue lights and the skull timing cover Lenny had slipped to me. I'd just have to make sure to ride where Bart wouldn't see me.

By the time I'd mounted all the pieces, it was almost two o'clock. If I was going to get any sleep at all I knew I'd better wake Howie. I pushed the bike back to the garage and walked up his steps, feeling exposed in the brightness. I wondered if the cops had made any extra passes by the house like Officer Meadows had promised.

"My turn, Princess?" Howie's face was creased with sleep.

"If you're up to it."

"I'll manage."

"You should know—it wasn't Hubert. Willard left a message saying Hu couldn't possibly have been here when the cows were killed. He's got witnesses to prove it."

"So that means—"

"Could be anybody."

Howie sighed. "Okay. Go get some sleep."

Back in my house, I de-greased with Fast Orange soap, dropped my dirty clothes in the washer, and fell into bed.

When my alarm went off I had a huge headache I decided to blame Nick for. I had plenty of other things to cause it, of course, but it was easiest to make him the scapegoat. I wasn't used to practical strangers—or even close friends—delving into my deeply personal life.

I pushed myself out of bed, did my bathroom business, and pulled on my milking clothes, still half asleep. I turned on the "All News, All the Time" station on the radio and listened to a story about a businessman who had bought out a trucking company on the verge of bankruptcy, revamped it, and made it a commercial success.

It was only at the end of the segment I realized they were talking about Turner Enterprises. Seemed Sonny had done it again—he'd taken a floundering business and made millions on it. I wondered if he could do the same thing with my farm. Or Pam's. Or at least our borough's budget.

The newscaster went on to spout Accu-Weather's forecast. Nothing new about what they were now calling the "Killer Fungus Illness." I snapped the radio off.

My orange juice—not made from fresh local produce—and Cheerios didn't have much taste, but I forced myself to eat them, and by the time I was done I felt a little more human.

I turned the floodlights off and opened the side door to listen, hoping to hear the patter of Queenie's feet on the gravel drive. The morning was silent and still. No excited yelping or panting, no cold nose rooting in my palm. I walked down the steps and headed toward the garage, trying to have hope for my faithful collie, but worried as hell the madman plaguing my farm had gotten her.

I glanced up at Howie's apartment and saw the reassuring light outside his door. He left it on every night, just in case I needed him. I had always told him I could handle anything on my own, but he was as hard-headed as I was, and during the past few years I'd done some growing up and wasn't afraid to ask for help once in a while.

Underneath the light sat Howie, playing solitaire and whistling.

"Morning," I said.

"Morning. Want help milking?"

"Nah. You go back to bed. Wouldn't you know, the night we stay up nothing happens."

"Maybe that's why nothing happened."

"Could be. See you in a few hours."

The walk to the barn felt lonely without Queenie, so I tried to focus on my job and the things I needed to do. Unfortunately, Queenie always made herself a part of the morning chores, whether helping or getting in the way, and my ache for her grew stronger with every moment.

I stepped into the parlor and switched on the lights, half afraid I'd find a dead cow or some other catastrophe waiting for me. What greeted me was the sight of a few very alive cows lounging in stalls, so I breathed a sigh of relief and went back out and around the barn to get into the lower floor. I took one step into the room and stopped.

"Oh, man," I said.

The entire floor was covered with water, and looking at the legs of the cows standing in it, I'd say there was a good six inches of it. Water was spraying out of one of the pipes that came down from the ceiling and led to the cows' water fountain, filling up the barn floor and making a muddy, manurey mess.

"Oh, *man*." I swept my eyes across the room, hoping I hadn't forgotten and left a bag of feed or something on the floor, when I noticed the pile of straw bales on the other side, where Zach had shown off the new kittens just yesterday.

"Oh, no." I waded quickly through the water, dreading what I would find. Zach would absolutely blacklist me if those kittens had drowned on my watch.

I reached the site where the cozy nest had been and peered into the hole. In the pale light it was hard to make anything out. I assumed I would at least be able to see the mother above the water, and there was nothing showing. I stuck my hand into the dark mess and let out my breath when I found no wet, furry creatures.

I straightened up and looked around, wondering where the cat could have taken her little family. I soon saw the smart mama on top of a stack of burlap sacks, her four dry and very squirmy offspring suckling at her belly.

"Good *girl*," I said emphatically.

I splashed over to her and slowly offered my hand. She checked me out for a moment, shot visual daggers at me for allowing her home to be flooded, then deigned to let me pat her head. I should've known she'd have those babies out of there at the first sign of danger.

Satisfied the cats were safe and Zach wouldn't want my head on a platter, I turned my attention back to the mess I had to deal with. I was thankful an Amishman I knew had come to take away Cleopatra's remains the evening before so I didn't have cow innards floating around, but there was still plenty to clean up. Howie wouldn't get to sleep after all.

First off, though, I made my way across the room, found the spigot on the pipe which came from outside and led to the fountain, and turned off the water supply. The water continued to spray out for a few seconds, but soon slowed to a trickle, and then to just drips. I took a quick look to see if something had been tampered with, but couldn't get a good enough vantage point. I'd come back in a minute.

I sloshed my way to the door, got onto relatively dry land, and trudged back up the hill to Howie's place. His light was now off since the sun had started to rise, and he came to the door as soon as I knocked.

"What'd they do now?" he asked, fear in his voice.

"Don't know if it's Them or not."

"What is it?"

"We've got the Shit Sea in the basement of the barn. Pipe burst on the water fountain."

"For real?"

"I think so. I'll check it out to be sure."

"At least it's something fixable." He pulled on some boots. "Want me to get on the cleanup?"

"Actually, how 'bout we get the girls going in the parlor, then I'll take care of the water while you take care of them."

"I'll do the water," Howie said. "You've been doing all the crappy jobs the last couple days. And it's your birthday and all."

"It's not my birthday anymore. And you've done the crap jobs all your life."

He made a sound and I held up my hand. "I'm doing it. No arguments."

"Fine." He slammed the door in my face, and I trotted down his steps, smiling. Howie and I were very good at fighting.

I went back to the basement of the barn, and by the time Howie appeared I had shooed all the cows up the hill without landing face first in the muck.

"Over it?" I asked him.

He glared at me.

"Seen Queenie yet?" I asked.

His face changed. "Nope. God, Stella. You don't think They got her, too?"

I shrugged and my chest constricted. I couldn't think about it.

"You hear about the fungus?" I asked. A cow bumped into me and I pushed her toward an empty stall.

"Yeah. Isn't aflatoxin something that attacks peanuts?"

"Don't know. But we don't have local of those, so it can't be that. I think they test field corn for it sometimes."

"Huh. I'm just glad they figured out something. If that's really it."

I looked at him sharply. "You're having doubts, too?"

He put a hand on a nearby haunch and patted it while he talked. "It seems too easy. I mean, you can't tell me all them kids are eating their vegetables."

We stared at each other uneasily for a few moments before getting back to work. He was right. Normal kids just don't eat fresh tomatoes and green beans. Corn on the cob, maybe.

We got the cows clipped in and pumping, and without saying anything more I went down to the watery mess. I took a look at it, sighed louder than necessary, straightened my shoulders, and went to work.

First, I waded over to the straw bales where the cats used to be housed. I took one of the already broken bales and started spreading it around. One bale doesn't go a long way in that mess, so when I had that pile distributed I had to go upstairs and grab some more.

Eight bales and a lot of energy later, I stood beside the water fountain and tried to figure out what had happened. Pipes, unfortunately, don't often get the attention they need or deserve, and they crack, corrode, and rust. They freeze and thaw in the winter, and sweat in the summer. These pipes looked like they'd been left alone for a little too long, and, from what I could see, I had only myself to blame. Well, I could've blamed Howie, but that wouldn't have been fair.

The pipe in question had apparently rusted through, and as soon as a tiny fissure had appeared, it was all over. There are forty pounds of water pressure surging through the pipes at all times, and when it finds a leak, no matter how small, it's like a little army breaking through an enemy's wall. There are valves in the water fountain itself which close and open as the cows drink and the water level changes. They allow water to fill up the trough as need be, and keep it in the pipes when the fountain is full. They were no help at all with a hole like this.

The straw needed time to soak up the water before I could scrape the mess out of the barn, so I headed to my office and called Granger's Welding. They were usually open by seven, so I figured someone would be around. I was right.

"Granger's," Jethro said. He sounded chipper.

"It's Stella. How's Zach?"

"No worse, no better. Mallory, too. But doc says they'll be better by this evening, and I'm counting on it."

I wasn't about to contradict him. "Does that mean you got a free hand?"

"What's up?"

"I need a new pipe in the barn. I figured you guys know a little about welding, maybe you could fix it."

"Sure. I learned a lot when I re-did our bathroom last year. Can it wait an hour or so? I got a trailer needs fixing, and they want it this morning. I'm kinda behind from the last coupl'a days."

"An hour's fine. I gotta let the straw do its work, anyway, before I can clean it up. I'll try to have it ready for you by… say…nine?"

"Sounds good. See you then."

I hung up, then reconsidered and looked up Pam Moyer's number.

"Hello?" Pam's father sounded weary.

"Mr. Moyer. Stella Crown here. Your daughter around?"

He cleared his throat. "Sorry, honey, she's not home right now. She's out working with those doctors and whatever."

"Right. Sorry to bother you. Can you please let her know I called?"

"No problem, sweetheart."

I hesitated. "You doing okay over there, Mr. Moyer?"

He coughed into the phone. "Sorry, darlin', just haven't talked much yet this morning. Sure, I'm doing just fine, just fine."

"Keeping your gate closed against those developers?"

"Aw, shucks, they ain't no match for me."

I laughed, because he seemed to expect it. "Well, you take care of yourself, now."

"Oh, I will, honey. And you keep them cows healthy."

I said good-bye and went out into the parlor. Howie was on the last cows, and they had all been fed, so I unclipped the first few, got them out of their stalls, and picked up the pitchfork.

"You still mad I'm taking care of the flood?" I asked Howie.

"Nah," he said amicably. "I suppose you can use the experience. Being a girl and all."

Chapter Thirteen

I restrained myself from throwing my pitchfork at Howie, and we got the stalls cleaned out in relative peace. I soon exchanged my pitchfork for the broom, and grabbed the lime.

"Thanks for helping out, Howie. I wish you could've slept, instead."

He made grumbling noises, but I was pretty sure he'd missed milking the night before and was glad to get back in the parlor again. He probably also felt guilty that Gus had died while he was off getting stitches, and wanted to do some penance. For myself, Howie was a heck of a lot better company than Miss Fancy Pants.

"You calling the cops about the water?" Howie asked.

"I don't think it was Them. We would've heard something last night. I think it really was just the pipe."

He was silent, sweeping rhythmically.

"You think I should?"

"What?"

"Call the cops."

"You maybe want to at least mention it to Willard when he calls."

"Okay, I will." I felt my shoulders seizing, and stopped sweeping. "God, Howie, what are we doing? We're going on like everything's normal, but it just isn't. How do we know they're not out there right now planning something else?"

He propped his broom against the wall and mopped his forehead with a handkerchief. When he glanced up at me, his face looked old.

"What can we do, Princess? We can't afford professional protection. We can't hardly pay ourselves. Although we're somehow finding money for the eye candy working on the heifer barn."

I felt my face flush. "He's tons cheaper than security, and you know it."

He continued, ignoring me. "We stay in touch with the cops, take turns guarding at night, and keep our eyes open during the day. What else is there?"

I swept another patch. "I thought of asking the Grangers to help guard, but if they're not at their jobs they're sick or taking care of sick kids. I'm not asking them here till I know this new aflatoxin theory is it. Maybe I'll try Bart and Lenny again today."

Howie shoved his hanky back in his pocket. "I'm with you about the Grangers. Bart or Lenny would be great. Scare folks off just by bein' here." He looked like he was going to say more, but didn't.

We were almost done sweeping lime onto the floor when Howie stopped and gave me a forced grin. "Remember you got the co-op dinner tonight."

"Tonight? Since when?"

"Since they sent you that invitation two weeks ago. Don't tell me you forgot." He became more and more amused as I tried to think of excuses I couldn't go.

"You're coming with me, right?" I finally asked.

"Now, Stella, think back a few minutes. Are we really going to leave the farm unattended so I can attend a co-op meeting?"

I stared at him. He just smiled.

"Do I really have to go?" I asked.

"You're the farm owner. It's your responsibility."

"At least tell me it's at a good restaurant."

"Meyer's."

"Well, I guess I'll get something decent to eat…not frou-frou salads and crap like that."

Howie started to whistle along with the radio and ducked the roll of paper towels I grabbed off a shelf and threw at his head.

Co-op meetings were important, but I never liked having to take the time to go. Especially when I've got more pressing business at home.

The co-op is the marketing agent of the dairy farmer—they make sure our milk is picked up and taken where it needs to go. Sometimes the milk from my farm ends up in Florida, if that's where it's needed. Sounds crazy, but that's the way it works. I never have to worry about getting a milk check, and the buyers are getting the amount of milk they need. The best part is I don't need to know anything other than how to farm—the co-op takes care of the rest. They even use direct deposit, so the money appears in my account without me having a chance to mess things up in between the mailbox and the bank.

The co-op meetings, no matter how tedious, tell me where the market has been and where it's going. We, as dairy farmers, actually own the co-op, so it's in our best interest to know where we stand with the government, finances, and marketing. I'd prefer not to deal with any numbers at all, but to be a responsible farmer I at least need to show my face at the meetings.

Howie was just headed out the door when he froze. "Who's that?"

I hadn't heard a car pull up, since Queenie wasn't around to announce it, so I was surprised to see a man standing in the middle of the driveway. He stood by a white Lincoln Continental, staring up at the house. Nick's truck sat to one side of the lane, but he wasn't anywhere in view. I was a little less eager than usual to see him after our intimate conversation the night before.

The guy, a youngish fellow wearing a suit and shiny shoes, held a folded-up umbrella looped around his wrist. Howie and I exchanged glances. Maybe this weirdo had been the one jinxing the weather—we hadn't had rain for at least two weeks. In his hands, the guy had a notepad and pen and was making notes while he looked around.

"Hmm." I laid down my pitchfork and made my way outside, where I leaned against the barn, crossing my arms over my chest. I watched the suit as he casually walked from building to building, making notes and peeking around corners. He didn't look dangerous, but then the last thing we needed was someone casing the place for more ways to wreak havoc.

Nick had appeared at the heifer barn and was now six feet off the ground on a ladder with a hammer and a tool belt. The guy approached him, and we could see him gesture with his pen at the house. Nick looked where the guy was pointing and shrugged, probably explaining he didn't own the place. When the guy had his nose in his notebook, Nick looked my way. I put my finger to my lips and Nick nodded.

Howie soon joined me, and together we watched the guy pick his way around the garage. I could feel Howie's tension as his home was being examined, and it transferred to me when the guy walked up and began looking in my windows.

"Down, girl," Howie whispered. It took a lot of will power to keep myself from running over and grabbing the guy's throat.

After an incredibly stupid eternity, Mister Bad Manners noticed us standing at the barn. He looked over his shoulder, as if hoping for back up, and eventually made his way down to us.

"Miss Crown?" he said. He stuck out his hand. I saw him notice the tattoo on my neck, and could tell he was trying very hard not to stare at it.

"What of it?" I said.

Flustered, he angled his hand toward Howie, who suddenly found something more interesting to look at toward the road.

"Um, Richard Cramer," the guy said. He dropped his hand and dug around in his suit pockets until he came up with a card that he held out to me. I didn't take it, but got a look at it, even though it was shaking ever so slightly.

"Real estate lawyer?" I said. "Do I need one?"

"You've got a lot of money in this farm, Miss Crown. You would be smart to have someone like me on your side going into negotiations."

"Negotiations?"

"For the sale of your property."

I remained completely still except for my left eyebrow, which raised half an inch. Cramer stumbled on.

"I came to offer my services, which I hope...." He stopped and looked at me with growing horror. His Adam's apple bobbed up and down.

"Hubert sent you, didn't he?" I said. I had no doubt—as I had with the dead cows—that this was Hubert's doing.

"Well, uh, he, uh—"

I snapped the card from Cramer's hand and without looking gave it to Howie, who stuck it in his shirt pocket. I put my hands down at my sides and stepped so close to Cramer I could almost feel the sweat spouting from his pores. I leaned over so my mouth was right by his ear. His jugular pounded at the speed of light as he braced himself.

"Hubert Purcell was found in a Dumpster and raised by barn cats," I said.

I stood back and Cramer looked at me like I was a lunatic. I smiled and waited a few moments until he felt comfortable enough to give me a wavering smile in return.

Still smiling, I said, "You tell Hubert Purcell that the next person he sends onto my farm is going to return with a backside that's become very familiar with my twenty-two."

Cramer's smile froze.

"Think you can give him that message?"

Cramer nodded.

"Then you can leave."

Cramer swallowed and stumbled over his feet, backing all the way to his car. The Lincoln didn't start on the first try and Cramer put his head down and closed his eyes until it finally did. I think he was praying.

Chapter Fourteen

A woman answered at the Biker Barn.

"Where's Bart?" I asked. "He's not sick, is he?"

"No. Him and Lenny are in Jersey at a swap meet till tomorrow morning."

Great. Guess they wouldn't be helping to guard my farm.

"You want I should give them a message?" she asked.

"No, thanks. I'll call tomorrow." When Howie and I were the walking dead and wouldn't be able to stay awake another night.

I was in the middle of supposedly doing paperwork in my office after a few hours of scraping wet straw out of the barn and watching Jethro fix the pipe, but in actuality I was cursing the day Hubert—or any developer, for that matter—was born. So he wasn't sabotaging my farm. He was still a pain in the ass. I hung up the phone and was staring at the new aerial photo on my wall when I heard someone come in.

"That better not be you, Hubert," I said, "or my lunch menu just got bigger."

"Sounds inviting," Nick said.

I spun my chair around and took in the view. "I hope you're not here to ask more deep, dark secrets."

"Nothing so interesting. I just wanted to know how you'd like to work things with supplies. Should I get things on my own and bill you at the end, or do you have a tab somewhere?"

"Tab. Go to Schlectic's, down the pike. Little mom and pop store. They'll have paint and whatever else you need."

He jutted his chin at the photograph. "That new? I noticed it when I came by the other day, but it wasn't on the wall yet."

"Yeah, got it on Saturday. My birthday."

"Happy birthday."

"Whatever. I think it's beautiful."

"Your family picture."

I gave him a sharp glance, but he was checking out the photo.

"So where were we last night?" he asked.

I wasn't sure exactly which aspect of the evening he was referring to, so I made a choice and stood to run my finger down the field's irrigation row to somewhere off the picture. "Above the frame, about here." I slid my finger along the wall in a big rectangle. "The whole property would really take up this much space."

He stepped closer, and I could feel his breath on my neck. I pretended to look at something on the photo until I realized he wasn't looking at the photo either, but was running his finger along the lines of my cow skull tattoo. I shivered.

"Sorry," he said.

I turned to go back to my desk, but he didn't move. "Stella, I know we hardly know each other—"

He stopped talking, because I kissed him. I kissed him because I didn't want to hear the rest of what he was going to say. Well, also because I'd been dying to ever since the moment he walked into my office two days before.

"Wow," he said when I broke away. He slid his arms around my waist and kissed me back. Completely and thoroughly. I am far from twenty-nine-and-never-been-kissed, although not as far as I might like. Howie always said my dates—few that they were—were afraid to touch me for fear I might break their legs. I don't know where he got that idea.

Anyway, my back must be connected to my lungs, because Nick's hands were starting to run up and down my spine in a way that made it awfully hard to breathe. I was starting to return the favor when I heard someone calling my name.

"Damn," I said, and pulled away. "I wish I knew where Queenie was. Our alarm system's gone without her."

"Stella?" the voice said.

"Oh, God." I had just enough time to push Nick away, get to my chair, and smooth out my shirt before Abe was standing in the doorway.

"Hey, Abe," I said, trying not to sound out of breath.

Abe looked from me to Nick, taking in my face—which I'm sure was flushed—and Nick's casual air and wicked smile. Nick was leaning against the filing cabinet, his arms crossed in front of him, looking like nothing so much as a gorgeous kid caught cleaning up the cake.

I compared the two men in front of me—Nick with his Nordic, playboy look, and Abe with his darker, serious one. Complete opposites in every way, as far as I could tell. Except that both made my insides do calisthenics.

"Um, Abe, this is Nick. Nick—Abe."

Abe gave Nick a short nod. Nick continued to smile.

"What's up?" I said.

"Just thought I'd stop by to see what's going on." With this he shot Nick another quick look through narrowed eyes. "And to say thanks for showing Missy the ropes last night."

"She okay? Things got a bit messy—in more ways than one."

"She's fine." From his look I could tell she'd told him about our fight. "Where's Queenie? She didn't meet my car."

I felt a twinge in my temple. "I don't know. I wish I did."

He looked at me, concerned. "I hear Jethro was out here today."

"Exciting news travels fast."

"He get everything fixed up?"

"Good as new."

We stared at each other for a few moments before he spoke again. "You talk to Zach today?"

"I've stayed away—I'm not his favorite person right now."

Abe nodded. "He's pretty upset." He stood there, apparently not quite sure what else to say.

I steepled my hands in front of my face, resting my elbows on the desk. "So did you stop by *hoping* to make me feel more guilty? Gee, thanks a lot."

"No, I...." He eyes flicked to Nick, then back to me. "I was wondering if you wanted to go out for ice cream tonight. Catch up."

I hesitated. The idea of having some time alone with Abe sounded great. But we probably wouldn't be alone. Abe's new *girlfriend* would probably be there.

"We'd love that, Abe," I finally said, "but there's a co-op dinner. Nick and I probably won't be back until late."

"Oh." He looked at Nick one more time. "I guess you've got plans then."

Nick kept on smiling, going along with my story, thank God.

Abe's face hardened and he pulled his car keys out of his pocket. "I'll get going, then. I can see you're in the middle of something."

He caught my eye for a long, searching gaze, and was gone before I could think of anything else to say.

Silence descended for a moment before I spun my chair toward Nick.

"So. Want to go to a dinner?"

Chapter Fifteen

I spent a long hour driving around after Abe left, again hoping I wouldn't find Queenie lying alongside the road, but praying I'd catch a glimpse of her somewhere. No luck. My head had begun to throb like I hadn't gotten enough sleep. Then I remembered I hadn't.

I arrived back at the house at the same time Detective Willard was pulling out. He stopped his car beside my truck and I opened my window. I was surprised to see Pam Moyer in the passenger seat. She looked tired and a little green. I wondered if that was from working through the night with the doctors, worrying about her dad, or if she was coming down with the aflatoxin sickness herself.

"Sorry about the calf," Willard said. "You get my message last night?"

"Yeah. I'm not quite sure how to feel about it. You're sure Hubert couldn't have been involved any other way?"

"You mean like hire somebody?"

I shrugged.

"I checked him out pretty well," Willard said. "No past history of violence. Sticks to the law as far as I can tell. Really has never had any trouble. Sonny Turner tells me Hubert's got enough on his plate these days, with zoning hearings and building permits, the last thing he needs is another land purchase."

Pam and I glanced at each other. We both knew full well Hubert would take whatever land he could get his slimy little hands on.

I leaned into the window. "So, Pam, what're you doing with the detective here? I talked to your dad this morning and he thought you were with the Department of Health people."

"Yeah, I was, but they finally kicked me out since I'm not official. The CDC's here, too, so they really don't need extra people hanging around. Sonny suggested I take a ride with the detective today, see what he does."

"What for?"

Willard chuckled. "The Town Council president oversees the police department. At least, we're accountable to him."

"But—"

"And it looks to me like Sonny wants Pam here to take over when he retires. I think he was just waiting for someone like her to come along."

I raised my eyebrows at Pam and she blushed, adding red to her face's greenish tinge and making her skin an interesting puce color. "I'm not quite sure what they see in me, but it sounds like a job I'd be interested in. Be a good platform to help farmers."

"Sure would."

She closed her eyes and swallowed. I hoped she wasn't going to heave right there onto her pants.

She opened her eyes. "Sorry about your calf. Is it the one from the other morning?"

"Yeah. The one we'd just done a C-section for. And I'm sorry to hear about the Bergeys. I don't suppose your dad's figured out yet how to replace the land?"

She shook her head slowly. "Nothing around to replace it with. I guess he'll just have to be happy with his own eighty."

Which wouldn't be enough to keep him safe from foreclosure. And we all knew it.

I looked back at Willard. "See anything back there at the hutches that might help us catch the guy?"

"Nothing to see. No fingerprints I could find, anyway. And not much else to go on."

Damn. "Hope it didn't matter we went ahead and buried him."

"Nah. Not much I could've seen from that, probably."

I took in his sunken eyes and decided not to complain about Officer Meadows' inference that I was making things up. "Your boy any better since they figured out this aflatoxin thing?"

Pam made a sympathetic sound and shook her head, putting her fingers to her mouth.

"Maybe a bit," Willard said. "I'm hoping." He didn't sound convinced.

"So the Department of Health has helped already, huh?" I said. "By finding the aflatoxin?"

Pam made a face. "Actually, the county coroner did the autopsy and discovered the fungus trace. Nobody expected to find *that*."

"That's why I called you this morning. Does what they're saying make any sense? Kids are getting sick because of something they ate?"

She stared out the windshield for a moment. "Unfortunately, it's probably true. Now everybody's working like mad to find the source of it."

"Well, good luck to them." I turned back to Willard. "Thanks for coming out."

"Sure. Your farmhand told me about the water problem. I took a look at it, but didn't see anything."

"I'm pretty sure it was natural causes."

"That's what he said." He paused. "Wish there was more I could do." He started to roll up his window. "I hope I don't hear from you about any new problems. I'll let you know as soon as we come up with something."

"Thanks. See ya, Pam."

She gave a weak smile and nodded.

They eased away, swerving around Wayne, who was waiting at the end of the lane in the milk truck. I hoped Pam made it to their next stop before puking.

Wayne drove up, parked, and stepped down from the cab. Exhaustion was apparent in his every move.

"Ma'am," he said, not quite meeting my eyes.

"Wayne. It's all there for ya. Need any help?"

"I think I can handle it. Although it has only been ten years I've been hauling your milk."

"Guess I can trust you, then."

"I should think so."

I tilted my head, studying him. "You all right? You don't look so good."

He fidgeted, then thrust his hands into his pockets. A sheen of sweat shone on his forehead.

"God, Wayne. You're not getting sick, are you?"

He gave me a strange look. "No, no. It's Flo."

"Your wife?"

"She…she's got MS, you know."

That's right. "She okay?"

He swallowed. "Having a few problems. Nothing we can't fix, I don't think."

"Hope you get it taken care of soon."

He gave me a smile that didn't reach his eyes. "Thanks. Appreciate it."

"Go to it, then. And have a good lunch." He had to be hungry, since we were the last stop of his busy morning run.

I left him and was standing at the kitchen sink wolfing down an apple—imported from North Carolina—and a PB&J when Carla drove up the drive. I brushed my hands off, washed my food down with water from the sink, and went out to join her.

"Where's your greeter?" she asked, looking around for Queenie.

"I wish I knew. I haven't seen her since yesterday."

Carla watched me steadily. She knows how much Queenie means to me—knows how much *anybody's* dog means to them—and I could see the fears written on her face. She'd told me before that dogs often go off when they know they're going to die, in order to find a quiet place to do it. She also knew I'd had a cow murdered just a couple days before. I looked away.

"What can I help carry?" I asked.

"Nothing, Stella. You know the drill."

Each month Carla comes for a monthly herd inspection. She checks for pregnancies, doles out medicine, and looks at any problems I point out to her. It takes time, but it's worth it to know everything is as it should be.

As it should be. Didn't I wish.

I jogged to my office, grabbed a folder that had seen better days and threatened to spill its load should I give it half a chance, and got back to Carla's truck. I sat on the bumper and watched while she pulled on her "check-up gear," which consists of coveralls, the same biceps-high gloves she'd used for the C-section and autopsy, and high rubber boots.

I smiled to myself, watching her dress. Carla is my exact opposite. She is small and round and soft in all the places a woman should be, plus a few more. She says if God had meant her to be thin, she wouldn't have been born with a craving for dairy products—pure dairy, that is. To her, skim milk is un-holy water, frozen yogurt is sinful, and non-fat cheese is an abomination in the eyes of the Lord. Carla is very religious about her fat.

She suddenly froze, her eyes catching on something. "Am I on my way to heaven, or is there really a man of unlimited beauty walking this way?"

"You ain't dying, sister," I said. "Your eyes are seeing true."

"How long have you been keeping this a secret? Here I've been taking another long look at my same old Abs of Iron calendar."

I laughed. "Sorry, Carla. He was covered up when you were here yesterday. You're welcome to come and observe any time."

She waggled her eyebrows, but behaved herself once Nick reached us.

"I'm off for the afternoon," he said. "What time should I be here for dinner?"

I could sense Carla looking at me and hoped I didn't betray any discomfort. "Five-thirty, I guess. Dinner starts at six, boring speeches at seven."

"I'll bring a book to read." He smiled and looked at Carla, who showed him her teeth in return.

"Sorry," I said. "Carla, this is Nick Hathaway. Nick, Doctor Carla Beaumont—she keeps my cows happy and healthy."

They shook hands, which Carla enjoyed entirely too much, and made all of the appropriate "glad to meet you" noises.

Looking at Nick, I made a sudden decision. "Can I ask a favor, Nick?"

"Sure, what do you need?"

"Howie and I have to go to a funeral this afternoon, and we'd appreciate it if you could hang around for a couple of hours after lunch. Keep an eye on the place."

I could feel Carla's eyes boring into me, and Nick looked at me in confusion.

"What do you mean?"

I wondered how much I should say. "Somebody's been playing pranks on us and it's gotten out of hand. I hate to leave the place unguarded."

He looked at his watch. "Sure, I guess I can do that. What time do you need me?"

"Say, two-ish? The funeral's at two-thirty."

"No problem. See you then."

Carla and I both kept a close watch as he walked to his truck, got in it, and drive off.

"You sure know how to pick 'em, girl," Carla said.

"The good Lord planted him in my path."

"Well, then, praise God." She turned to me. "Should I ask about the 'pranks,' or was that just your way of not telling him you had a cow murdered?"

"Make that two cows, and a messed up manure lagoon."

"Two? You didn't call me about the second."

"No need to. He was hanged in his hutch."

"Oh, no. Not Zach's calf?"

"'Fraid so."

"But that hardly ever happens."

"Bingo."

"Good lord," she said. "What kind of creep would do something like that? How are you handling the threat?"

I told her about the cops and keeping the lights on at night, along with Howie and me taking shifts, and our false hope that we'd gotten Hubert into a corner. She shook her head, understanding more than most how vulnerable we were. "Let me know if I can help somehow, but I wouldn't be too good at guard duty. I'd fall asleep on my shift." She finished pulling up the zipper of her coveralls and picked up her tool kit. When she stood, she suddenly took a deep breath and leaned on the truck, setting her kit back on the ground and resting her head on her arm.

"You okay?" I asked, stepping toward her.

She held up a hand. "I'll be fine. I'm still fighting this cold, and I've been getting these head rushes."

"You're sure it's not this aflatoxin thing?"

"I don't eat fresh vegetables. You know I'm a closet non-vegetarian."

"You pregnant?"

"If I am, I'll start a new Church of Immaculate Conception." She straightened up, her face starting to regain its color. "Where to, boss?"

"If you're sure...."

"I'm sure."

"Okay. Let's start out with the possibly pregnant cows. I want to know how many actually took."

I looked in my folder to see how many cows Carla had hopefully impregnated last month. That's not as kinky as it sounds, believe me. Carla uses a long tube that looks kind of like a turkey baster, and—forgive me—sticks it up the cow's vagina and forces sperm to the hopefully awaiting egg. A few days before that I give the cows a hormone called Prosta, which puts them in heat.

Not as fun as the typical way of getting pregnant, but the odds are a lot better.

Artificial insemination is a big thing in farming these days, just like genetically modified foods. You get to pick from a bank of semen after seeing which DNA fits your needs. Need milk with higher milkfat content? Choose semen from a bull who's had offspring with it. Need wider hips? More milk production? You got a problem, you try to fix it with good genes. Some might say we're playing God, but those folks aren't trying to make a living by farming.

Carla had her hand up the back end of a cow when Wayne stuck his head around the corner.

"I'll see ya, Stella. All done for today."

"Great. Tell Flo to feel better soon."

His eyes teared up and he looked away. "I'll tell her. Thanks."

"Isn't he usually much more cheerful?" Carla asked when he'd left.

"Yeah. But his wife's sick. Sicker than usual, I mean. She's got MS. Anyway, he has a right to be crabby since he hasn't had lunch."

"That's just because *you're* crabby when you haven't had lunch."

"Gee, thanks."

Carla grinned and pulled her arm out of the cow. "Preggers. That's how many now? Four?"

"Five. Five out of seven ain't bad. And that's the last one."

"But I was having so much fun."

"That's life."

"Well, if I can't do that any more, I want to see the cow I cut the calf out of the other day." She looked suddenly sad, and we both took a moment to wish Gus was still alive.

On our way to the barn we saw Howie and Wayne talking by the tank truck. Wayne was shaking his head, his hand on the truck door, and Howie didn't look too happy. I wondered if I should see what the problem was, but Carla had already headed into the barn, so I followed. I found her standing beside Wendy.

"Healing up nicely," she said, giving the cow a pat.

I grunted. "At least she can do something right."

Carla stretched her back. "Got anything else?"

"A sore foot, and a couple that are way pregnant."

Carla checked on the soon-to-be-mamas and said they were doing just fine and should have their babies in two weeks or less. This may not seem like a long time, but it sounded way too long to me, seeing as how I can't milk them at all once they're seven months into their nine of gestation.

"Any trouble with the newly freshened cows?" Carla asked. She was referring to the mamas of the two calves who had been Gus' neighbors in the hutches.

"They're fine. Howie moved the calves to an empty storage room in the heifer barn last night, just to be safe. They join the yearlings today."

"Great. Just show me that foot yet."

I took her to where Howie had tied the lame cow, and she checked the problem hoof.

"Yup, exactly what I thought. It's an abscess. Here, give me a hand."

Together we pulled the foot up with a rope tied around the ankle and slung over a beam above the cow. Carla got the foot between her knees and started shaving away layers of hoof. I held onto the end of the rope so the foot wouldn't move.

"So what's this about dinner with the hunk, Stella?"

I sighed. I had known she wouldn't let it go. "Howie can't go to the co-op meeting tonight, so I asked Nick to go. No big deal."

She paused and looked up at me, studying my face, and then went back to the hoof. "What about Abe?"

"What about him?"

"Ah, there we are. Look at that beautiful infection."

"I have never understood your obsession with pus." I watched the white mess ooze out of the foot.

"That means I got to the heart of it. Here. Hand me that bottle. No, the one with the copper top. Thanks."

She sprayed the cleaned-out foot and unstraddled the hoof.

"You know what about him," she said, going back to Abe.

"He came home with Miss Macy's. That should end any further speculation on your part."

"Whatever you say." She packed up her bag. "That it? If so, I'm going to go grab some lunch."

"If you don't want more than a PB&J you can eat here."

She considered that for about a nano-second. "Sorry, babe. I'm going to enjoy my lunch—not cram it down like you do."

We were walking out to her truck when Marty Hoffman pulled up in his truck. Once again, no Queenie to bark at the tires.

"Hey, Hoffman," I said. "What's up?" It had been just the day before I'd seen him at the Derstines', and I hoped he didn't have bad news. It was unusual for him to drop by in the middle of a work day.

He stepped out of his truck and hitched up his jeans. In his fifties, Marty had yet to gather the love handles most men his age acquire. Therefore, he had trouble keeping up his pants, and he refused, for some reason, to wear suspenders.

"Rochelle made some apple pies this morning," Marty said. "Thought you might like one."

I breathed a quick sigh of relief that it was just a neighborly call, and could see Carla eyeing the pie he held out.

"Thanks, Marty," I said. "That's really nice. Be sure to tell Rochelle it'll probably be gone today. Before Carla leaves, in fact."

Instead of denying it, Carla asked, "Do you have vanilla ice cream?"

Marty laughed, hitched up his pants again, and climbed back in his truck. He leaned out the window. "You going to the co-op dinner tonight?"

"Yeah."

"Then you can thank Rochelle for the pie in person. We'll try to sit with you."

"That would save the evening."

We waved as he drove off. I wondered if he'd be at Toby's funeral, too, but hadn't wanted to bring it up.

"So, do ya have ice cream?" Carla asked. "It doesn't matter if it's not Breyers."

Chapter Sixteen

After Carla, Howie, and I had demolished most of the pie, I tried calling Jude again. This time someone picked up.

"Hey, Marianne, it's Stella. Jude around?"

"No. He's at the welding shop. The guys think they know what happened to the combine."

"Sorry about that."

"Yeah. Well."

I waited for her to say more, but she didn't.

"I guess you could tell me," I said. "Has Jude been working in the field at nights?"

"No. He doesn't like to. Why?"

"Someone saw lights in the west field the other night. I didn't think it would be Jude, but I don't know who else it would've been."

She was quiet for a moment. "I can't help you with that."

"That's all right. Could you have Jude give me a call if he has any idea who it was?"

"Sure. I'll ask him."

I hesitated, not sure if I should say anything about her being at a fertility clinic the day before, and decided I'd better not. I didn't want to get Jethro into hot water. So I simply said good-bye.

Instead of hanging up, I punched the flash key and dialed the metal shop. Jermaine answered.

"Granger's."

"Hey, Jermaine."

"Oh, hi, Marianne. Jude's here. Want me to get him?"

"Jermaine, it's Stella."

"Oh, sorry. Jude's expecting Marianne to call. Your mower break again? Your pipes burst? Or maybe it's your truck decided to conk out."

"Ha ha. What's up with Jude's combine?"

"Fried. Found two nice little holes in the air cleaner."

I groaned. I knew what damage that could do—the smallest of holes would allow dust and grit and all sorts of nasty things into the cylinder and do its best sandpaper imitation on the delicate innards. This would wear the rings, which in turn would cause the combine to lose compression and burn oil, causing power loss. The dirt would also get into the engine oil and cause bearing failure. If you don't understand any of that, it doesn't matter. All you need to know is that Jude's combine was completely and expensively screwed.

"So where's Jude now?" I asked.

"On the phone with his insurance agent."

"Lost cause."

"You're telling me. His agent won't touch it with her ten-foot Chrysler."

"Tell him he can use my tractor and pull-type combine if he wants. I told him, but I don't think it registered."

"Will do."

I hung up and shook my head. Poor Jude. I didn't know what kind of financial situation he and Marianne were in, but the last thing any farmer needs is for his most important machine to crap out on him in the middle of oat harvest.

For the next half-hour I looked around the farm for Queenie, calling her name and checking all of her old hiding places. I walked out into the fields around the house in case she'd gotten caught somewhere, and looked up and down the road. No luck. I was feeling desperate, but didn't know what else to do. If the person who killed Cleopatra had Queenie, there was no way to find her. I just couldn't make myself believe the teen-agers I'd turned down for jobs would stoop to animal abuse as revenge. They could always get a job bagging at the grocery store. And since Hubert was now just a remote possibility, I was completely stumped as to who else might have a motive.

On my way back to the house to change for the funeral I caught up with Howie, who was standing at the door of the yearling pen, observing while the two new calves insinuated themselves into the group.

"You about ready to head to Toby's funeral?" I asked.

He shook his head, not looking at me. "Figured one of us better stay here."

"I took care of that already."

He looked at me, and I caught my breath at the expression of sadness on his face.

"You okay?" I asked.

He turned back to the calves. "I'm not sure. I— What do you mean you took care of it?"

"Nick's going to come while we're gone."

He gave a glance toward our big barn, then rubbed his eyes. "A stranger's gonna protect our farm?"

"No more of a stranger than an expensive security guard."

"I don't know—"

"It's just for an hour or two. In the middle of the day."

"Gus got killed in the middle of the day."

"I know. But I can't imagine they'll try that again. You want to tell me what's wrong?"

He watched the two calves for another minute. "I'll meet you out front in a bit."

So he wasn't going to tell me. Since he was as hardheaded as me, I let it go.

I was waiting on the side steps in clean clothes when Nick pulled in and parked in his usual spot. He came sauntering over in his work clothes, and I tried not to stare. I still hadn't gotten used to how good he looked walking around my property.

"You ready to play farm-sitter?" I asked.

"Sure. Figured I'd get a little work in, too, if that's okay."

"Great. I just want these jerks to see someone around so they don't try anything else."

"Like kill another cow?"

I looked at him. "How'd you know they did that?"

He shrugged. "Didn't think electrocution or a calf getting hung were usual things. And if it was just something like soaping your windows you wouldn't have these new stress lines in between your eyebrows." He reached a hand out and touched my forehead, making me shiver.

Howie came down his steps and frowned when he saw us. I stood up, and Nick took his hand away.

"Thanks," I said. "I wish I didn't have to go to this, but...."

"I know. I've been there, too."

I was about to ask for details when Howie blew his horn. I waved at him, irritated.

"Well," Nick said. "See you in an hour or so."

I trotted over to Howie's truck and got in the passenger side. "Was that absolutely necessary? I was on the verge of learning an actual fact about Nick's life."

Howie grunted and started down the lane. "Didn't think you cared about his life. Just his pretty ass."

I studied Howie's stern expression. "Just how shallow do you think I am?"

His lips twitched. "Just shallow enough to enjoy the resident stud muffin."

"You got it." I tried to believe it, but something niggled at my insides. Nick was a gorgeous addition to farm life, but if I wasn't careful, he'd soon be more than that. An image of Abe flickered through my mind, and I pushed it aside. If I thought about him, I might as well think about Missy, too. No thanks.

The parking lot was packed when we got to the little Mennonite church, and we had to leave the truck in the grass next to the blacktop. We weren't the first ones to make our own spaces, and if the vehicles were any indication, the sanctuary was going to be packed. I looked around the lot for familiar cars and couldn't help seeing a Town Car taking up more than its fair share of space, the CHP logo looking as gauche as always. Hubert better not try to talk to me, I thought, or I'd have to smack him for his pathetic lawyer stunt.

Howie and I squeezed into the foyer of the church, wondering what the hold-up was.

"Oh, crap," I said. "I didn't even think about viewing hours."

The line we found ourselves following led to Tom and Claire, who stood by the tiniest coffin I'd ever seen. My stomach rumbled, and I looked at Howie. "We need to do this part?"

His expression was stony, and again I saw a deep sadness sweep across his face before he covered it. "It's a show of support. You don't have to look at Toby if you don't want to."

I didn't want to, but when we got to the head of the line twenty minutes later, my eyes were drawn to him. I reached out to touch his hand, and images flashed through my mind of the little guy giving me a thumbs-up from his front window as I rode by on my bike. Damn it, sweet kids weren't supposed to die this way.

"Stella, thanks for coming," Tom said. His handshake was firm, but his eyes were bloodshot, and I guessed he hadn't had more than a couple hours of sleep in the past few days.

Claire gave me a blank look, her eyes glassed over. Her skin was pasty and puffy, and I wasn't sure whether or not to put out my hand. I did, but when she didn't reach for it, I let it drop.

By the time Howie and I made it to the sanctuary, every seat was filled. We found a few feet of wall space in the back, and took it. I scanned the crowd and caught glimpses of some familiar faces. Marty and Rochelle Hoffman sat about halfway up, squished between folks I didn't know. Some of the other homeowners from my stretch of road were sprinkled amongst the crowd, and I saw a couple of the Grangers—Jethro and Belle, and Jordan. Two rows ahead of them sat Ma, a serene look on her face, eyes closed. Probably praying.

Beside Ma sat Abe, and he suddenly turned as if he'd felt my eyes on him. We stared at each other for a few seconds, till I realized his arm was around the back of the pew, and nestled into the crook of it was Missy. He looked down at his elbow, his face registering something—embarrassment?—then back at me. Feeling a little sick, I turned my attention toward the front of the church, where Toby's casket was being wheeled. The service was starting almost a half-hour late.

The funeral wasn't at all what I expected. I'd been afraid Howie and I would find ourselves surrounded by sobbing women and children, but was surprised to find the tone of the service more hopeful than tragic. Women cried some silent tears, as did some of the men, but the children who were present looked more interested than mournful. Posters adorned the walls, drawings of playgrounds and suns, and a photo of a smiling Toby sat on top of his now-closed casket. My throat tightened, and I had to just listen through the hymns that were sung.

Music over, the church's minister said a few words, then introduced Sonny Turner. I looked where Sonny was getting up, all decked out in suit and tie, and was able to see Pam squeezed into the bench beside him. She didn't look green anymore. Now her face was red and puffy, like she'd been crying. It wouldn't have taken too much for me to break down, either.

Sonny spoke the usual platitudes, offering the family sympathy and brotherhood, then gave a little pep talk about how the culprit of the sickness had been found, thanks to Toby's sacrifice. I was sure all the other parents in the room were feeling more than a little guilt, and a whole lot of relief, that their children had been spared. I even saw Jethro give Belle a tight smile and squeeze her shoulders with his arm.

I couldn't help but think everybody was jumping the gun. I hadn't heard yet about anybody's kids actually getting better. Until I heard good news, I was going to expect the worst.

When the service was over, a few speakers and a couple songs later, Howie turned to me. "You want to stay to talk to anybody?"

I thought of Ma, but figured I'd have to endure Missy and Abe's closeness at the same time. I also didn't want to chance running into Hubert, who I hadn't yet spotted in the packed room. "Let's go home."

Not so simple. The crowd was crammed into the little church, and movement toward the door was painstaking. I was taking shuffling steps, people pressed all around me, when the claustrophobic feeling I'd had at the Derstines came rushing back. Howie was now three people in front of me, and I couldn't reach him to grab his elbow and gain some stability. Panic edged into my breathing, and I fought back toward the wall. I finally reached it and was pressing my forehead against it, glad to find something solid, when an arm went around my waist.

"Come on, Stella." Abe used his other arm to block for me, and we pushed our way across the wall to the door. As soon as we were in the foyer the crowd thinned out, but Abe stayed by me and got me outside. He led me down the steps and to the side, where I was finally able to take a few deep breaths. His arm was still around my waist, and he kept it there while he put his other hand on my cheek and gently turned my face toward him.

"You all right?"

I took another shaky breath. "Yeah. I'm not sure what happened in there. Not enough space, I guess."

"You're not getting sick?"

"No. No, I don't think so."

We stood silently, inches apart, his hand on my face. My breath went shallow again, and the lightheadedness returned.

"Stella," he finally said, "are you—" He looked over my shoulder and suddenly dropped his arms. "Hey, Missy. Lost you in there."

She looked from him to me. "Yeah. I guess so."

I took a deep breath and thankfully felt my steadiness returning. Fainting in front of Missy was the last thing I needed.

Howie sauntered up and completed our little circle. "You ready, Princess?" His expression said he knew I needed to get away.

"Ready." I turned to Abe to say thanks, but Missy had already regained his attention, and I felt like a third wheel. "Let's go."

We were walking toward the truck when I noticed Detective Willard leaning against his car at the far side of the parking lot, scanning faces as people passed.

"Hang on a sec," I said to Howie. He followed me as I made my way down the row toward the Caprice Classic. Willard looked awful. Worse than even that morning when he'd stopped by the farm.

"Oh, hell," I said, and quickened my pace. Willard looked at me when I reached him, and I knew my instinct was right. "Not your son?" I asked.

Willard shook his head slowly. "Boy in the next bed."

"When?"

"About two hours ago."

Howie looked from me to Willard. "What are you talking about?"

"He died, Mr. Archer. Another child has died."

Chapter Seventeen

"How am I supposed to sit through a ridiculous, boring meeting when I'm terrified Zach might die? Or Mallory? Or any of the rest of them?"

Howie sat silent behind the wheel of the truck. We were in our driveway, watching Nick pack up his stuff. Wishing Queenie was there, barking at the tires.

"What are you going to do if you stay here?" he said. "Helping me milk won't make any difference to those kids." His voice cracked, and he looked away.

I knew he was right, but I felt so useless, just waiting for another child to die. A child I loved like family. After getting the news from Willard I had found Jethro in the mass of people and insisted he tell me Zach's condition. The same, he'd said, as before. No better, no worse.

Not good enough.

"What are you going to do, Princess?" Howie asked again. "You're not a doctor."

I hit the dashboard. "I don't know, dammit."

Nick got his stuff stashed in his truck and was making his way toward us. I opened my door and got out.

"I'm going to go change," he said. "Five-thirty?"

I stared at him, my mind whirling. Howie was right, of course. I had no way of curing those sick kids. I was as useless to them as I had been to poor Gus.

"You still want me to go?" Nick asked.

I tried to smile. "Yes. Five-thirty." I glanced at Howie, but he was busy getting out of the truck. "Everything quiet while we were gone?" I asked Nick.

"As quiet as drying paint."

He was soon gone, and Howie was off to clean out the heifer barn. I stood in the driveway, frustrated and frightened, then finally walked toward my office where I intended to do the bookkeeping I'd ignored that morning. As I went, I remembered Howie and Wayne talking by the milk truck, and wondered if that had anything to do with Howie's somber mood. I almost changed course to go ask him, but decided it could wait. If he really wanted to talk about it, he'd find me.

I spent the next few minutes trying to forget about Zach and my vulnerable farm by paying bills, but by the time the computer spreadsheets came up, I realized I was trying to escape one kind of vulnerability by studying another. Even without balancing the checkbook I knew that if unexpected expenses came up anytime soon, I'd have to look at yet another loan to cover the ones I already had. Not for the first time, I regretted my adolescent impulse to hire Nick.

I closed out the financial files and went on-line, knowing if I didn't at least think about the aflatoxin problem, I'd drive myself crazy wondering what was going on.

Aflatoxin came up with so many Google hits I wasn't sure where to start. I clicked on the first few and read about the problem fungus in peanuts—all kinds of nuts, really—hay, corn, cottonseed, you name it. Most of the research findings were about sick animals, and since animals weren't the ones dying, it seemed irrelevant.

I found one article that mentioned an antidote to aflatoxin poisoning. N-acetylecisteine. No wonder Jethro couldn't remember the name.

I clicked on another site. And froze. This site stated that a group of terrorists had admitted to experimenting with aflatoxin as biological warfare. They had gone so far as to fill several warheads with the toxin. The site's experts couldn't understand why the terrorists had used this fungus when its effects were so long-term—liver damage, cancer, kidney malfunction. There was a chart showing how much aflatoxin would have to be taken in for immediate reactions, and the amount was ridiculous. The dose would have to be huge, and I knew no terrorists had dropped a bomb on our little burg recently.

The symptoms of long-term aflatoxin ingestion included everything the locals had suffered—nausea, headaches, rashes. And they had found the substance in Toby Derstine's intestines. If I was reading everything correctly, that meant people in our town were being exposed to the poison over an extended period of time, rather than in one big dose. What did that mean?

There were two options: either aflatoxin had found a nearby place to thrive and was infiltrating people's bodies somehow, or someone was poisoning people on purpose. I shook my head. The idea of terrorists targeting our town was crazy. We had no major industry and no government power to speak of. We were just a little hometown, a peaceful kind of place.

I heard a clank from the milking parlor and glanced at the clock. I was surprised to see it was almost five. Nick was going to arrive in half an hour and I wanted to be ready to go. It wouldn't feel right to have him sitting downstairs waiting while I was upstairs naked in the shower. I had put on clean clothes for the funeral, but felt like I needed to actually wash up before going on a date. If you could call a co-op dinner a date. I turned off the computer and office lights, and shut the door behind me.

"Ready to go get pretty?" Howie said. He was in the feed room of the parlor, filling up the grain wagon and opening some hay bales to get ready for milking. "That'll be a welcome change."

"Shove it, buster," I said.

He grunted, but didn't say anything more. I stopped in the doorway. "Come on, Howie. Something's bugging you. Something from before the second boy died. Want to talk about it?"

He concentrated on getting a stalk of hay out of his boot, then said, "What? Oh, sorry. This hay is just so much more interesting than you."

So he was going to play that game. Fine.

"At least I have a date while you're stuck here on the farm," I said.

"Yeah. I feel sorry for the guy already."

I blew him a kiss and went into the house, shedding my clothes as I walked by the washer. I dropped them in and walked in the buff up the stairs to the bathroom. Exactly why I could never see myself wanting a roommate.

I was grabbing a towel when my eye caught on the only pink thing in my whole house. The fancy gift bag that came from Abe and Missy sat in the corner where I had stashed it after my birthday party. I eyed it with something approaching fear, but ended up carrying it with me into the bathroom. I was going on a date—I may as well break all traditions at once and do something feminine.

I would never have admitted it, but the shower gel did smell good, and the fluffy wash thing felt nice. I almost didn't recognize myself once I'd washed, shampooed, shaved my legs, and lotioned all with "Strawberry Dream." Too bad I didn't have long hair I could fling and leave the smell in its wake.

I hunted through my closet for something appropriate to wear, which is harder than it sounds. I have about five pairs of jeans, six flannel shirts, riding boots, farm boots, fancy leather boots with heels and a chain around the ankle, old tennies, and T-shirts. The dress Ma Granger made me for church many years ago—the only dress I've ever owned—was about six sizes too small and boxed up in the attic somewhere, heaven knows why.

I finally settled on a pair of black jeans, a red and black flannel shirt with silver snaps—one of my birthday presents—and my fancy boots. It would have to do. I wasn't sure exactly what had come over me—if I'd had any make-up around, I might have used it.

I did find some lip balm, which gave my mouth a slight shine. I realized this would be gone once I even glanced at the salad, but it was my small attempt at looking remotely girly.

Nick showed up with five minutes to spare, and I was downstairs ready and waiting. My hormones suddenly remembered why I'd hired the man. He looked good enough to eat, or at least lick a lot, in his khakis, blue and tan striped button-down shirt, and loafers. I considered for a moment that we would really clash, but decided it didn't matter. He was the only one I was looking at, and I didn't care what anyone else thought. He held up a dark blue tie.

"Should I wear this?"

I regarded the tie, and realized that if he put it on he would have to button up his shirt and hide his throat.

"No," I said.

Attire question answered, Nick tried to lead me to his truck, but I couldn't stomach the thought of showing up in front of the other farmers in the passenger seat, so I veered off toward my F250 and he followed without complaining. I saw a grin start which he wisely wiped off his face before getting in.

"Still no Queenie?" he asked.

"I don't want to talk about it."

"And your little farmhand's illness?"

"Same answer."

"Okay."

We had just started rolling when Howie stepped into the parlor doorway, looking serious. I waved at him, but he didn't respond. Oh well. If he'd wanted to talk, I'd given him the opening. For now, I'd just assume he was being the father-type, watching his daughter-type go off with another man.

"So I'm to expect nothing but food and boring speeches?" Nick asked.

"You mean at the dinner or after?" I asked, suddenly remembering what Abe had interrupted that afternoon.

Nick smiled and my insides did the little two-step that was becoming familiar.

"I meant the dinner," he said.

"Well, the speeches are the official part of the evening. The fun part—if any part of it is fun—is talking to the other farmers. Marty Hoffman, another dairy farmer, said he and his wife would try to sit with us, which would make the evening go a lot faster."

"Great. Just tell me what to do."

I glanced at him. "Do whatever you want to do."

He shrugged and started to grin again. I ignored him.

"So how's the barn coming?" I asked, after I'd ignored him long enough.

"I should be done power washing tomorrow. I've already started repairs on the front and the east side. I replaced a few rotten boards, closed up a hole where squirrels were getting in, and got rid of a hornets nest—which was no fun, let me tell you. The building's actually in pretty good shape, for an old barn."

"Glad to hear it."

"I should be able to start painting in a few days."

"Great. It'll be nice to have it protected for the winter."

Report given, we were silent the rest of the ride, not sure what to talk about and wanting to avoid the more personal areas we'd stumbled into the night before.

I greeted other farmers as we parked and went in to dinner, and Nick followed, smiling at the appropriate times and saying very little. Conversations swirled around us, most of them about the aflatoxin poisonings. Now that another child had died, no one believed a cure was close at hand, even with the antidote available. The tension was as thick as a good prime rib, but a hell of a lot tougher.

"We know goddamned well it's them terrorists," another farmer said to me. "They're probably poisoning our water. I told Norma to turn off the supply to our house. We ain't even taking a bath unless the water's store-bought."

I nodded my head, wondering if the guy could be right—if extreme—and turned away, just to run into another farmer from across town.

"It's not terrorists. It's airborne. There must be a huge crop of the fungus growing somewhere, and the wind is transporting it. That's why it's just our town. Air can only carry it so far."

Nick and I finally got to the dining hall, what appetite I'd had now completely gone. I spotted Marty and Rochelle across the room and headed toward them. Rochelle saw me coming and gave a little smile and a wave.

Rochelle is one of those women who naturally exude warmth and hospitality. I could feel it even as we walked toward her. Her silver hair was brushed into what for her was as neat as it got, and her lavender dress looked at home on her short, stocky body. She was an attractive woman, and Marty had often said so within her hearing, which—although nauseating at times—was pretty sweet.

"Hey, Stella." Pam stood at my elbow.

"Hey, Doctor Moyer."

She looked pained. "Oh, please...."

"Just a joke. You okay?"

She didn't look okay. Her eyes were bloodshot, and veins showed through her skin she was so pale. "You're not getting this sickness, are you?"

She blinked. "No, no, I'm sure it's not that. I just haven't been getting much sleep with all that's going on. Sonny's working me overtime, trying to get me on board with everything. And I've been helping Dad on the farm. God, I don't know how he's been doing it all by himself." Her face tightened. "And would you believe a real estate lawyer stopped by today, just to 'offer his services'?" She ran a hand over her eyes. "After the fiasco with the Bergeys, I thought Dad was going to have a stroke."

"Realtor came to my place this morning, too," I said. "Hubert sent him. Skinny guy with an umbrella?"

She shook her head. "Short guy with a goatee."

Blood pounded in my ears. It looked like Hubert had planned the lawyer attack carefully, sending them at the same time so we couldn't warn each other.

"So what's your agenda here?" I asked Pam. "Seeing how you're not dairy."

She shrugged. "Part of my town council thing. Sonny hooked me up with Robert Rockefeller. You know, the owner of Rockefeller Dairy?"

"Sure. Nice man." I grinned. "Rich man. And a widower."

She slapped my arm. "He's also old enough to be my father." Her face sagged. "And my dad's seeming really old these days."

We stood quietly for a moment.

"Have you thought about taking over the farm?" I finally asked.

She didn't answer, because she was looking behind me with interest. I glanced over my shoulder, then pulled Nick up beside me. The farmer he'd been chatting with drifted away.

"Nick," I said. "This is Pam Moyer, an old friend from school days. Pam, Nick Hathaway. He's painting my heifer barn."

They shook hands, and the defeated light in Pam's eyes diminished for just a moment.

I suddenly noticed we were about the only ones standing. "Guess we'll find our seats, Pam. See you later."

She waved and headed toward Rockefeller's table.

Marty and Rochelle had saved two seats at their four-person table, and admitted surprise that I'd showed up with Nick. Marty was more than a little amused.

"Howie couldn't come," I said.

"Right," Rochelle said. "You mean he's going to sit on his couch and watch TV, laughing that you're here and he's not."

Or guard our farm to make sure no nutcases destroyed anything else. "You're probably right. Anyway, Nick here was gracious enough to come along, even though I warned him about the speeches."

"Brave man," Marty said. "And I don't mean because of the speeches."

I gave him a gentle slug on the shoulder at the same time Rochelle slapped his hand that was sitting on the table.

"If you don't have something nice to say...."

Marty grinned at her and sat back in his chair as a server put a salad down in front of him. "Saw you talking to Pam Moyer. She around again for good?"

I spooned ranch dressing onto my salad. "Yeah, I guess. Saw her the other day for the first time in years. She's done with school and is living at the farm, commuting down to the city a few days a week to work at Penn."

"How come she's here tonight?" Marty asked. "Her dad hasn't taken up milking."

I explained her new position on the town council, and Sonny Turner's hopes for a retirement replacement.

"I can think of a few people who won't be too happy about that," Rochelle said. "Tippy Benson's been on the council for years. And Warren Wycoff."

"I think it's because she went to Penn," I said. "'Our own Ivy Leaguer.'"

"That's not all," Marty said. "Turner Enterprises funded her scholarship."

I stopped in the middle of buttering a roll. "Really?"

"Sure. Sonny's been donating a scholarship to Penn for years, and was thrilled when he could give it to 'one of his own.' So it's no wonder if he wants her active on the council."

"Well, I hope she gets the job," I said. "She would do some good stuff for us farmers."

"But she's so young," Rochelle said. "She shouldn't be able to just waltz right in."

Marty patted her shoulder. "Don't get worked up yet, hon. He can't possibly retire now. He just bought out another company."

"So how many does that make?" I asked.

"Well, let's see…there's the meat packing plant, that chain of grocery stores—"

"Don't forget his car dealership has a new store in Quakertown to add to the ones in Souderton and Lansdale," Rochelle said. "But maybe he wants to quit being council president because he's too busy otherwise?" She swiveled her fork around in her salad. "It seems people should get to vote on who gets the spot next."

"Oh, who cares how someone gets the position?" Marty said. "Politics are too disgusting to pay attention to. I have other stuff to worry about."

"You're right about that," I said.

Nick glanced at me, and I knew he was thinking of the sabotage on my farm. I wasn't sure I was ready to share that with the Hoffmans, so I changed the subject. "What do you think they'll tell us here tonight?"

Marty's grin faded. "About the same as last year, I guess." Rochelle took his hand and pulled it onto her lap.

"Great," I said.

Nick perked up and looked at us with interest. "What's going on?"

"We're a dying breed, son," Marty said. "Stella here is one of the younger folks left. Our family businesses are in dire straits."

"Maybe your town council president-elect can help," Nick said, smiling.

"This isn't a joke, young man," Marty said. "Believe you me."

I looked at Rochelle and she raised her eyebrows in a "What am I supposed to do?" gesture. We knew Marty was off and running and nothing we could do, besides dragging him away, would stop him from telling Nick everything he knew. He leaned toward Nick.

"Would you believe the average age of dairy farmers is fifty-six? What's going to happen in ten years when we all retire? Our *kids* sure aren't taking over the farms—not that we'd want them to around here, the way things are going. Twenty-some years ago there were three hundred thousand of us, and now there are only eighty-three thousand. The government has no idea how things are going to crash and burn if they don't do something, and soon."

Nick looked astonished, but I wasn't sure if that was because of the information, or the fact that Marty was getting completely worked up. And he wasn't finished.

"In 1977, when I started in this business, I was getting four-teen dollars and fifty cents a hundred weight for my milk."

"Every hundred pounds," I murmured to Nick.

"Today I get twelve-fifty for the same amount! We've been socked by inflation everywhere we turn, but the money we *get* has *de*flated! We work eighty hours a week and where has it gotten us? Lower on the totem pole, that's where. The public has no idea what's behind their plastic milk jugs. They just pick 'em up at the store like they pick up a loaf of Wonder Bread. And our bank accounts sure don't show our hard work."

"Isn't there some program that pays farmers to keep their place a farm forever?" Nick asked.

"You know how long I've been on that list?" Marty said. "Six years. I applied as soon as I heard about it. But the money's run out now—a hundred million dollars. Why don't you take up smoking?"

Nick blinked. "What?"

"Two cents from every pack goes toward the program. That's how they're saving the farms now. Smokers."

"A lot of people smoke."

"Would you believe it brings in twenty-five million a year?"

"So why are you still waiting? That's a lot of money."

"There are a lot of farms, and they look at soil quality, farm size, location. And really, it's *not* that much money. They give up to ten thousand an acre, so say I got in the program. My ninety acres would get me almost a million dollars. Twenty-five farms later, they're out of money again, and a down-and-out farmer's only option is to sell out to a developer, who doesn't give a damn what happens to the land so long as his pockets get lined."

It seemed like divine intervention when the waitress came by to take our salad plates. None of us had eaten much, having been completely overtaken by Marty's speech, but I can't say I had much of an appetite left. Marty was usually such a sweet, unassuming guy, so his tirade was all the more disconcerting.

Marty threw down his napkin and abruptly left the table, leaving us open-mouthed and shell-shocked.

"I'm so sorry, Nick dear," Rochelle said.

"I'm the one who should be sorry," Nick said. "I didn't mean to start *that*." All pink had left his cheeks, and he looked more distraught than I would've expected.

"It's not your fault," Rochelle said. "It was bound to happen at some point. Perhaps now he'll be able to let us eat our main course in relative peace."

"Hello, Aunt Rochelle."

A man in a suit and tie stood beside her, looking out of place. His light gray suit was tailored and expensive-looking, and his hair was slicked into one of those styles where the short bangs stick up in the front. Classy, if you're at a four-star restaurant. Or if you're a teen-ager.

Rochelle put her hand on his arm. "Billy, how are you?"

"Um, I'm going by William now, Aunt Rochelle."

"Sorry, William. I keep forgetting."

Billy glanced at me briefly, then fixed his gaze on Nick. He turned a bit red, then looked back at Rochelle, who was trying not to laugh.

Sometime during high school I went to a church's youth group Halloween party with Billy because Rochelle begged me to. I think she wishes now she'd left it alone, because Billy refused to ever talk about the evening. It wasn't my fault he tried to put his hand up my shirt during the hayride. But I guess it was my fault he fell off the wagon and broke his arm.

"Hi, Billy," I said.

"It's—"

"William now. Right. Sorry." I tilted my head toward Nick. "This is Nick."

Nick got himself together enough to flash his outstanding teeth and hold out his hand. Billy took it because there was no way he couldn't and not look like a jerk.

"Billy is the accountant at Rockefeller Dairy," I told Nick. "He's been there for, what, two years now?"

Billy opened his mouth, probably to remind me to say William, but closed it and sighed, instead.

"It's two years next month, right, dear?" Rochelle said.

Billy nodded, then gave an unconvincing look at his watch. "I'd better sit down, Aunt Rochelle."

"Nice to see you, William."

We watched him make his way across the room to the table where Pam sat with Robert Rockefeller. It didn't look like Pam had touched her salad, either. She looked across the room at me and I made a face at Billy's back. She laughed silently and shook her head. She knew all about my high school adventures with Mister Billy.

"There's a story there, I take it," Nick said to me.

"Better left untold."

"Oh, here's Marty," Rochelle said. "He looks like he's calmed down some."

She was right, and the rest of the evening went by without another outburst from him, but it wasn't exactly enjoyable since we were all mulling over his words.

The representatives of the co-op got up during dessert to give us their report, and it was all pretty much as Marty had said. Nothing was getting any better, and besides the Bergeys, two other farms in our area had gone to developers, two out of the three to Hubert Purcell, himself. I could feel the restlessness in the room as we heard the news—everyone wondering who would be next. Kind of like the disciples at the Last Supper wondering which one among them would fall to the Devil.

Nick kept shooting me questioning looks, which for the life of me I couldn't decipher. Whatever he wanted to know would have to wait till our ride home.

When the reports were done and the last of the coffee was drunk, we stood up to go.

Marty grabbed Nick's wrist. "Sorry I went off like that, son."

Nick gave him a sad smile. "Please don't worry about it. I can see that to you—and the rest of the folks here—dairy farming is more than just a job. It's got to rip your heart out to see what's happening."

Marty let go of Nick's arm and nodded shortly. "We'll see where we are next year. Till then we keep on going."

Rochelle hugged me warmly, then reached for Nick. Surprise showed on his face, but he wrapped his arms around her and returned the gesture. When he stepped back, tears welled in his eyes. I looked away, not wanting to embarrass him, but wondered what the hell was going on.

A sudden reminder that I really knew nothing about the man except that he made me want to grab him and make a run for the hayloft.

When we got out to the truck, still not looking at each other, I slapped my hand on the hood. "Damn! I forgot to thank Rochelle for the pie."

"Want to go back in?"

"Not really."

He looked relieved. "Give her a call when you get home."

We got in the truck and I went to start it but paused with my hand on the keys. I had had a few pleasant expectations about the ending of the evening, but too many dark emotions were overwhelming me, along with questions about the man sitting next to me. I looked over at him and saw him studying my face.

"I don't feel like going home yet," I said.

"What do you feel like doing?"

What I felt like doing was taking an x-ray of his brain so I'd know what was going on in there. But perhaps a planned conversation could do the same thing. I forced a grin. "Ever since Abe mentioned going out for ice cream I've been thinking about a banana split." I didn't mention the ice cream I'd had at lunch with Rochelle's apple pie.

"After that dinner?"

"There's always room for ice cream. Didn't you know women have an extra compartment just for dessert?"

Nick laughed. "All right, then. Let's go."

Mom's Ice Cream Stand was open and hopping when we arrived at about eight-thirty, and I had to wonder what the business would be like if it were in my town. Here, in Hatfield, we were out of the danger zone of the illness, and kids were everywhere. Not exactly the private, quiet atmosphere I'd been hoping for.

The seating was all outside, and it looked like we might have to do without a table. We decided the ground was fine, so I got my banana split, Nick got a sinful-looking brownie delight, and we found a grassy place away from the crowd.

"I'd much rather be here than in that restaurant," I said, then corrected it. "I'd much rather be here than a lot of places."

He reached over and wiped a smear of whipped cream from my lip. "Here is a good place to be."

I took a breath to make my voice steady. "So where are you when you aren't here?"

He looked down at his sundae and swirled some fudge around his spoon. Without taking a bite, he raised his head and focused across the grass. "Stella, I—" His eyes widened. "I guess Abe was serious about going out for ice cream."

I followed his gaze and picked out Abe and Missy among the mostly teen-age mob. My heart sank. I remembered Abe's cut-off sentence at the funeral and figured it must've been my day for aborted conversations. Only those that seemed important, of course. "Maybe they won't see us."

But Missy's oh-so-observant eyes had already discovered us, and she poked Abe with her elbow. He saw us, too, and his face tightened. That dance club in my chest started up again, and this time it felt like something a little more active—like a polka. After the near-make-out-fiasco that afternoon, I wasn't sure I was ready to deal with him and Nick at the same time.

Nick didn't look too happy, either.

"I guess if we want to have an actual conversation we'll have to do it somewhere else," I said.

He studied his ice cream some more.

Abe and Missy got their orders, and once Missy had declared the grass dry, sat with us. Neither Nick nor I had much to say in welcome. I wasn't quite sure what to do with my hopping nerves. I hoped it wasn't obvious.

Missy, of course, broke the silence. "So where have you folks been?"

My mouth wouldn't open.

"At a dairy dinner," Nick finally said.

"Oh, what was it like?"

Nick was apparently out of words, so I scrounged one up. "Depressing."

Missy raised her eyebrows, but I didn't feel like expanding on the subject. I knew Abe's eyes were on me, so I finally met them.

"Bad news again?" he asked quietly.

"Nothing good. Damn developers are probably happy, though."

Nick made a strangled sound, but when I glanced at him, he hadn't looked up from his food.

"Tell me," Abe said.

So I did, and my heart sank lower and lower as I repeated all the buyout information we'd been given.

"Wow. Sounds bad," Missy said when I'd finished.

I turned to her, but Nick put a hand on my arm before I could reply.

"About time to get going?" he asked.

I looked down at my ice cream, now a melted mess, and fished out the cherry. I decided against eating it and pushed myself off the ground.

"Sure. Let's go."

"Stella…" Abe said.

I turned to him and for a moment the rest of the crowd—Nick and Missy included—disappeared. Until Missy opened her damned mouth again.

"If there's anything we can do," she said, "please let us know."

I closed my eyes, gave a quiet laugh, and walked away. Nick followed silently to the truck. I slammed my door behind me and gripped the steering wheel, resting my head on my hands.

"Stella…" Nick said.

I turned my face toward him. "When we get home, Nick, okay? Let's just get home."

We were about a quarter mile from the farm when I slammed on the brakes. The tires squealed and the truck fishtailed, skidding toward the drop-off at the side of the road. Nick grabbed the dashboard and planted his feet. I held onto the steering wheel with a death-grip, muttered some kind of prayer, and tried to keep from sliding into the ditch. The truck shuddered and screeched until coming to a complete stop about six inches from one of my cows, who stood calmly in the middle of the road, chewing her cud and looking at the grill of the truck like it was a fly about to sit on her back.

Chapter Eighteen

I jumped out of the truck and stood face to face with the cow. "What the hell do you think you're doing?"

She regarded me with her gentle brown eyes as if I'd just told her she was my blue ribbon winner.

For a moment I allowed myself to wonder how she got onto the road, but the possibilities were many, and in every scenario the quicker we got her home, the better. I looked back and forth from the cow to my truck, knowing I was going to have to entrust Nick with one of them. I figured it wouldn't be fair to saddle him with the cow, so I told him to take the truck the rest of the way home.

"Don't worry," he said. "I *have* driven a truck before."

He slid into the driver's seat and backed up the truck, keeping the lights on me and the cow. He flipped on the hazards and stayed there to warn any other traffic, showing more sense than I had at the moment. I waved him my thanks and began to try to get the piece of meat in front of me to move toward the farm.

After about five minutes of pulling the cow's chain, smacking her hind legs, and pleading uselessly, the cow decided on her own it was time to move. We paraded home slowly, me at the front, the cow taking up second, and Nick with my truck, backing us up.

We got into the farmyard to find barn lights blazing and Howie's truck parked in front of the paddock gate. I kept a firm hold on the cow and gestured to Nick to get out of the truck. He jumped out and trotted toward me.

"Find Howie, will ya?" I said. "See what's going on."

He was gone about five minutes before he came back. "Howie's in the feed barn. It's a mess in there—sacks everywhere, stuff all over the ground. He's got a cow cornered and is trying to pull her away from a pile of grain she's inhaling."

"Oh, that's just grand. What about his truck?"

"He said to move it to get this cow in, then put it back. Somehow the hook got broken off and the door swung open and he hasn't had a chance to fix it yet."

Somehow.

Furious, trying to keep a rein on my growing fear, I held onto the stupid cow while Nick moved Howie's truck out of the way. I somehow persuaded her she wanted to be back in the barnyard, and she slowly and deliberately walked in. I went back out into the driveway and Nick replaced the truck.

I jogged toward the feed barn and could hear Nick following me. I guessed that was good. He could help with the stubborn cow Howie was wrestling.

"Nice night, eh, Howie?" I said, trying to make light. "Glad you stayed home from the dinner?"

Howie gave the cow a good smack on the back, at which she merely tossed her head toward her shoulder.

"I've been working on her for a good fifteen minutes," Howie said. He looked at me tiredly. "Sure could use Queenie."

I took a deep breath and marched up to the cow. "Look, you. If you don't move your ass, you're going to the dog food factory in the morning."

She didn't seem to believe me, and stared at something over my left shoulder.

"I could get my twenty-two and scare her into moving," I said.

Howie grunted and went to the back of the cow, where he twisted her tail. That got her attention. I grabbed her chain while Howie twisted and pushed, and Nick ran out to move

Howie's truck again. When we finally got her in, Nick backed the truck up, and Howie excused himself to start cleaning up the destroyed grain.

I stood fuming, hands on my hips, and Nick came and stood in front of me.

"I guess this means our date is over?"

"What? Oh, yeah, I guess it does. Thanks for going along. And for helping with the cows." I started back toward the feed barn.

"So I'll see you tomorrow?"

Something in Nick's voice made me turn around and walk back to him. "I'm sorry. I really do appreciate your going with me tonight. I wish it hadn't turned out this way."

He shrugged, seeming embarrassed. "Hey, it's okay. I…You think we can talk tomorrow?" His face was tight, and he jammed his hands into his pockets.

"Sure," I said. "We can talk tomorrow."

He walked to his truck, looked at me one more time, and drove off. For once I was too preoccupied to enjoy watching his every move. I'd take time later to regret the way the evening ended.

I found Howie cleaning up what to me looked like cash thrown on the ground. In reality, it was several bags of feed—the kind I had to actually buy and not get from Jude—ripped open, tromped on, pooped on, peed on, and eaten.

I sank onto a couple of bags that had somehow survived the onslaught. "Can these jerks make anything else go wrong? Cows dying, shit everywhere, animals escaping…Good Lord."

Howie stopped what he was doing and came over to sit by me. He put his hands on his knees and sighed. His face looked tired and very old.

"You okay?" I asked. "You look terrible."

I thought of Pam's dad and wondered if he looked just as aged.

Howie slumped wearily. "It's just one thing after another, isn't it? Even without criminals messing with us."

"Someone broke the lock on the gate," I said. "I checked it just the other day and it was fine."

Howie shook his head. "I just can't imagine *why*."

I wondered where Howie had been that he hadn't seen whoever busted the lock, but didn't want to make him feel guiltier than he already did. We sat in silence for a few minutes, surveying the mess and grieving the money we'd just lost.

"I guess I'll call Detective Willard in the morning," I said. "I'm sure he's not in anymore tonight, and it's not like the guy's hanging around to get caught."

Howie nodded.

"All the cows in?" I asked. "I pulled one off the road where by some miracle she hadn't gotten hit."

"That should be the last one. Only six actually got out, if you can believe that, and I was just missing the one. Couldn't find her anywhere. She mustn't've been on the road very long."

"Loomed right up in our headlights, that's for sure. Scared the shit outta me."

Howie pushed himself up to do some more cleaning, but I couldn't make myself move.

"What are we doing, Howie? It seems every day something happens to set us back even more. If the market doesn't kill us, it's going to be all the little crap—or these stupid pranks—that does. Is it worth working twelve, fifteen hours a day to worry we can't pay the bills next month? Or the next? And maybe without Queenie?"

Howie leaned on his broom. "Bad news at the dinner again?"

"The Bergeys and two others, Howie." I looked around at the hay and the grain and the old wooden walls. "How long can we keep it going? How long till I have to have snot-nosed real estate guys come onto my property because I asked them here?"

"It may not come to that, Princess."

"You're right. It may not. But it sure as hell is looking more likely every day."

"We just have to keep going. We work hard, say our prayers, keep our fingers crossed. Nail these guys that are screwing with us. And don't you worry, Princess. I'll stay and fight with you till the cows come home."

I watched with affection as the old man went back to sweeping.

"Hey, Stella." Pam stood silhouetted in the doorway. "Saw your lights as I was driving past. Anything I can help with?"

I waved her in. "Howie, remember Pam? She went to school with me back in the day. Her dad's a crop farmer over on Harleysville Pike."

Howie put out his hand. "Sure. Chuckie Moyer's little gal, right?"

She grinned wearily and returned the handshake. "That's me."

"Park it on a bale," I said. "You look beat."

She plopped beside me. "Cows get in here or something?"

"Something." I stood and went to find another broom. "You stay sitting. With three of us we'd just get in each other's way."

She pulled her feet up onto the bale and clasped her hands around her knees. "Could you believe that news tonight? I knew about the Bergeys, of course, but two others?"

I tipped my head toward Howie. "I was just telling him. Damn developers."

She sighed and blew her hair off her forehead. "The problem is it's not all their fault."

I grunted. "You're right. But they're hovering like vultures. What we need is for one farmer to win the SuperBall when it's at two hundred mil and we'd all be saved."

Pam stared at me.

I shrugged. "I know it's a long shot."

"But worth hoping for." She closed her eyes and rested her head against the barn wall. "Do you remember as a kid watching your mom try to save money? God. My parents scrimped like crazy, only to end up further behind than they were to begin with. Every once in a while we'd have a bumper crop and I'd get an extra school outfit or two, but soon we'd be back to penny pinching."

She twirled a strand of hair in her fingers. "When I was a freshman in high school the first developer came. Norm Freeman down the road had just sold his farm for one point two million dollars. He'd never have to worry about anything again. Anything financial, anyway. My dad says Norm sort of lost his reason for living when they built the houses up around him.

"My folks swore it would never happen to us, and although Daddy was real polite to the developers, he made it clear they didn't need to bother coming back. But the next fall, after a drought summer, there they were. My dad's answer was still the same. He was keeping the farm for his little girl, and no one was going to take it away from him."

She choked up a bit, and Howie and I pretended not to notice. She eventually got herself under control.

"Each year Daddy said no, and each year Mom leaned a little more toward saying yes. When I finally got my scholarship to Penn, it was a relief to get away from the tension. I didn't know if I even *wanted* to take over the farm, and that was my dad's main plan."

I propped my broom in the corner and sat down next to Pam. "So what do you think now? You going to take it over?"

She shook her head thoughtfully. "I still haven't decided. I got my Ph.D. in Biology so I could help out farmers. I couldn't really do that if I was plowing and harvesting twenty-four/seven." A tear rolled down her cheek. "But then I get home and I see how the farm is a huge chunk of my dad's heart. He's this close to chapter eleven, but the only way he'll let go is if he's dead. I've got to at least keep him hoping while he's alive.

"Every day I look at him, and I just don't know how to tell him I'm not sure it's what I want for *me*. I only know I've got to help him keep the farm for *him*."

I patted her shoulder and stood up. I'd been saying basically the same things to Howie minutes before, and his words of wisdom came back out of my mouth. "That's the only thing we can do, Pam. We go day to day, hoping like hell each day isn't the last. We do whatever we can to survive."

Chapter Nineteen

Howie and I were watching Pam's car head down the road when Carla's truck pulled into the driveway.

Howie grunted. "Good thing we didn't go to bed at our usual time, the visitors we're getting. At this rate, we won't even have to take shifts guarding the farm."

Carla was smiling when she parked and jumped down from the cab of the F250. "I can't believe you're still up. But I'm glad."

"What's going on?" I said.

She smiled even broader. "Got something I think you'll want to see."

She opened the door on her extended cab and gestured inside. I stepped around her to peer in. Queenie was lying on the seat.

My breath caught in my throat, and my eyes stung. "Oh, *Howie.*"

He came up beside me and put a hand to his heart, then to the bridge of his nose. His eyes squeezed shut, and I clasped his arm, not quite believing what we were seeing.

Queenie was home.

I sank my hands into the fur around her neck and dropped my forehead against hers, inhaling her scent and feeling the oil of her hair. She panted lightly and licked my chin.

"You know she's glad to see you," Carla said. "She's just too tired to jump up and tell you."

I turned my face toward Carla, leaving my cheek against Queenie's head. "How did you find her?"

She grinned. "Didn't. Another one of my clients did, and called this evening, wondering what he should do. Seems Queenie wandered a little far off—Sellersville, actually, up towards the Ridge—and got a little too interested in a gopher hole. If I'm right, she's had her head stuck in the ground for a couple days. We're lucky she's a farm dog and the hole was in the shade, or she probably wouldn't have made it."

I studied my collie, looking for signs of injury. She looked okay except for being a little skinnier than when I'd last seen her. And there wasn't a speck of dirt on her.

"She's clean because I wanted to check her out before bringing her home," Carla said, reading my mind. "Figured I'd give her a bath in the bargain. She looks fine. A mite dehydrated, and a few pounds lighter, but hopefully wiser." She scratched Queenie's head. "You were a big dummy, weren't you, girl?"

Queenie thumped her tail on the seat.

"Thank you," I said.

Howie shook Carla's hand mutely.

She waved her arms and laughed. "Aw, shucks. Just doing my job. And I love this part of it."

I gently grabbed Queenie's ears and looked her in the eye. "We owe Doctor Beaumont big for this one, babe."

She panted, and I'd swear she smiled, her tongue lolling out the side of her mouth.

"So I can pick her up?" I asked.

Carla shrugged. "Like I said, she's fine. She can go back to her normal routine once she's rested up and hydrated."

I bent over Queenie and hefted her out of the truck. I looked at Howie. "She'll be sleeping with me tonight."

He nodded. "I'd hope so."

Carla looked back and forth at us. "What? Has something else happened?"

I told her about our most recent vandalism, and she bristled. "What is *wrong* with these people? Have they no brains at all? They could've killed somebody! Or lost you some good milkers!"

"Preaching to the off-key choir, Carla. I'll call the detective in the morning."

"*Idiots*," she muttered.

Howie patted her shoulder. "At least it turned out for the best."

"This time." She slammed the back door on her truck. "You'll let me know if I can do anything?"

I lowered my head toward Queenie. "You've done the best thing right here. Couldn't ask for more than this."

A smile twitched on her lips, and she reached out for a final pat. Queenie rubbed her nose against Carla's hand. "Like I said. Best part of my job." She stepped up into the truck and spoke to us through her window. "Now I know I'm an animal doctor, but people are animals, too, and all I'm going to say is this. You'se go to bed right now. All three of you look like you need to sleep for an entire week."

Chapter Twenty

I awoke to someone banging on my door.

Good God, I thought. *What now?*

It was two AM, and I had finally gotten myself and Queenie to bed around midnight. Howie insisted on taking the first guard shift, and I had fallen asleep in my underwear, having left the rest of my clothes by the washer. My shoulders were stiff from hauling now-useless grain to the Dumpster.

The knocking came again, louder and more urgent. Queenie opened her eyes but didn't move an inch from where she lay on a blanket under my window.

"You just sleep, girl," I told her.

I jumped out of bed, pulled on some jeans and a shirt, and ran down the stairs. Howie stood there, his hair on end and his eyes wide with panic.

"I called 911. They should be here anytime."

I shook my foggy head. "What?"

Howie dragged me out of the doorway so I could see the heifer barn, smoke and flames shooting out of the windows on its east side.

"Oh my God." I wrenched my arm from his grasp, leapt into the boots I'd left inside the door, and ran toward the barn. I searched frantically until I found a side door that wasn't on fire and threw myself into the smoke and chaos. Howie came running, screaming at me not to be a fool. But he followed me in.

I ran up to the heifers' gate and threw it open, making my way in amongst the panicked youngsters. I went to the back of the group and started smacking their rears and pushing them toward the entrance. The fire was still on the opposite side as the heifers, but not so far that we had more than a few minutes to get them out.

The cows ran into each other, rolling their eyes, stumbling over their own feet. I regretted the help Queenie could have given, and tried to calm myself enough to steer the heifers toward Howie, who stood holding the gate open, ready to shove the cows out into the night.

Finally, amidst their panic, the cows surged toward the entrance, pushing and getting stuck three across in the gate opening, until Howie could get them apart. Sweat poured down my face, and heat stung my skin. I breathed shallowly, but smoke burned my lungs and eyes, and I bent over to get to fresher air. The only light was from the fire, and I slipped and slid in manure and urine, falling several times when a cow would burst away from my hands.

I was chasing the final heifer toward the gate when I heard sirens and saw lights through the open door. Howie put a hand on my back and pushed me toward the barnyard. We ran outside and kept going until we were up by the house. I dropped to the ground, gasping for breath. Howie stood bent over, his hands on his knees, his breathing loud and forced.

A crash from the house startled me upright, and Queenie came barreling toward me from the screen door she'd bashed through. I caught her against my chest, making sure she hadn't cut her face or paws, then fell onto my back, breathing in the night air. It smelled of smoke, but it was pure compared to the inside of the barn. Queenie pranced around me, but couldn't get far with my fingers clasped around her collar.

Several fire trucks had arrived, as well as police cars, the fire chief, and an ambulance. A couple of EMTs ran up to us, carrying first aid kits.

"You folks okay?" one asked.

I gave him a weak thumbs-up, but Howie slumped onto the ground. Both paramedics rushed to his side. I let go of Queenie and started to crawl over to him, but it wasn't long before I heard him telling them to leave him alone. Satisfied, I went back to my collie, who lay down beside me and nuzzled my hand with her soft nose.

I forced myself to look at the heifer barn, now completely engulfed in flames. There wasn't any hope left for it, so the fire-fighters were doing their best to keep the blaze from spreading to the buildings around it. So far, it looked like they were being successful.

"Ms. Crown?" A man stood over me in fire gear. His black and yellow suit was covered with soot, his face as streaked as Howie's. Sweat plastered his dark hair to his head.

"That's me."

"Assistant Chief Downy. Any idea what started the fire?"

"Nope."

He sat beside me on the grass. "From what I could see, it looked like it started in the east corner there."

I nodded. "That's the first thing I saw. Flames shooting out those windows."

"Any electricity in that corner? Anybody smoking?"

"Neither. The only electric is for the lights and a couple plugs on the west side we use for space heaters in the winter. Neither Howie or I smoke."

"Your insurance up to date?"

I looked at him. "I won't take that personally."

"Good, because I don't mean it that way. Any reason someone else might want to burn down your barn?"

"Can't imagine any. There's no one who would benefit in any way. I won't benefit either, if you're looking at my insurance angle. I have to find a new place to house my heifers, and I lost all the hay and straw that was kept in there. Plus, I just hired someone this week to repair and paint the damned barn, and he's already put in two days work I'll have to pay him for."

With a start, I realized the heifers were still loose. They were cowering beneath the overhang of the main barn, milling about and shoving each other further into the corner, eyes wild and mouths foaming from their panic. I gave Queenie a final pat and pushed myself up from the ground.

"Anything else?" I asked.

Downy stood, too. "I'm going to call the county and ask them to bring in their arson dog. We'll find out what happened, Ms. Crown."

I nodded, and he clumped away in his big boots.

"I'm going to round up the heifers," I told Howie. "You stay here."

"But—"

"No, Howie. Besides, Queenie needs you."

He looked relieved at my insistence, and buried his hand in Queenie's fur. She leaned against him, and he planted a hand on the ground to keep himself from falling over.

I quickly counted the heifers by the barn and funneled them into the milking parlor where they'd be safe. Once they were secured, I ran out hunting for the two unaccounted for.

"Need some help?" A police officer trotted up to me, gun belt slapping against her hip. "Officer Stern, at your service."

"Got two runaways. Seen 'em?"

She shook her head. "I can help look."

"Great. I'm going around the house. You make sure they're not cornered somewhere in the midst of all these trucks."

She turned toward the vehicles, and I ran around the house. I went to the road first, remembering my encounter earlier in the evening. Fortunately, there were no cows lying alongside the road, having caused an accident. There was, however, a heifer in my yard, chewing on a young maple tree.

"Come on, darlin'," I said. I thought for a moment she was going to bolt, but I put up my hand slowly, and while she was studying it, got close enough to snatch her chain with my other hand. Unlike her older counterparts, she followed without a struggle.

I got her reunited with her friends and ran back out to look for the last escapee. In fifteen minutes I still hadn't found her, but a triumphant-looking Officer Stern came up, leading a docile heifer.

"Found her in that building over there," she said, pointing at the feed barn.

"Oh, great." Stern looked disappointed at my reaction, so I upped my enthusiasm. She didn't know what the feed barn had been through already that night. "Thanks a lot," I said. "I can't believe we didn't lose any of them."

"Kind of a miracle, I think. Glad I could help." She trotted back toward her car, probably to call in her successful rescue.

I got the heifer into the milking parlor and was leaning against the outside of the barn when I felt something brush against my leg. I automatically reached down and stroked Queenie's ears. She nudged my arm with her nose and I felt that her nose was wet. I was glad someone had the sense to give her some water.

Howie came over and slid down to the ground by Queenie. Together, the three of us watched the heroic efforts of the fire squad, while our partially refurbished heifer barn burned to the ground.

Three hours later the fire trucks had gone, having made a holy mess but leaving all buildings other than the heifer barn still standing. I probably should've been thankful for that, but at the moment I felt nothing but a cold, hard anger. An arson investigator with a big German shepherd was picking his way through the rubble, and I dreaded hearing what he found.

Unbelievably, it was almost five AM. Howie and I relocated the heifers to the back pasture—the one that had been manure-logged just days before in what seemed like another lifetime—so we could milk our completely freaked out herd. They may not have been directly involved in the fire, but they could smell the smoke and water-saturated wood, and had been kept awake by all the commotion.

It was wonderful to have Queenie back to help round them up, although she moved slower than usual and left off about halfway through to lie in her usual corner and fall asleep. She hadn't even had enough energy to be excited about the German shepherd sniffing through the barn's ashes. I gazed at her with a rush of love, thanking God I hadn't lost her.

Howie and I dragged ourselves through the milking, moving slowly from cow to cow, not saying a word. He seemed preoccupied and weary, but I figured that was to be expected after the night we'd had. He hadn't even gotten the two hours of sleep I'd managed.

Queenie woke up when Nick drove in about at about six o'clock, and Nick was so busy greeting her he didn't even notice the absence of the heifer barn or the arson guy's car that still sat in the drive. Talk about dense. I was watching him from the milking parlor when he turned around. His jaw literally dropped and he shook his head like he couldn't believe it.

He saw me looking at him through the window and came into the parlor. "What in the world...."

"It's just what it looks like, Nick."

He shook his head again and sat on a bale of straw, stunned. I went back to work until I saw him stand up.

"What can I do to help?" he asked.

"Not sure. Until the arson guy is finished we're not supposed to touch anything."

Nick opened his mouth to say something and then closed it.

"Why don't you take the day off?" I said. "Let me figure out what's going to happen."

He stuffed his hands in his pockets. "Sure I can't help around here?"

Two days ago I would have jumped at his offer, just to see him move around, but after hearing that certain tone in his voice last night I was a bit nervous about where our relationship was headed. His help would be nice, but my sanity was more important.

"Thanks for the offer," I said. "I'll let you know later if we can use you."

"Okay," he said, not sounding sure that it was. "Glad to see Queenie's back."

"Me, too."

He patted Queenie again and went outside.

Howie gave me a look which told me he knew what I was thinking about Nick. I ignored him, and we continued working in silence. When the last few cows were milked and let outside, and the milker was going through its cleaning routine, we sank onto the floor, resting our backs against the wall.

"The stalls are just going to have to stay dirty for a bit," I said.

Howie grunted and closed his eyes. I tried closing mine, too, but my mind was spinning too fast to drift off.

"This is crazy, Howie. No matter how I think about the past few days, I can't imagine who would be messing with us. The only person who has any kind of a motive is Hubert, and he's pretty much been shoved out of the picture. Besides, he couldn't stomach *this*. Cut off electricity, punch holes in the manure lagoon, maybe. Come to think of it, he could've let the cows out, too. But burn down a barn? With livestock in it? Sending the dweebie real estate lawyer is much more his style."

My fried brain couldn't take any more creative thinking. I stuck with facts.

"We can be pretty damn sure someone deliberately set fire to the barn."

Howie rolled his head toward me and opened his eyes. "I guess we'll find out for certain when that guy's done out there."

I pounded the floor with my fist. "What have we ever done to anybody?"

Howie looked away, but I could tell he had an opinion.

"What, Howie?"

He shook his head. "Nothing for sure. But I've been check-ing into—"

The arson investigator suddenly loomed over us. His face was grim.

"What?" I asked.

"I think you already know."

I put my head between my knees.

Someone had burned down my barn.

Chapter Twenty-One

By eight o'clock I had eaten a piece of toast, tried to force one down Howie—who excused himself and went up to his apartment—left a message for my insurance agent, called Belle to make sure Zach was okay, and taken a long shower. I used my Lever 2000.

At eight-thirty I was standing in the muddy and fire-engine-rutted driveway trying to decide where to start cleaning up, when Queenie started to bark and a couple-year-old Taurus pulled up. It was Richard Snyder, my insurance rep.

"Hey, Richard," I said. "Thanks for getting here so fast."

"Stella." He put his briefcase on the ground and stood beside me, taking in the damage. His face was pinched and pale.

"Thank God for insurance," I said. "I guess those premiums weren't a waste of money, after all."

He looked me up and down, taking in my heat-scorched face and the bags under my eyes, and I tried out a smile. It mustn't have worked, because he looked even more disturbed.

"I hope your new rep will take care of you as well as I would have," he said. "And why call me? Where's your new guy?"

"What new guy? You're the only guy for me."

His eyes widened. "Stella, what about your phone call the other day?"

"What phone call? The last time we talked was when we went over the schedule of insured items in May."

He paled even more, and I was suddenly afraid he was going to be sick on my shoes. I backed up a step.

"Stella." He ran a hand through his hair. "You called the other day and told me you found cheaper and more comprehensive insurance. You canceled your insurance with me."

I opened my mouth to deny it, and the consequences of what he was telling me hit home. Then I felt like *I* was going to throw up. "I never called you."

"Then who was it?" Richard no longer acted like he was going to puke, but still looked terrorized.

I put my hand over my mouth and walked a few steps away. Queenie followed, whimpering. I patted her head and turned back to Richard.

"What does this mean? I never signed any cancellation."

He shook his head. "I don't know. This has never happened to me before."

"Well, you'd better find out. Because I need that money."

He nodded, speechless.

"I *have to have* it."

He picked up his briefcase and clutched it to his chest. "I'll go back and check my logs. There's got to be an explanation."

"I'm sure there is one. But it's not going to be one I'm happy about."

Richard scuttled to his car, gave me one last glance over his shoulder, and drove off. He'd been gone about ten minutes before I could make myself walk to my office. Once there, I pulled out my insurance file to make sure all was in order from my end of things. It was.

Without letting myself think about it too much, I picked up the phone and called Abe. Ma answered and knew by my tone of voice I wasn't calling for a chat. Abe was instantly on the line.

"I might need a lawyer," I said.

"What? What happened?"

I explained the situation, somehow without throwing anything at my office wall. "I figured you might know somebody.

Only lawyer I ever had was when my mom died, and he bit the dust several years ago."

"I'll find you someone. Give me an hour or two."

I hesitated, wanting to say more. "Thanks, Abe."

"Glad to help."

It got to be nine-thirty without a call from Abe or Richard, so I forced myself to go out and take care of things that had to be done. Howie wasn't in appearance, so I assumed he was getting some much-deserved sleep. I wasn't about to wake him with more bad news.

I spent an hour hauling hay and water down to the pasture for the heifers, then checked my answering machine. Still no message from Richard, but Abe had called to say that Brigham Bergey, a lawyer from Lansdale, would be waiting for my call. I wanted to wait to talk with him till I'd heard back from Richard, so I went back out and used the skid loader to scrape up the mud the firefighters had created in the barnyard.

Once the mud was cleared away I went back to the office and found the message light blinking. I called Richard back immediately.

"Well?" I said.

"It's all here. Documented and dated. I got a call at three-thirty in the afternoon, three days ago, canceling your insurance."

"It wasn't me."

"I know. I believe you."

"Good."

I heard him take a deep breath. "But my bosses don't."

I froze. "*What?*"

"They think you canceled your insurance, then your barn burned, and now you want to renege."

I threw the receiver down on my desk and stared unseeing out my window until I was calm enough to talk again. I picked up the phone.

"Okay, Richard. Supposedly I told you I was going with another insurance carrier. Who are they? And why would I come back to you?"

"I told you, I believe you. You don't have to convince me."

"Well, that's great. It just doesn't help me a whole hell of a lot if you can't convince the rest of them."

"What do you want me to do?"

"What do you think I want you to do? Get my insurance back."

"No need to be snide. I'm doing my best."

"Sorry. I'm just very…upset." I was going to say something stronger, but was afraid I might *offend* him.

"How about the phone number?" I asked.

"What phone number?"

"The one of whoever called you." *You idiot.*

"How am I supposed to know that?"

"Caller ID. Don't you have it?"

"Sure, but since I get so many calls it doesn't save things longer than a day if I don't lock them in."

"So you don't have the number."

"No. I checked."

"Well, how do we get it?"

"Look, Stella, I'm doing everything I can from my end. I don't have the phone number, I don't have a photographic memory, and I don't have a recording of the call. I can't do anything else."

"Fine. Just do whatever you can to get your stupid superiors to believe me. I *have* to have that money."

"I told you. I'm on your side. I'll keep after them."

"Great. I really do appreciate it, Richard. And my lawyer will be calling you."

"Oh. Okay."

I pushed the flash button and dialed the number Abe had given me. Brigham Bergey was with a client, but his secretary said she'd have him call as soon as he could. Great.

I pushed the flash button again and called the police station, hoping to leave Willard a message. I had told Howie the night before that I would, after the cows were let out, and now seemed as good a time as any. Plus I had a lot more to tell him.

"Police Department, Detective Willard speaking."

"I wasn't expecting you to be there."

"And this is?"

"Sorry. Stella Crown. I figured you'd be with your son."

"Nothing I can do there. And he's holding steady. No better, no worse."

Seemed to be the parent mantra these days.

"Heard about your barn," Willard said. "I was at the hospital last night, or I would've come. Arson investigation team's on it, right?"

"Right. And today I found out someone canceled my insurance."

"What? How'd they do that?"

"Over the phone."

"The agent took the cancellation?"

"I know, you don't have to tell me. He's a moron. But he really thought it was me."

"So what can I do for you?"

"The home office of the insurance company doesn't believe me, even though Richard does. I need to find out who called him. Can you get a list of phone numbers or something?"

"When was this?"

"Two days ago."

He was quiet for so long, I thought we'd been cut off.

"You there?" I asked.

"Sorry, just thinking."

"Can you think a little faster? I'm about to blow up here."

"I'm not sure I can help you."

"What? Can't you get a court order or something?"

He sighed. "I'll see. But phone companies are notoriously difficult to work with on things like this. Don't get your hopes up."

"Gee, thanks."

"It's the best I can do."

"Something else. Somebody let my cows out last night. Cut the padlock on the barnyard gate and set half a dozen of them free. Probably the same person that burned down my barn."

"Good grief. Don't they know when to stop?"

"Apparently not."

"There's a large fine for that offense."

"I don't care about that. I just want these assholes caught."

"As do I. Anything left for me to look at in regards to the lock they cut?"

"I saved the lock. Tried not to handle it too much."

"Great. I'll come get it sometime this afternoon."

"After you check on the phone numbers."

"After that."

"All right. Thanks." I hung up and leaned my head on my hands. On top of everything else, I now had a headache bigger than a tanker truck.

Chapter Twenty-Two

I wasn't sure what else to do, and I didn't have screening to replace the door Queenie had busted through, so I forced myself to go into the house and eat something. There wasn't much there, so I scrambled up an egg, slapped two pieces of bread around it, and called it lunch. While I ate, I sat at the table and stared blankly at the twelve o'clock news on my little black-and-white. The voices droned on, floating past my ears in unintelligible blurbs, until I heard a voice I recognized. I blinked and sat back with surprise. Pam Moyer was on television.

"The illness has become a menace as frightening as the plague," she was saying. "We know the partial cause of illness, but the Department of Health has yet to come up with the source." She stood behind a podium at a press conference, looking professional and neat, but also about ready to keel over. I hoped she'd soon be able to get some sleep. I wondered why on earth Sonny wasn't doing the press conference, and figured he was too busy managing his conglomeration of businesses.

"The dedicated Department of Health and Centers for Disease Control are working around the clock, trying to save our children," Pam said. "We feel confident a cure will soon be found, and the culprit—the aflatoxin—negated. We have the antidote to the poison, but it unfortunately can't keep new cases from developing, and some cases need more than a simple cure. This situation is absolutely our highest priority."

I would hope so. I grabbed the phone and dialed Jethro and Belle. There was no answer, so I left a message.

The news was now back to the regular broadcaster. He oozed concern. "Doctor appointments in the small borough and surrounding areas have become almost impossible to schedule, and we're still no closer to finding the cure for the geographically centered problem. The two children who died had both been suffering from severe allergies prior to contracting the illness, and doctors surmise this was the final factor in their deaths. Stay tuned to this station for the most up-to-date information."

I dusted the crumbs off the table and rolled my rock-hard shoulders. I wondered how Richard was getting on with the home office. Hopefully he was a little more assertive than he had sounded. If he didn't get on the ball, I'd have my new lawyer—well, once he called back—get on him.

I also wondered how Detective Willard was doing with tracking down the phone number of the fake who had called Richard. It had been at least a half-hour since I talked with him. My kitchen phone is a throwback that still has a cord, and I stood and pulled the receiver over to the table so I could sit again. When the phone was ringing at the police station I realized I had left the TV on, but didn't feel like getting up again and dragging the phone cord across the room, so I tried to ignore it.

"Police, Officer Meadows speaking."

Oh great. Mister Rude. "Detective Willard, please."

"Who's calling?"

"Stella Crown. I talked to the detective a little bit ago and he was checking on something for me."

"The phone stuff?"

"Yeah, the phone stuff."

"Hang on."

I heard a click and a few seconds of some weird music before Willard got on the phone.

"Detective Willard speaking."

"Stella Crown here. Find anything out about that phone number?"

"Boy, you expect fast work. But I actually do have an answer for you. Unfortunately."

My heart sank. I thought it had already reached the low point, but I must have been wrong.

"Unfortunately why?"

"Because it's basically impossible to track the number. First off, there's the privacy issue—"

"If there's been a crime—"

"I know, Ms. Crown. Please let me finish. Besides the privacy issue, the number is vanished by now. After a day or so it's practically impossible to track, and local calls are most likely not captured, anyway. The phone company says there's really no way they can help us."

"And you believe them?"

"I have no choice but to believe them. They can, however, check phones for local calls that originated *there*. So they could check *your* phone to ascertain you didn't call the insurance company."

"Like I don't know that already."

"It might clear you with the insurance company."

"They'd just say I called from somewhere else."

He sighed loudly. "I didn't say it was a brilliant plan. I said the phone company thought of it."

"Well, thanks for nothing."

"A lot of times, nothing is what I do best."

Even in my condition, I laughed.

He continued to talk, but I didn't hear him. Hubert Purcell, that slimy, pathetic developer, was on TV.

"Gotta go," I said, and jumped to hang up the phone. I turned up the volume on the TV and leaned against the table to watch.

Hubert sat in a leather executive chair, probably in his own office, wearing a very nice, dark blue suit, his hair slicked back. He was smiling his nauseating smile that always drove me nuts. I hoped my egg sandwich wouldn't end up on the floor.

The interviewer was out of sight, asking intelligent questions for which she hoped to get interesting, if not always truthful, answers. The segment was part of a series called "Get to Know Your Business Neighbors." I guess they mistook Hubert for a human being.

"What do you consider your finest achievement?" the reporter asked in her low, full voice.

Hubert smiled even wider and my stomach heaved.

"I would have to say all of the communities I've started where people can find friends and…well…community. Thousands of people in this county have found a new, warmer lifestyle because of the homes I've built. I'm very proud of that."

"The houses," the reporter said. "What can you tell us about them?"

"They're built of the finest materials, from the most detailed blueprints, and the most updated technology. The team I've gotten together is the best in the business, from electricians, to roofers, to interior designers. When you buy a Hubert Purcell home, you know you're getting only the best."

Now my cookies were really at risk for being tossed. Howie and I always joked about people falling through the floor in one of Hubert's houses and ending up in their basement, or finding that all the electricity is hooked up to one fuse. Anyone who had any brains knew that Hubert used waferboard for his sub floors and the carpet manufacturers refused to put warranties on anything laid on them. And there was always the one complete side of the house with no windows, to save money. Great view. Sub par roofing materials, unsanded drywall—don't get me started.

Hubert was still smiling, but that diminished when the reporter got serious.

"What about the people who say our farmland is being swallowed up by developers and we'll soon have no room left to breathe?"

Hubert took a deep breath, as if testing the amount of air around him, and put on a show of concern. "Let's be realistic.

We have thousands of people moving into this area every year. We need to put them somewhere, and that means unless we want to turn families away we need to build more homes. As for the farmers…what can I say? They have a hard life and a hard job to do. Some of the smaller ones are finding themselves out-dated and maybe a bit redundant at the same time as their finances are dwindling and the commercial farms are taking the business. Most farmers I know are hanging on by their fingernails, and if there are any wrenches thrown at them—say, machinery that breaks down, livestock that dies, insurance that's unreliable—that can put them in a downward spiral that takes them nowhere but bankruptcy, and they're happy to have someone like me to rescue them."

"People have accused you—"

I snapped off the TV and breathed evenly through my mouth. I couldn't believe it. My doubt of Hubert's criminal abilities had been wrong. Willard's belief that Hubert's alibis had cleared him had been wrong. We were both incredibly, *fatally* wrong.

Hubert, in his pathetic attempt to identify himself with the farmers' plight, had given himself away.

Chapter Twenty-Three

I jumped into my truck and pulled out of the drive so fast I spun my tires and kicked gravel into the yard. I pounded the steering wheel with my fist until my hand started to bruise, then switched to shouting curses instead. I turned toward Hubert's office and floored it.

It wasn't until I almost hit a young mother pushing a stroller that I realized I was driving blind. Blinded by rage, frustration, and disappointment. I had known Hubert was scum, but hadn't realized to what magnitude. I pulled into the next drive to put my head on the steering wheel and take a few deep breaths.

What was I planning to do when I got to Hubert's office? Beat him to a pulp? It might feel good, but it wouldn't exactly help me in the long run. I sat up and looked out the windshield, not really seeing the house where I'd pulled in.

If I followed my heart, Hubert would look like hamburger in fifteen minutes. If I followed my head, I'd go back to the farm and tell Howie what happened. See what he'd say. He'd probably say I should call Detective Willard, but I wasn't sure I could do that this time. I had no proof. Nothing but my instincts.

I backed out of the drive, making sure the young mother wasn't behind me, and drove home like a sane person.

Howie still wasn't in sight when I got back to the farm, but Jethro was, along with Jermaine and Jordan. They all stood staring at the black space where my heifer barn used to be.

Seeing them, I was suddenly struck by an idea for dealing with Hubert.

Jethro suffocated me with one of his bear hugs when I stepped down from my truck. I patted him on the shoulder, knowing the zeal with which he hugged me wasn't only for my troubles.

"Thanks," I said. Jethro finally let go and I stepped back.

"Anything we can do?" Jordan asked.

"Not much to do until the insurance comes through."

"You know what happened?"

"Someone soaked a rag in gas, lit it, and threw it into my hay mow."

They looked at me, aghast.

"How do you know that?" Jethro asked.

"Arson dog found the place where the gas had soaked into the dirt. We knew the area where the fire started, and the investigator didn't have much trouble finding the evidence."

"Holy cow," Jethro said.

"You know who did it?" Jordan asked.

"I do." I pointed at Jermaine. "And you're going to help me pay him back."

◇◇◇

The guys left after extracting promises I'd call them once we could start cleaning up and rebuilding the barn. I watched them go, and Queenie dug her nose into my thigh.

"Where's Howie, Queenie? I haven't seen him all day."

She trotted toward the garage as if she'd understood my question. I followed her up the stairs and knocked. Howie came to the door looking just as awful—if not worse—than when I last saw him that morning.

"You okay, Howie?"

"Hey, Princess. I'm okay. Just doing a little research."

"Research? On what?"

"You remember I was telling you I was looking into something and— What's up with you? You're looking crazy."

I wanted to hear what he had to say, but my news was about to fry my brain. "I know who's been sabotaging the farm."

"What? But I—"

"It's Hubert, the little rat. I saw him on TV. He was schmoozing with the reporter and mentioned everything that's happened to us so far."

Howie looked at his socks for a minute. "But he's got alibis—"

"So he paid somebody. I'm telling you, Howie, it's *got* to be him. And he's going to be sorry." I told Howie my plan.

Howie sat down on the top step and rubbed his hands on his knees, looking around the farm, studying it. I sat beside him and watched him think. He finally had to laugh. "So all you're asking is that I do the evening milking by myself."

"That's it."

His face got serious but still held remnants of his laughter. "Even if you're wrong, he can always use a little bullying. I wish I could see his face when you show up."

"I'll take a picture."

Howie patted me on the shoulder and stood up.

"What about your research?" I asked. "What are you thinking?"

He put his hands in his pockets and looked toward the main barn. "I'll tell you when you get back. That'll give me a little more time to check on some stuff."

"You sure?"

He wouldn't look me in the eye, but nodded. "I'm sure." He turned to go, and I suddenly had a terrible thought.

"You're not getting the sickness are you?"

He kept his back to me. "Just tired, Princess. Just tired." He disappeared into his apartment.

After an anxious minute spent worrying about his health, I went to my office to finish my planning. The light on the answering machine was blinking. I punched play.

"Stella, it's Nick. Just wanted to see if you were ready for some help, or something. I'll call again later."

I sat back and thought about how different my life had been when he'd showed up three days ago. I wished I could still feel that just seeing his face—well, the rest of him, too—could make my day complete. All that beauty wasted.

A second message started to play.

"Brigham Bergey here. Sorry I missed you. Abraham Granger gave me a call and said you might need some help. Give me a call at your convenience and I'll see what I can do."

I dialed the number he left, but now the lawyer was out for lunch.

"I can leave him a detailed message, if you like," the secretary said.

I liked. I gave her Richard's name and number, the number of the main insurance company, and an explanation of what had happened. She promised to give it to her boss as soon as he came in.

I hung up, took a deep breath, and called Hubert's office. His receptionist answered.

"CHP, may I help you?"

"Stella Crown here. I'd like to speak to Hubert."

"One moment." I heard a split second of Muzak before Hubert picked up.

"Stella?"

"It's me, Hubert."

"The farmer of my dreams."

Nightmares, maybe. "I've been doing a lot of thinking. Things aren't going so well here, and I want to find out about my options."

He was quiet. If he were smart, he'd realize I would never capitulate and my call had to be bogus. But greed can make a person stupid.

"How can I help, Stella?"

"Is there any way you'd have some time later to go over some things with me?"

I could visualize dollar signs popping out of Hubert's head.

"Sure, Stella. Whenever is convenient for you."

"How about six? At your office?"

"You got it. I'll be here. Say, would you like to do dinner, instead? We could meet at—"

"I don't think so, Hubert. I really haven't got much of an appetite."

"Right, right. Okay, then, see you here around six."

"Thanks so much, Hubert." Might as well envelop him in charm. I'd eradicate it soon enough.

I made another call, got a promise that more help was on the way, and decided I'd better do a little work around the farm until it was time to go deal with Hubert.

By five o'clock I had scraped the paddock, emptied all the manure into the lagoon, and fed the heifers and yearlings. Once I stopped working long enough to stand still I could feel my fury beginning to emerge from where I'd shoved it for the afternoon.

I went into the house, did my usual stripping routine, and took a long, hot shower. Once I had thoroughly steamed up the bathroom, I stepped out and began the process of deciding exactly what to wear. It was much more fun than picking out clothes for the co-op dinner.

When I was dressed and primped, I checked the final result in my mirror. I was wearing my fancy boots, seeing as how they had higher heels and bore the nice, thick chain. My black jeans were partially covered by my fringed leather chaps, which matched the vest I'd snapped over my black tank top. For good measure, I put on my riding gloves—leather over the palms with the fingers cut out—and tied a red bandanna around my throat. My tattoo showed up nicely on my neck, and the one on my arm looked great. I gave myself a thumbs-up. I might get hot, but the effect was worth it.

I went out to the garage to pull out my bike and shine it up with a rag. It didn't take much to make it sparkle since I'd just washed it the other day. Around five-thirty I heard some throaty rumbling, and two more Harleys pulled into the drive. I went to meet them.

"Hey, guys," I said, once the motors were off.

That last call I'd made had been to the Biker Barn, where I'd found Bart and Lenny back from their swap meet and eager to help. They were some of the nicest guys I knew, and when I'd told them about my plan, they'd laughed.

"You want us to be the big, bad bikers and scare the crap outta that cheap bastard?" Bart had said. "Count us in. We'll try to look mean."

Now, Lenny stepped off his ride and gave me the peace sign. I checked him out and nodded my approval. If I were Miss Ordinary Citizen I wouldn't want to meet Lenny anywhere except a very public place at high noon. His red hair was still wild, sticking out from under his almost non-existent—and definitely not DOT approved—helmet, but his beard had been tamed into a braid that reached down to touch his chest. Under his black vest he wore a black T-shirt tucked into his jeans. His riding boots looked heavy and huge.

Bart's look was just as good, although his was more a wiry threat, while Lenny's was bulk. Bart was decked out in all black, with the addition of a wallet with a chain that hooked onto his belt loop, and a sheathed knife I wasn't sure was legal.

"Nice timing cover," he said.

I glanced at the grinning skull. In all the excitement I'd forgotten it was an under-the-table gift from Lenny.

"Oops," I said.

Bart looked at me and then at Lenny. Neither of us confessed. Bart turned his face to the sky, hands raised. "Lord, why do you send me these trials?"

"Dressed like this, I'd never guess you were a churchman," I said.

He dropped his hands. "Hey, so was John the Baptist—and everybody was scared of him."

"Are we it?" Lenny asked.

"One more."

A couple of seconds later we heard what sounded like a really pissed off thunderstorm. Jermaine appeared, sitting low and large on his Fat Boy.

"Oh, man," Lenny said. "Hubert's gonna wet his pants."

Jermaine pulled up and cut his engine, giving us all the once over.

I smiled and yelled, "Howie!"

Howie appeared in the door of the milking parlor, where he had just gotten the herd clipped in.

"What do you think?" I asked.

His grim face broke into a smile, and he walked out to get a close-up view, Queenie at his heels. "What I think is that Hubert Purcell will be the least of our worries after tonight. He won't even want to *imagine* you, for fear he'll die." He gave me a hug. Then, holding his hand on the back of my neck, he looked solemnly into my eyes.

"You be careful, okay, Princess? I'll be waiting to hear the whole story when you get back."

"You got it, partner."

He gave my neck a light slap and stepped back while we mounted our bikes. The sound of all four bikes starting was enough to send Queenie hustling back into the barn. I held up my hand, gave the go ahead sign, and led my trusty hunters to our kill.

We cut our engines about half a block from Hubert's office, coasting to a stop in front of the building. I sat for a moment and considered what we were about to do. I hoped it was the right thing, and guessed I'd know in a little bit if it was. If Hubert wasn't ready to give me his first-born when we left, then I should've done something else.

We got off our bikes and left our helmets on the ground beside them. Lenny pulled a leather skull cap over his head, and Jermaine decided to leave his sunglasses on. I approved of both.

Hubert's receptionist, a little-bitty blonde thing held over to announce Hubert's important visitor, looked up with something approaching terror when I entered the lobby. I could tell when the guys got in the door because she dropped her pen and actually started to shake.

"Hubert's expecting me," I said. "No need to call back."

I don't think the poor girl had the wits left to remember her boss' name, let alone call him, so I walked past her toward Hubert's door. I rapped on it with my knuckles.

"Come on in," Hubert said.

I opened his door and went in. He stood and looked at me for a moment, taking in my clothes, and forced a smile. He never did approve of my biker leanings.

"So nice to see you, Stella. Please have a seat." He gestured to a chair in front of the desk and sat back down in the leather executive chair I'd just seen on TV.

"I hope you don't mind I brought someone with me," I said.

"Not at all, not at all. I thought you might bring Howie, since he has a lot invested in your farm, too."

"Oh, I didn't bring Howie."

I waved to the guys, and they walked in to fill up the space.

A look of utter horror swept over Hubert's face as Bart and Lenny entered the room, but that was nothing compared to the squeak he gave out when Jermaine dipped his head under the doorjamb and squeezed through the door.

I sat in the chair Hubert had offered. "Like I said, I hope you don't mind I brought support."

Hubert stammered for a moment before shutting his mouth. Bart sat beside me on the other chair, while Lenny and Jermaine drifted toward opposite sides of Hubert's desk.

I shook my head and clicked my tongue. "Hubert, Hubert, Hubert. I know we've never been the best of friends. I know we've actually leaned toward hostilities. But violence? Deceit? I thought your level of scumminess was above that."

His eyes rolled. "I don't know what you're talking about. What *are* you talking about?"

I leaned back in my chair, crossing my right ankle onto my left knee, and played with the chain on my boot. Jermaine found something interesting on the desk and leaned toward Hubert to look at it. A bead of sweat rolled down Hubert's face, and his ears started to turn red.

"Let's see," I said. "Shall I list your latest accomplishments, or do you want to do the honors?"

He seemed incapable of speech, so I ticked off the items on my fingers.

"Okay, first we have my manure lagoon. Not much danger. Not much work to do. The worst that can happen is I have to shell out some of my pollution liability insurance. But I caught it in time, even though you'd already made the call to Pam Moyer.

"Second, one of my cows drops dead in the pasture, electrocuted. What did your lackey use? Battery charger? Portable generator? The lost money is a problem, but the thought of the cruelty is what really gets my goat.

"Third, my electricity goes out. I know, that does happen naturally sometimes, but really, how often does a squirrel actually make a nest and feed on the wires in the main box? Too bad for you, my generator worked like a top. Didn't think of screwing that up, huh?

"What was next? Oh yeah, Zach Granger's calf is hung in his hutch. It's such a rare occurrence I knew there was outside help. God, Hubert, you're sick."

He looked like he was going to say something, but Jermaine made a low growling noise, and Hubert's mouth shut with a pop.

"Okay, what else could go wrong?" I said. I was beginning to enjoy myself. "How else could we screw up Stella's farm so she'll want to give in? There's got to be something a little different. Something not mechanical. I know, let's let the cows out. It will make a mess, be a lot of work to round them up, and maybe we'll get lucky and one of them will cause a terrible accident by getting on the road and killing some innocent people.

"But that wasn't enough, was it? I wasn't taking the bait. Or else you just wanted to completely stack things your way. How 'bout we burn down Stella's barn, after canceling insurance on it, perhaps killing all forty of her heifers, and maybe her and Howie, if we're lucky?"

I held up my hands, fingers splayed. "That's six nasty items, Hubert. And I didn't even mention the fresh-faced real estate lawyer you sicced on me. Oh, here's his card in case you forgot about him." I pulled it from my pocket and placed it on his desk. "I hope he gave you my message, by the way. Are there more things I have yet to discover?"

He opened and closed his mouth a few times, making him look like the large-mouthed bass Jethro had mounted above his fireplace, but no sounds came out except for a high, breathy whistle.

I leaned forward in my chair and smiled. "Now, Hubert." I tried to sound sweet, which is hard for me at the best of times. "Have you anything to say for yourself?"

Hubert swallowed forcefully and glanced up at Jermaine, who seemed to find Hubert very intriguing.

"It's okay, Hu," I said. "You have permission to speak."

He cleared his throat and forced himself to look at me. "Okay, I did the manure lagoon. Like you said, how much harm could it do?" He looked at me expectantly, but I stayed silent. "And the electricity, it seemed harmless. I figured you'd have a generator. And letting the cows out—I just thought it would be a pain, not that it could kill anybody. But I swear, that's all I know about. I don't know anything about any dead cow, or calf, or, for God's sake, your barn. I wouldn't *do* something like that."

I looked at him, saw the desperation in his eyes, and thought he just might be telling the truth. "If that's true, how come animals have died? How come Howie and I had to risk our lives to save others? I gotta tell you, Hubert, it's getting old."

His face flushed, and he sputtered. "I *told* her to stop—" He clamped his mouth shut and looked horrified.

My insides tightened, but I made myself retain an outer show of calm. "*Her?*"

Hubert looked down at the desk, above my shoulders, anywhere but at my face. "I can't...."

"Jermaine," I said. "Hammer."

Jermaine straightened and looked a good three feet down at Hubert. Lenny put a hand on Hubert's shoulder and gave him a pat and a smile. It wasn't a pretty smile.

"I think you can tell me, Hubert," I said. "I can't imagine that, whoever she is, she's either as big or as persuasive as my friends here."

"Oh, *God*." Hubert put his head down on his desk and started to sob. I let him go for a minute, then made an encouraging sound.

"It was never supposed to come to this," he said. He took his fist and pounded it on the desktop. I looked at the guys and they gave me looks of amusement compounded with rage.

"Spill it, Hu," I said. "You'll feel much better once you do. Believe me."

His sobs stopped, but he remained face down on the desk.

"Who is she, Hubert?"

He lifted his tear-swollen face and took a couple of shivering breaths.

"Come *on*," I said.

"It was Marianne. Okay? Marianne Granger."

I sat with my mouth open, and blood pounded in my ears. I glanced at Jermaine, who looked as dumbstruck as I felt.

"*Marianne?*" I said. "Marianne killed Zach's calf? And burned down my barn?"

Hubert nodded miserably. "She first came to me just wanting to put you back a little. She figured if you sold your farm Jude would have less land to work, and he might be so disheartened he'd be willing to give up farming. You know how it is finding land to rent around here. Impossible."

I suddenly had a flashback from the day before, when Jermaine had mistaken me for Marianne on the phone. No wonder my insurance rep thought I'd called him. I only talked to him twice a year, usually, so Marianne could have easily faked being me. The sneaky little bitch.

"So Marianne wasn't ready to stop harassing me when you were, huh, Hu?" I said.

He shook his head. "She's desperate. I don't know why. She said she'd do whatever it took, whether I went along or not." He looked at me, a glimmer of hope in his eyes. "I told her just last night I'd have nothing else to do with it. I'd wait until you were ready to sell. I couldn't deal with any more sabotage. I don't want to go to jail."

I stared into Hubert's eyes, trying to understand where he'd derailed. I'd told him unlimited times, in unquestionable ways, that he would never get my land. And yet here he was, gazing at me hopefully. I closed my eyes, then leaned my elbows on his desk. I sighed and looked at him.

"I know you want my farm, Hubert. Your participation in this...little scheme shows me just how desperate you are. But, you know, I have friends. You've now met some of them. And I don't think you have friends like I have friends. So, let's make a little agreement."

He closed his mouth again and managed what I chose to interpret as a nod.

"Good. Here's the agreement. You stay so far away from me, my farm, and anything remotely attached to it, that it would never occur to me to think of you, ever. Okay? Oh, what do you get from our agreement? You will keep the use of your legs. You will continue breathing. You will not wake up to find yourself holed up in a burning barn. Have we got ourselves a deal?"

A tear made its way slowly down Hubert's face, and for a moment I was afraid I was going to begin laughing hysterically. I controlled myself and stood up. Bart stood beside me, and Hubert was caught looking up at the four of us.

"You also will not contact Marianne Granger ever again," I said. "That means you are not to warn her once we are out this door. If you do, I *will* find out."

I stuck out my hand and Hubert winced so forcefully I was afraid he'd gotten whiplash.

"Have we got ourselves a deal?"

Hubert held out his hand, which, to his credit, shook so slightly I could hardly see it, and I gripped it as hard as I could.

"So glad we could do business together." I turned and walked out of the room. Bart followed, but Lenny and Jermaine held out a moment longer before crowding into the lobby. The receptionist, not surprisingly, had fled.

"So did he?" Bart asked Lenny.

"I think so. I stole a glance at his pants and they weren't looking any too dry."

We got out to our bikes and I sank onto mine, trying to take in the meaning of what Hubert had said.

"So my sister-in-law is a psycho," Jermaine said. He stood in front of me, pretty much blocking all other sights.

"So she is."

He pounded a fist into his other hand. "Is she next?"

I shook my head. "We can't go after her like this."

"Why not?" Bart said. "Sounds like she deserves it worse than Purcell."

"She does," Jermaine said.

"She does," I agreed. "But she's also married to your brother."

Jermaine stared at me for a couple of seconds before looping his thumbs over his belt and heaving a huge sigh.

"So what's the plan?" Lenny asked.

"I'm not sure, but I *am* sure that I need to do it alone."

All three made sputtering noises, and I put up my hand. "She may have been able to kill Cleopatra and a little calf, but she's no match for me."

They looked at me.

"That's true," Bart said.

Jermaine frowned. "I don't like it."

"I'll be fine."

He fidgeted a bit, but he could see I wasn't open to options. "Okay. But I want a call when you get home safe."

"That I can do."

He finally shrugged and swung his leg over his scooter.

When we started the bikes I could see the glass on Hubert's front door vibrating, but Hubert failed to make an appearance.

We let the bikes idle while I hopped off mine and shook all their hands, giving them slaps on their backs.

"Thanks, guys," I yelled.

Lenny grinned. "Our pleasure."

"You know I'm going to have to say about fifty Hail Marys for this," Bart said.

Lenny pointed at me. "You be careful, now."

I gave him a thumbs-up, and he and Bart waved and took off for home.

Jermaine reached over and gave me a hard hug around my waist. "You gonna be okay?"

"I'll be a lot more okay once it's dealt with."

"You sure you won't let me come along?"

"I'm sure. You get on home to your wife and baby."

"You're the boss."

I swung my leg over my bike and flipped up the kickstand. Jermaine stayed until I was on the road, then turned and went the other way.

Chapter Twenty-Four

"Hey, Jude," I said.

"Hey."

He had a sandwich in one hand and held the door open with the other. His face looked less ashen than it had the last time I'd seen him, when he was practically comatose beside his defunct combine. He gestured me in, glancing at my leathers but not commenting on them. From his lack of excitement and concern, I assumed he had yet to hear about my barn.

I stepped into the living room and Jerry Seinfeld smiled out at me from a little TV. Jude must have been settled on the sofa for supper, because there was a glass sitting on the end table, making a ring, along with a bag of chips. I sat on the edge of the La-Z-Boy, resting my elbows on my knees, and looked at the floor. I was afraid Jude would be able to read my eyes if I looked at him.

"I decided to hire a guy to harvest my oats," Jude said. "So I won't need your tractor. Thanks, though."

I nodded, still not looking at him.

"Marianne in?" I asked the carpet.

"Upstairs. Taking a nap."

"Any idea how long she'll sleep?"

Before he could answer we heard a creak on the stairs. I looked up, waiting. Marianne came around the corner and stopped short when she saw me.

"Hello, Stella," she said. "Did you come to find out if Jude knew who was in your field the other night? I asked him, but he didn't know."

I said nothing. Just looked at her. She stared right back.

"I'm going to grab some supper," she said. "Would you like anything?"

I continued to look at her. She made a move toward the kitchen.

"You didn't have to ask Jude about those lights in my field," I said, "because you knew who it was. It was Hubert, sabotaging my manure lagoon."

She stopped, her back stiff and her head high. I continued.

"That was just the beginning. The manure lagoon was kids' play compared to what came next. Animal abuse. Arson. Now, I know from the way you acted when you saw Zach's calf and the new kittens that you really don't care about animals, but surely *human* life means something to you?"

She didn't move. Jude sat gawking at me. "What in the Sam Hill are you talking about, Stella?"

"Ask your wife. Ask her how come the day after my barn burns down I find out I have no insurance. Ask her how come wires in my electrical box were cut through, or why cows were wandering onto the road last night. Ask her how it is that Zach's little calf got hung in its hutch and another full-grown cow was electrocuted in the middle of a field."

"*What?*"

"Marianne," I said, "did you ever stop to think that Howie or I would die ourselves before we let our heifers get burned alive? Or that Gus' death would be traumatic to your nephew, who doesn't need anything further to compromise his health?"

My pulse beat at the side of my throat, and my breath came in quick bursts. I made myself stay sitting and tried to exude nothing but calm. A thought hit me like a thunderbolt.

"And I can't be certain, but I'm pretty sure my dog wouldn't wander several miles away on her own."

Marianne's shoulders twitched in response, but Jude cut off her reply by jumping up from the sofa. His hands clenched, and he rocked on the balls of his feet.

"I don't know what you're talking about, Stella, but you can just get the hell out of my house."

I sighed and looked down at my hands, hanging between my knees. "What are you gonna do, Jude? Pick me up and throw me out? Break my legs because I'm giving your wife a hard time? Come on."

"Who do you think—"

"Stop, Jude." Marianne's quiet command echoed in the small room. Slowly, she turned toward me, avoiding eye contact with her husband.

"What happened?" she asked. I knew she wasn't asking about the barn or Queenie—she obviously didn't care about either.

"I just had a little talk with Hubert," I said. "He was a bit flustered and said more than he should have."

She stood as if frozen, her eyes never leaving my face, her jaw tight.

"*Why*, Marianne? I know you've never loved farming, but *this?*"

"Would someone tell me what's going on?" Jude still stood over me, but he was no longer a threat. Marianne didn't respond to him, but I wasn't about to explain her transgressions. I wanted him to hear it from her own lips.

"Tell him, Marianne."

She kept staring at me, not moving except for a slight trembling that had begun in her lips and moved on to her hands. I might have missed it if I hadn't been looking for something to give away her tension.

Jude went to her and tried to take her hands in his. She shook him off and strode to the other side of the room, where she stood looking out the window. The room was dead silent for at least a minute before she spoke.

"I can't stand it anymore. This life. Farming. Not knowing if next month will be the one when the phone gets turned off. Depending on the weather for how stingy we have to be this winter. Wearing the same clothes over and over until they're practically threadbare, just so we can put gas in the combine. I can't *stand* it." She turned and looked at me. "That's why."

I completely understood what she was saying, as I had said practically identical words to Howie the night before. I snuck a look at Jude and he stood like a man paralyzed. He either hadn't been reading Marianne's signals or had chosen to ignore them.

"You're not happy?" he asked, his voice small.

"Oh, Jude." Marianne clutched her head. "Are you completely dense? Have my needs been so secondary you've completely blocked them out? I married you under the impression that farming was something you were going to try out. That eventually something else would catch your fancy. Year after year I hoped it would be the last."

Jude stared at her, his face starting to harden. "Farming is my life. It always has been, and you know it. If you thought different, you were dreaming."

Marianne spun away from him, her nostrils flaring. Jude took a step toward her.

"You did all those things yourself? You killed Zach's calf?" He looked at me, suddenly realizing what I'd said. "You burned down Stella's *barn?*"

"And," she said slowly, "messed up your combine."

Jude made a choking sound, and Marianne turned cold eyes on him. "Did you really think those holes got in the air filter on their own? The way you baby your machines? I swear you care more about that hunk of metal than about our family. All I did was try to preserve what little we have left going for us. I can see now how little it really is. You're just a stupid boy in a big man's body."

Jude made a move toward her, and I jumped up and got in between them. The last thing Jude needed was to have charges brought against him for battery.

"Jude, why don't you give Belle and Jethro a call? See if they can come over for a while?"

"I don't want them here."

"I know you don't. But I think it may be better for you if they were."

He locked eyes with me for a long time before leaving the room to find a phone.

Marianne snorted. "So now you're going to protect me? Be my knight in shining armor?"

I swung around, grabbed her shirt, and knocked her up against the wall, her feet dangling. I put my face so close to hers our noses were touching.

"I will never, ever, in my whole life, do anything to protect you, help you, or aid you. Understand? Jude is the one who has my loyalty, and I will do everything in my power to see that you are prosecuted for everything you've done. You've killed—"

"*Animals.*"

I pulled her away from the wall and banged her against it again.

"You have killed, vandalized, and sabotaged. I just hope Jude gets away from you before you destroy him, too."

She laughed and I breathed in through my nose to keep from hitting her again. Jude came back into the room and stopped when he saw us.

"You want to know why I decided to do this now?" Marianne said, her voice tight from being held against the wall. "After all this time?"

I stared at her, not sure I really wanted to know. I could feel Jude's tension behind me. Marianne laughed again.

"I'm pregnant."

Chapter Twenty-Five

The shock in the room was tangible.

Jude bent over at the waist like someone had punched him, and I dropped Marianne, not wanting to touch her. She smoothed out her blouse, smirking, and I went to the other side of the room before I did something I'd regret.

After ten years, Jethro and Belle arrived. I watched them park and walk slowly toward the house, not sure what to expect. Keeping an eye on Jude and Marianne, I opened the front door.

"What's happening?" Belle whispered. She eyed my biker outfit curiously.

Jethro pushed himself in. "What the hell is going on? That's the strangest phone call I've ever gotten. 'Come over before I kill my wife'?" He gestured wildly, looking from Jude to Marianne, then finally at me.

"It was my idea," I said.

"That he kills Marianne?" Spittle flew from Jethro's mouth.

"Of course not." *Although that may not be such a bad idea.* "I meant that he called you. It seemed the best thing at the time."

He opened his mouth to speak again, but Belle put her hand on his arm. "I think we should sit down and hear what they have to say."

She pulled Jethro over to the sofa and pushed him into it. Jude was too tense to sit, and stood like a statue where he was. Marianne, a strange smile on her face, slowly walked to the

La-Z-Boy and sank into it, looking intently at something down toward her feet.

"So?" Jethro said.

Jude looked at me, but I held up my hands. "Not my ball game anymore, Jude."

"But—"

"No. I have problems of my own to take care of. Thanks to your wife."

Jethro and Belle looked at me with confusion, but Marianne didn't react at all, keeping her eyes focused on something I couldn't see. Jude sighed and turned toward the wall, leaning his forehead against it.

"They have a story to tell," I said.

Marianne finally raised her head. "You know all those trips to the fertility clinic?"

If that was her opening, I didn't want to hear the rest. I slipped out the front door.

The whole way home I tried to feel relieved and grateful that the sabotage was over. I had found the culprits. I would give Detective Willard a call, and they would be prosecuted. No matter how much I wanted to grab my twenty-two and take care of them myself, I figured I'd be better off letting the law do its thing. By the last mile of the ride, I was beginning to feel pleased with myself for having put the pieces together and taken care of my farm.

The fresh sight of my flattened heifer barn drove any feelings of success completely away. I might have stopped the sabotage, but I still had a lot of work to do to fix it all.

I drove up to the garage and parked the bike, leaving it out to cool. I set my helmet down, pulled off my biking gloves, and dropped my vest and chaps onto the seat. The lights were still on in the barn, so I figured I'd help Howie finish the after-milking clean-up.

I walked into the barn and was surprised to see the cows still clipped in. The stalls should've been empty and almost cleaned out by that time. Besides the cows' presence, something else seemed strange, too, but I couldn't put my finger on it.

"Howie?"

I looked at the cows, either licking up the last of their grain or lying in their stalls, and was suddenly struck by the oddity. The cows' udders were still full. The guys and I had left Howie at the start of milking almost two hours before and it looked like only the first few cows had been emptied. The milking hoses lay on the ground underneath the depleted sacks, and I could hear the motor running, but no milk was shooting through the transparent tubing.

"Howie?" I said again, a little louder.

I peered down each aisle, afraid I'd find Howie lying among the cows, having been kicked in the head or struck down by a heart attack, but he wasn't there. A whining sound came from behind me and I suddenly realized Queenie hadn't met me in the drive.

I turned to walk into the feed room and almost tripped over Howie, who was lying on the floor with a gaping hole in his stomach. Blood was everywhere, spattered on the walls, the feed bins, even Queenie, who lay with her face on her paws right by Howie's head.

"Oh, my God," I breathed.

I dropped to my knees by Howie and looked into his glassy, still eyes. Trying to stem my panic, I put my face by his mouth and after a few horrible seconds could feel the barest of breath.

"Howie, you ugly old bastard," I said. "Don't you dare die on me." My voice shook.

I looked around frantically. One of my flannel shirts was hanging by a nail on the wall and I yanked it down and wadded it up on Howie's stomach. I talked to keep myself from crumbling.

"You're not old enough to retire, Howie, but I would've let you have a vacation. If that's what this is all about."

Howie made a choking sound, and for a petrifying moment I thought he'd stopped breathing. I leaned down into his face and hoped I wasn't imagining the fluttery air on my cheeks. He didn't seem to see me, but the choking sound could've been in response to my voice. I kept up my patter, knowing I should call 911, but afraid to leave him.

"Dammit, Howie. Can't I let you for an hour or two? Do I have to hire Mallory to come baby-sit when I go away?"

Queenie's ears perked up and I heard someone drive in the lane. The vehicle's door opened and closed.

"Help!" I screamed. "Whoever's out there! Help!"

I heard footsteps coming toward the barn. "Stella?"

"Call 911!"

Nick came running into the barn and followed my voice. When he looked around the corner, the blood drained from his face and he stopped still.

"Call 911!" I yelled. He still didn't move. "Nick!" I threw a handful of grain at him, and he sputtered. "Call from my office!"

Nick shivered, then turned and sprinted away. I could hear him clattering around, opening my door, and then the staccato of his voice on the phone.

I sneaked a look under the now blood-soaked shirt at Howie's stomach and tried to assess the damage. From what I could see, Howie didn't have much of an abdomen left. His insides were all mixed together, along with blood, grain, and straw from the floor. I put the shirt back and started to say the only prayer I could remember. "Now I lay me down to sleep—"

Nick came running back to the feed room. "They're on their way. My God, what happened?"

I shook my head. "I think...I think he's been shot." Nick put his hand on my shoulder and squeezed. A sob fought its way up my throat and I forced myself to take a deep, shuddering breath.

"Go out and wait for them," I said. "I want them in here right away."

"Sure." He gave my shoulder another squeeze and ran outside.

Queenie whimpered, and I stroked her head. She was lying on the opposite side of Howie, and she laid her head back onto her paws, her nose at Howie's cheek. I lay down, too, and put my mouth by Howie's ear, wrapping my arm around his chest and holding him tightly.

"You should've seen Hubert. I swear he pissed his pants when Jermaine walked in. He looked at us like he'd been kidnapped by the Hell's Angels. If he'd known Bart's a regular churchman and Jermaine's got the sweetest baby daughter in the world, our plan wouldn't have worked."

My voice broke and I pushed my face into Howie's neck. I got myself together and continued.

"He didn't really admit to it all, but I guess I didn't give him much of a chance. All I know is he wouldn't come near us now at gunpoint."

That stopped me cold.

"But Hubert's not it, Howie. You'll never believe it. It was Marianne who did the worst of it. Zach's calf, Cleopatra, the barn."

Howie gurgled, and my heartbeat was skyrocketing when I finally heard sirens—for the second time in less than twenty-four hours. It was the sweetest sound in the world. I heard doors opening and closing, and Nick's voice, then feet running toward us.

The tiny room filled with paramedics, and claustrophobia came roaring out of nowhere. One of the guys grabbed at my arm on Howie's chest, and I kicked him in the shin. Another tried to move my legs, but I fought and kicked until he let go, and I laid my head back down by Howie's ear.

"Hey," Nick said gently. I felt his hand on my back. "These folks want to help Howie, but they can't unless they can get to him."

My muscles relaxed slightly, but I didn't let go of Howie.

"You and Queenie have taken care of him up to now," Nick said. "It's time to let these people have a turn. Okay?"

I took a deep breath and turned my head to look at him. His face was kind and serious, and I suddenly realized I was acting like a crazy person. I got up on my elbow, stroked Howie's face with my hand, and put my mouth down to his ear.

"Don't you die, Howie, old man." I pressed my cheek against his. "Queenie and I love you."

I took Nick's hand and let him help me up. "C'mon, Queenie." I didn't think she'd obey, but she finally came to my outstretched hand.

As soon as we were out of the room I heard lots of noise, and before I knew what was happening, Howie was on a stretcher, being hustled out to the ambulance. I ran after them and tried to get in the back, but the doors slammed before I could get in.

"Wait!" I screamed, but the ambulance was already hurtling down the driveway, siren blaring.

Nick came up beside me and I grabbed him, forcing him toward his truck. I threw him in the passenger's side and pushed him toward the steering wheel, then jumped in after him. "Follow them!"

Nick got the truck started and floored it. We caught up to the ambulance and stayed right behind them, running the traffic lights and avoiding other cars, all the way to the hospital. I had the door open before the truck had stopped, and was as close as they'd let me get while they pushed Howie into the emergency room. I followed until we arrived at some double doors where two orderlies were standing guard.

"Sorry, Miss," one said. "This is as far as you go."

I took a step toward the door, and he put a hand on my arm. I looked down at his thick fingers and how they firmly grasped my elbow. Resigned, I pulled away and dropped onto a vinyl couch to wait.

A few minutes later, Nick came in and sat by me. I hadn't even missed him. He just sat there, not speaking, not touching me. He was just there.

Every few minutes I broke the monotony of the sitcom on the wall-mounted TV by jumping up and pacing the room until I felt even worse, so I'd sit again. Nick didn't say anything or try to stop me.

"Stella!" Abe came running into the waiting room during one of my "up" stages and stopped in front of me, looking at my clothes. I glanced down and was shocked at all the blood. I was also surprised to see I was still in my blacks and boots.

"You okay?" Abe asked.

"No, I'm not, Abe."

"Sorry. Stupid thing to say."

"What are you doing here?"

"Nick called and told me what happened. He thought you might want me here."

I turned to Nick and he looked away, studying the tile on the floor. The man kept surprising me.

"Anything I can do?" Abe asked.

"Nothing much *to* do. We're just…waiting."

Abe sat in one of the other vinyl chairs and became a part of the vigil. The guys sat, and I alternated between sitting and pacing, until the double doors opened and a man in a blue surgical outfit came out, looking serious and sad.

"No," I said.

He shook his head. "I'm sorry."

I turned and walked out of the emergency room. I didn't know where I was going, except out of the hospital. I somehow got to the road and kept walking. In the midst of my fog, Nick soon pulled his truck ahead of me and stopped. He stepped out and opened the passenger door. I got in.

He drove around for a while, taking a couple of secluded, country roads, and eventually headed back to my place. I sat in the truck, my head resting against the side window, and watched the fields, traffic, and houses go by, until the house I finally saw was my own.

Chapter Twenty-Six

We sat in the driveway for a few minutes, saying nothing and sitting completely still, until I noticed we weren't alone. There were at least three police cars, an unmarked van, and two other cars crowded into my driveway.

"Oh, God," I said. "This is really happening, isn't it?"

After few more minutes of frozen silence, I took a deep breath and stepped down from the truck. Queenie came slinking up and I knelt and put my arms around her neck, burying my face in her fur. I sat there until I felt Nick's hand on my shoulder.

"Looks like you've got more company."

A cherry-red VW Bug pulled up and Missy got out, accompanied by a skinny and pale Zach. They stood by the car, behind the doors, seemingly unsure how I'd react to seeing them. I stood up and looked from one to the other.

"We hear the cows are in need of milking," Missy said. Her eyes flicked to Nick, and I was sure he'd been the one who'd made the call.

I turned to Zach. His shoulders jumped in a kind of agreement, but he didn't look at me.

"They are," I said. I had forgotten all about them standing in their stalls, udders tight and unforgiving.

Missy waved toward the barn. "We're here to help."

"You sure you feel up to it?" I asked Zach.

His shoulders moved again, and I took that for a yes.

Nick gave me a gentle push, and I used the momentum to send me toward my house. Zach was sneaking peeks at my bloody clothes, and I knew I needed to change.

"I'll be out in a minute."

Missy nodded and they shut the car doors. I went in, stripped off my jeans and shirt, and shoved them into the trash can. The washer wouldn't be able to get out everything I needed it to.

A few minutes later I was in different pants and a tank top. Missy and Zach followed me to the milkhouse, where Officer Rude stopped me.

"You can't come in here."

I took a deep breath and stepped closer to him. He straightened up, but didn't back away.

"Listen, Meadows," I said. "If you don't let me in, these cows are going to riot. They have extremely full udders, and if I don't milk them, they will get sick, contract mastitis, and end up with other sicknesses I don't have the time to explain to you, but will blame you for. Besides, if you don't let me by, I will personally take your nightstick and beat your head in."

"Just a minute—"

"It's okay, Officer Meadows." Detective Willard stepped up and put a restraining hand on the policeman's shoulder.

"You?" I said.

He looked terrible, gray and fatigued, but I didn't have the energy to feel sorry for him. He met my eyes and tilted his head toward the cows. "You need to get these girls milked, don't you, Ms. Crown?"

I nodded shortly.

He pulled Meadows aside and stepped in front of him. "All I ask is that you stay out of the feed room and anywhere else you don't absolutely have to be, okay? You work around us, and we'll work around you."

I considered this request and even in my numb state decided it was reasonable. "Okay."

Willard stepped aside and I went in, flanked by my two self-appointed assistants. Officer Meadows glowered. The two people collecting evidence in the feed room and parlor didn't even look up. Missy and Zach stood in front of me, and I finally realized they needed instructions.

"Zach, go get some feed from the feed barn. Start with the hay. Missy, grab the paper towels and a bucket and start cleaning off the teats."

Silently, they both did my bidding. I stood by the first cow—one of the few who had been milked—and rested my forehead on her back. I breathed in her smell and warmth, listening to the thumping of her heart until my brain started to work again. I pushed off of her and began putting the milkers on the cows Missy had prepared.

Zach had finished with hay and was pouring out grain, and Missy was halfway done with cleaning, when Detective Willard showed up beside me.

"Any chance I could steal you away for a few minutes?"

I was shaking my head when Missy spoke. "I think I could handle this part. I did it last time, remember?"

She must have seen doubt on my face, because she added, "Besides, Zach's here if I need help. He's done this hundreds of times."

I looked at Zach over the cows' backs, and he finally made eye contact with me. I raised my eyebrows and he jerked his head yes.

"Okay. Looks like I've got enough back-up. Let's go to my office."

"Well, um, we've kind of already gotten set up in there."

I stared at Willard and he looked embarrassed. "We needed a phone and a desk to work on. I'm sorry. I should've asked."

"Damn straight."

I marched in front of him to my office and flung open the door. The first thing I noticed was Pam Moyer sitting in one of the chairs. I ignored her, because Officer Meadows was sitting in my chair, using my phone, and writing with my pen on a piece of paper taken from my printer. I walked over to him, took the receiver from his hand and replaced it on the cradle. Then

I slid my pen out of his fingers, lifted him by the armpits, and dumped him on the floor. I floated the piece of paper over his head and he snatched at it before it hit the ground.

"Thank you, Officer," I said, and sat down. "Have a seat, Detective."

Meadows stood up, sputtering and angry, until he noticed the detective and Pam were simply staring at him, not offering any sympathy. He shut his mouth.

"That will be all for now, Officer Meadows," Willard said.

"But—"

"I'll let you know when you're needed."

Meadows stomped out of the room, slamming the door on his way out.

I looked at Pam. She held her hands out, then let them drop to her lap. "God, Stella, I'm so sorry."

I swallowed. "Thank you."

"I just...I stopped by to see if there's anything I can help with."

Her eyes started to water, and I pushed my fingers against my own. "I can't think of anything right now. Maybe later."

She studied my face for a few moments, then stood and turned to Willard. "If you don't need me, Detective, I'll get out of the way. But please give me a call if something comes up that I can do."

She left, closing the door quietly.

Willard looked at me, his eyes sad.

I spun my chair away from him and focused on the photograph of my farm. Anything to keep my thoughts off of Howie lying on the feed room floor. I could feel Willard scrutinizing me. He dove right in.

"You're Mr. Archer's next of kin, am I right?"

"Not exactly," I said to the photograph. "But the closest either of us had. He's been the farmhand here ever since I can remember. Helped me keep the place going when my mother died. Been here ever since."

"And you're the daughter he never had."

"We never talked about it that way."

"Okay. Tell me what happened today."

I took a deep breath and my brain locked up. I didn't want to remember what had happened that day, even though I figured it somehow had to do with everything that had been going on. Apparently, talking with Marianne and scaring the shit out of Hubert hadn't solved anything.

"Please, Ms. Crown."

"Well, you know about the dead cows, the manure lagoon, and that phone call I asked you to trace. I thought I'd figured out the puzzle." I swung my chair around to his surprised face. "I thought I'd taken care of it, too."

Ten minutes later I had outlined everything that had happened that afternoon, and stopped at the point where I pulled into the drive after visiting Hubert and Marianne. My throat closed.

Willard must have seen it happen, because he said, "I'll be right back," and left the office, closing the door gently behind him. I laid my head face-down on the desk and concentrated on my breathing until I heard the door open. Willard set a glass of water in front of me.

"Take your time." He left the room again.

At first I sipped at the water, then had a bout of thirst and guzzled the whole thing. By the time Willard came back in, I was pacing the room.

"It doesn't make any sense," I said. "Hubert, other than being a horse's ass, is harmless. I wouldn't mind if he'd get run over by a truck, but that's just because he's annoying and pathetic. And however sick it was of Marianne to kill those cows, that's still not the same as killing another person. Besides, I was with them both this evening, while Howie was...." I couldn't go on.

"Either one could've hired somebody."

"I don't think so." I stopped in front of the wall and pounded on it. "It seems wrong, somehow. Why would they want Howie dead? They both know me well enough to realize that losing him will just make me work all the harder to keep my farm."

"Which means—"

"Which means that someone else is fucking with me. Someone else had a reason for Howie to be dead." I pounded the wall again. "And whoever it is better be keeping a watch out for me."

Chapter Twenty-Seven

I stormed out of my office, but halted once I'd shut the door. I had no idea who had shot Howie, and nowhere to start looking. My brain was paralyzed, and I walked stiffly back to the parlor. I automatically avoided the feed room.

Missy and Zach both noticed my arrival, but neither said anything. I fit myself back into the routine and tried to work on auto-pilot. My fingers shook, but eventually I got into the rhythm of putting on milkers and taking them off.

If only I had called the police instead of storming off after Hubert, Howie would be alive. I would've been home to protect him.

And I might be dead, too.

A truck came speeding up the lane, narrowly avoiding the law enforcement vehicles, sending dust flying. Jethro's Dually. I sighed, knowing what was coming, but went outside anyway.

Jethro jumped out of the truck and smashed me with a hug. Belle came scurrying right behind.

"You will come stay with us, won't you?" she said tearfully.

I freed my face from Jethro's shoulder. "No, I won't."

"Then I'll stay here."

"No, you won't."

"But—"

"Look, I appreciate the offer. Really. But I need to be here. You have two sick kids to take care of. I'll be okay."

Jethro looked around at the vehicles and bustle. "But, Stella, what *happened?*" His voice broke.

"I left Howie alone and someone killed him."

His head snapped toward me. "It's *not* your fault. You were taking care of business. Nasty business caused by *our* family."

"Marianne didn't kill Howie, Jethro." At least I didn't think so.

"But still...."

Belle put her hand on Jethro's arm. "Jethro, stop."

He shoved his hands in his pockets and stared angrily toward the back field.

Belle tore her gaze from his stony face and raised a hand toward me. "You'll call if you need us?"

"You're on my speed dial."

Without another word, Jethro stomped to his truck, where he opened the back door and gently helped Ma step down. I hadn't seen her through the high window.

She walked over to me and put her hands on my face. "You're going to be all right, Stella."

"I hope so, Ma."

"There may be a point when you feel your soul breaking. But you'll get through it. Just trust and the strength will come."

"Thanks, Ma."

"I'll be praying."

She'd be praying. Having Ma pray for you was like having the Pope as your cousin, so I felt a little more confident about toughing out the next difficult days.

Ma looked steadily into my eyes. "And I'm so sorry about... about Jude's *wife*." Without waiting for a reply, she turned and went back to the truck, where Jethro lifted her in. They left without the usual parting waves.

Zach, Missy, and I were close to done with the milking stage when Abe drove in the lane. His headlights shined in the parlor windows, making me squint. He came right in.

"Where have you been?" I asked.

"The hospital. I wanted to see what I could find out."

"And?"

"It was…pretty straightforward. A gunshot directly to the stomach. He never really had a chance, even if you would've found him right after it happened."

I let out a huge breath. I'd been kicking myself for getting to Howie too late.

"The doctor said he wouldn't have suffered much," Abe said. "He most likely went into shock immediately after he was shot."

"Bullshit."

"Stella!"

"You think you could get a fatal shot to the stomach and not suffer? Save me the sentimental doctor speeches."

Abe lifted his hands and let them drop. "Whatever. I thought you'd want to know." He gave Missy a look, and that was enough to send me over the edge.

"Okay, everybody out."

Missy blinked. "What?"

"Thanks for coming to help, but now I need to be alone."

"You're not alone," Abe said dryly, gesturing toward the drive.

"Cops aren't company," I said.

"Not just cops." He tilted his head and I looked out the window. Nick was sitting on the side yard brushing Queenie.

I looked at Abe steadily, my emotions so tumbled I couldn't untangle them just then.

Without another word he walked out of the barn, got back into his car and drove away. I stood still, waiting, until Missy flicked a few errant pieces of hay off her pants and left. Zach didn't even bother to glance my way as he followed.

I took up where we'd left off, and soon finished up the milking. I unclipped the herd, then watched them blankly as they made their way out of the parlor. They seemed a bit bewildered by the darkness outside, but that didn't keep them from heading there.

I left the radio on Temple's station, wanting the soothing tones of classical music, and slowly began the clean-up process. I worked meticulously, knowing that as soon as I finished I'd have time to think. I was spreading lime on the walkways when Willard came in.

"Little later than usual, huh?" He leaned against the doorjamb, looking as tired as I felt.

"It's keeping me busy."

"Work's a good antidote to worry."

I stopped sweeping. "Then I guess you haven't been thinking about your son at all, huh?"

"Right." He pushed himself off the door. "You going to be okay here tonight? You have people to call?"

"I'll survive. And I've got plenty of back-up should I need it."

"You feel safe? I can send someone to watch the place for tonight."

I thought about that. "I think I'll be okay. They…they came after Howie when I was gone. They could've waited around till I got back."

He nodded. "All right, then. I'm off, and I'm taking my menagerie with me. Call if you need to."

I watched as the officers and whoever they all were packed themselves and their equipment into their various vehicles. As they left, I was struck by how many times I'd stood in that exact place during the last few days. It seemed people were always leaving my farm.

When I turned around, I realized Nick was still there. He sat on the side steps of the house, Queenie at his feet. I went and sat beside him for several minutes until he said something I didn't hear.

"What?" I asked.

"What can I do?"

"Nothing, Nick. I'll see you tomorrow."

"You sure?"

"Please."

He gave me a look that was both tender and exasperated. "Okay. I'll check in sometime tomorrow." He started to say something else, then stopped.

"What?"

"Just a second." He jogged to his truck, messed around inside for a minute, then came back. He held out a piece of paper. "Here. It's a number where you can reach me if you need to."

I looked at it. "You mean I hired you and never bothered to get your number?"

He shrugged.

I took the paper. "Cell phone?"

A look of embarrassment flitted across his face.

"It's okay," I said. "People have them."

"You sure I can't stay?"

"I'm sure."

He brushed his fingers over my hair, got into his Ranger, and drove away.

So I was alone. Alone, confused, and determined.

"It's you and me, girl," I said to Queenie. "What do we do now?"

I looked around at the farm, silent and stately in the glow of the dusk-to-dawn light. The heifer barn was gone, but the cows were safe and Queenie was beside me.

And Howie was dead.

I started sinking into a black hole when I remembered what Howie had said only that morning.

"I'm just doing a little research."

Research? What would he be studying? More to the point, could what he was doing have gotten him killed?

My God, he'd tried different times to tell me about something and had been interrupted every time. I felt a surge of panic, and pushed it down. Could I have saved Howie if only I'd listened? Would whoever it was be coming after me?

"C'mon, Queenie," I said, my voice shaking. "We're going where no one has gone before—at least since I was six."

We went over to the garage. I stood at the bottom of Howie's stairs and looked up at the darkened doorway. My throat tightened. Every night Howie had turned on that damned light. Well, tonight, his light was out. Tears pushed at the back of my eyes at the thought of that gentle man lying broken on the feed room floor. I breathed forcefully through my nose, straightened my shoulders, and walked up the steps, feeling like I was breaking and entering. I was a bit nervous that Willard might show up and ask what I was up to, but I had every right to be there. I did own it, after all.

The door was unlocked and swung open easily when I turned the knob. I flipped on the outside light and felt better once that nightly ritual was in place. Illuminating the inside was different, and I hesitated before hitting the switch.

The lights came up on a surprisingly clean and tidy apartment. The police had been searching, but had either been neatniks or didn't have much to mess up. A few spots of fingerprint dust, but other than that, nothing looked out of place. Not that I would've known.

Queenie trotted in and started sniffing around, but I stood in the doorway, struck by how small the apartment actually was. When I was up there as a child to bring Howie a fresh apple pie my mother had baked, the rooms had seemed much bigger.

Now, the bachelor pad seemed like just that—something a college kid should have before he can afford a real place. I stepped into a combined living room/dining room that had a small kitchen off the end. I walked down and looked in there, shocked at the lack of space. Maybe two feet of counter, one of those stoves that seems too small to cook anything, and a skinny, short refrigerator. Sitting on a small table jammed against the wall was a small microwave. Big enough for a plate of food and nothing more.

I returned to the main area and crossed to the only other door. This led to his bedroom, which was no bigger than it needed to be. A bed, a dresser, and a closet, with a small bathroom just outside the door. Shower, no bath.

Back in the living room, I stood and tried to get a feel for Howie. I quickly stopped myself, knowing the tears that had threatened minutes before were still there, waiting to spring forth. I looked around.

Behind me was a small couch, the only sitting space in the room, and in front of me was a small color TV and VCR. I felt a pang as I thought about the movies Howie had liked to watch. Old movies and action/adventure. When I was a teen-ager, *Terminator* had been a truly bonding experience.

Stashed in the corner of the living room were a battered desk and folding chair. On top of the desk was the only thing of much value I'd found in the entire apartment—and a real surprise. Sitting there like a trophy was a blue iMac. What was the correct name? Blueberry? I dropped into the folding chair, shocked. I didn't know Howie *used* computers, let alone *owned* one. And a *blue* one? Good grief.

I booted up the computer and watched as the smiling Mac icon came on the screen. The computer beeped and groaned, and finally the desktop appeared. I looked at the folders that came up, and they all seemed to be for software he had installed.

I clicked on the hard drive icon and studied the folders. Mostly software, systems folders, and other computer-oriented files. There were a couple of extras—solitaire and Myst. And one personal folder. It simply said, "My stuff." I opened it. The folder was sparse. Just a list of material possessions Howie owned. Which weren't numerous. I felt a pain in my chest, wondering how much Howie had sacrificed for me in the past fifteen years.

I suddenly couldn't be in Howie's apartment another minute.

"C'mon, girl," I said, and Queenie followed me obediently out the door.

When I got to the bottom of the stairs, I was at a loss. I didn't want to go into my house, but I couldn't just stand there all night, either. I looked at the barn.

"I'm not going in there," I said. Queenie looked up at me. "I'm not."

But I did.

The milking parlor was silent and dark when we walked in. I grabbed Queenie by the collar so she wouldn't go running into the off-limits feed room. We stood outside the tape and surveyed the mess of blood, straw, and grain that was smeared on the floor and walls. My stomach was trying to find its way out of my body, so I tugged Queenie's collar and walked quickly away before I decided to lie down on the floor and not get up.

In the office, I shut the door. Queenie lay down by the desk and put her nose on her paws. I put my hands over my face, then rubbed my forehead, eyes, and cheeks to get my blood moving. When I opened my eyes, I was staring at the aerial photo. Something looked weird. I cocked my head first to the left, then to the right. The photo was crooked, that was all.

I tilted the photo to the right to straighten it, but as soon as I let go, it tilted back to the left. I tried it again, but it seemed to be stuck on leaning. I grabbed the sides of the frame and pulled it off the wall to see if the hanging wire had gotten caught somehow. But that wasn't the problem at all. There was a manila envelope taped to the back of the picture.

I set the photo on the ground, tore the envelope off the backing, put it carefully on the desk, then hung the picture back up on the wall. It hung straight.

I sat and squinted at the envelope.

"What is this, Queenie?"

She looked at me without raising her head and made a groaning sound.

There was no writing on the outside of the envelope, and it wasn't sealed. It was just closed with the metal clasp. I bent the tabs up and three things fell out. A green spiral notebook and two stapled stacks of printed sheets. I started with one of those.

It was information about where our milk was sent—a list of all the markets which bought product from co-op members. I could see from the small printing at the top of the page that Howie had downloaded it from the co-op's web site. Buyers ranged from small to large, and hailed from places practically next door and places a thousand miles away. According to the information, our milk had gone to just about every one of the markets in all the years we'd been producing. Until this year. I looked through the entire stack, but could find nothing at all for where our milk had been going for the past twelve months. What the hell?

The second stack of paper looked like Howie had found our milk hauler's web site and downloaded whatever he could find, which wasn't much—the history of the company, their mission, vague schedules, and contact information.

I put it aside and picked up the notebook.

Like the envelope, there was no writing on the cover. I flipped to the first page and immediately recognized Howie's handwriting, staring at me in blue ink. I fanned through the pages. He had written on about a dozen of them. I went back to the first page and read it.

What Howie had written wasn't organized—just scribbled notes. He must have been brainstorming, for there were lots of things which didn't make much sense. After several pages, I thought maybe I'd found a pattern, and was surprised that the gist of his thinking was about Wayne.

Until I remembered that furtive conversation they'd had by the truck the other day when Carla was doing herd check. I never had found out what they'd been discussing.

Howie wrote questions like, "Why did Wayne get so defensive when I asked him where our milk was going?" and "Who is Wayne really working for?"

I wondered why Howie didn't just call the co-op and ask them where our milk was going. It would have been easy enough. I'd never done it, choosing to let them worry about the milk once it was out of my hands. Just so long as the money got deposited in my account, I was happy, and I'd never missed one payment.

And Wayne obviously worked for the co-op. He drove their truck. Wore their uniform.

I tucked those thoughts aside and looked through the rest of the notebook. There were notes about all that had happened over the last several days, with question marks, dashes, and lines drawn from place to place. He'd imagined about every scenario, a lot of them not making any sense at all.

Then I found one that sent my head spinning.

Nick had appeared at the farm the very day the manure lagoon overflowed—the first sign of sabotage. Everything else had happened after I hired him. "Where did he come from?" Howie's notes said. "What is he doing here?"

At first I tossed the idea off as irrelevant. We knew who had sabotaged our farm. Hubert had now crawled into his hole, and, along with Marianne, would be visited by the police at any time. The sabotage was all wrapped up.

But Howie's death wasn't.

My body went cold, and my brain tried to wrap around several disturbing questions. Where had Nick been this evening while I was at Hubert's and Marianne's? How convenient that he showed up right after I'd found Howie in the feed room. And the arson? Did Marianne really do that? She hadn't actually admitted it, had she? Nick had every opportunity to set something up so the heifer barn would burn. He was getting to know the place inside and out. Did he know I was gone to Hubert's? Had he come by and found Howie alone?

"But Queenie likes him," I said out loud.

Queenie heard her name and thumped her tail on the floor.

"Could we both be that wrong?" I asked her.

I thought through every encounter I'd had with Nick, from the first time he walked into my office, to the way he'd supported me at the hospital. He'd asked some very personal questions the first night he'd been around, and he'd learned a lot about my life at the co-op dinner, both of which now made me very nervous. Was it all an act, for some unimaginable reason? He'd been wanting to tell me something the past couple of days, but we'd always been interrupted. I had no idea what he could possibly have to say.

Dammit, my hormones had taken me over from the moment I'd laid eyes on him, and now I was paying for it.

Perhaps that had been the plan.

Angry with myself for falling victim so easily, I swore and threw Howie's notebook across the room, where it smacked the wall and fell to the floor. Queenie jumped up, scared by my outburst.

"Sorry, girl," I said. "Come here."

She whined and walked over to lay her head on my leg. I put my hand under her chin and lifted her nose up to look into her eyes. I wished she could tell me what she'd seen tonight. Thank God whoever it was hadn't shot her, too. I stroked her nose, then stopped suddenly. Queenie had been splattered with blood and other things I couldn't think about when I'd come home from Jude's. Now she was clean and fluffy. Had Nick given her a bath while I'd been milking? He'd been brushing her when I'd looked out at him.

I immediately felt a whole lot better. Queenie would never have allowed him to care for her if he'd been the one who killed Howie.

A sudden desire to see Nick swept over me. Just to assure myself I hadn't been a complete sucker. I pulled the slip of paper with his phone number from my pocket. I shook my head when I thought I'd been so bowled over I'd never even asked him for it when I'd hired him. Maybe I really was a sucker.

I punched buttons and the phone rang on the other end, but after three rings I got his voice mail saying he was so sorry he was unavailable, and if it was an emergency I was to please call this number. I really didn't want to leave a message.

I dialed the emergency number, and again there was no answer. And I got a different answering machine.

"Hello. You've reached Das Homestead, your home away from home. Please leave a message and we'll—"

I slammed down the phone. Das Homestead. The rich person's home away from home. The B and B Howie and I made fun of, betting on which expensive vehicles would be in the parking lot. Assuming no one we knew would ever have the resources to stay there.

I guess I was a sucker, after all.

Chapter Twenty-Eight

Nick's truck sat bathed in the B and B's motion detector lights, between a Lexus and a Ground-Pounder—a custom chopper that'll run you thirty grand, minimum.

I sat in my truck alongside the road, an ugly feeling of betrayal flooding my body. A barn painter. Right.

A light went out in one of the bedrooms and I wondered if it was his. I rested my elbow on the steering wheel and rubbed my temples. I wanted to storm the place, demand some answers, but had enough smarts to know it would be a mistake. Even if Queenie and I were right, and he wasn't a killer, he wasn't a blue collar Joe either. So who the hell was he?

I took off the emergency brake and eased away, going somewhere I knew I'd be welcome.

Rochelle Hoffman pulled me into her house and held both of my hands in her own. Her eyes filled with tears, and oddly, I found myself doing the comforting while we stood hugging in her foyer. She pulled away and wiped her eyes with a handkerchief.

"I'm sorry, Stella. I just...." Her lip quivered and she put her hanky over her mouth.

"Okay if Queenie comes in?" I asked.

She got a hold of herself and nodded. "Of course."

"Come, Queenie!"

Queenie trotted into the house, claws clicking on the marbled tile. Rochelle knelt and let Queenie lick her face.

"Marty around?" I asked.

"He's out in the barn, doing something or other. Couldn't sleep after he heard about Howie. We drove by your place a little while ago, but it was all dark, so we thought maybe you were trying to get some sleep. We should've stopped in."

"It's okay, Rochelle."

"Oh, Billy—I mean, William—wanted me to tell you how sorry he is. He was here for supper when…when we got the call about Howie."

"Thanks." I looked at the wall for a moment to stop the tears that threatened. "You want Queenie to stay with you while I go out to the barn?"

"Sure. Come on, girl. I've got some treats in the kitchen."

You'd think Queenie understood English the way she took off ahead of Rochelle.

Marty was in his milking parlor, scrubbing the outside of the milking tubes. Not something that gets done every day. Or every year, for that matter.

"Hey," I said.

He looked at me silently for a moment before climbing down his ladder and hanging his rag on one of the rungs.

"You okay?" he said.

"Not really. Got a minute?"

"Got more than one."

He led me into his office, which was really just an old storage room with a desk and a fridge, and we sat down. He opened the fridge and took out a fresh jug of chocolate milk. He poured some and handed me a mug. I took a sip and was sent back to my shorts and tennies, braids stuck on the sides of my head. The milk was creamy and thick—the kind that feels like it leaves a coat of fat all along your esophagus and stomach. Heavenly.

We sat in silence for a few minutes until visions of Howie on the feed room floor began floating in front of me.

"Tell me again how the co-op decides where our milk's going," I said.

He raised his eyebrows. "It's not rocket science. Markets call to say they need so-and-so amount of milk, and the haulers take it there." He shrugged. "You never know where it might end up. My milk ends up going as far as Texas sometimes, or as close as Philly. Depends who needs it. Why?"

I shook my head. "I'm not sure. I was going through some stuff of Howie's—" I stopped to clear my throat. "And he seemed to be very concerned about who was getting our milk. The co-op had no records of where our milk has gone for the past year."

Marty perked up. "What? That's not good."

"I know. But I've been getting milk checks, so obviously the milk's going somewhere. Howie downloaded a list of the co-op's markets, our records from past years, and stuff from the haulers. He was even wondering about the guy who drives the truck."

"Wayne?"

"Yeah." I stood up and started to pace. "We've been having trouble with sabotage—"

"Heard about that."

Once again I was taken aback by the speed and thoroughness of the farming grapevine.

"Anyway, this evening Howie was milking while I was…dealing with the situation." I looked at him to see if he knew what I meant, but he didn't give any indication one way or another. "So I don't think those folks had anything to do with what happened to Howie. Those notes of his are my only lead."

"Don't the police have ideas?"

I dropped into the chair, exasperated. "I don't know. I hope. They didn't take his computer, but there was really nothing on it except personal files and games. I suppose I need to tell them about this notebook and stuff, but I have to do some thinking on my own or I'll go crazy."

"Well, a conspiracy with the co-op and milk haulers sounds pretty crazy itself. I can't see what the idea would be. I mean, who cares, really, whose milk they get, or where your milk ends up?"

"Obviously, Howie did."

Marty nodded. "All I can say is you could give the co-op a call tomorrow. Or ask Wayne yourself."

"I thought of that, but so did Howie, apparently. He seemed to think Wayne didn't know. Or didn't want to tell him."

As I thought about Howie's conversation with Wayne, I realized it was after that when I noticed Howie looking older and worried. I had figured at the time it was all the sabotage that was getting to him, but he'd never had a chance to tell me what he was thinking. And all along, he'd been scribbling down thoughts in his little green notebook.

"What?" Marty said, seeing my face change.

I shook my head. "Just something I remember. I'll call the co-op tomorrow to see what they can tell me about the past year."

I stared down into my empty mug and felt the milk rumble around in my gut. I had to keep myself from thinking about Howie. At least from thinking about the fact that he wouldn't be home when I got back.

I looked up when I felt Marty's eyes boring into the top of my head.

"Sorry I can't help you more," he said.

"Forget it. I think I really just needed to get away from home for a bit."

"You can stay here if you want. Get some sleep. You look exhausted."

I rubbed my eyes. "I didn't get much sleep the last couple nights, between the electricity going out, the cows getting loose, and the fire."

"Didn't know your cows got out. What happened?"

"Part of the sabotage story. Tell you later?"

"Or never. You get some rest, Stella."

"I'll do my best."

Marty walked me back to the house, where I gathered up Queenie and the bag of food Rochelle hoisted on me. The Hoffmans let me go, extracting one of the many promises I'd given people that I'd call if I needed anything.

When I got home I carefully avoided looking at the garage, not wanting to see the meaningless light by Howie's door. My Harley was still outside and I knew I should put it in, but I figured one night out wouldn't kill it. I couldn't stomach getting that close to Howie's place again. Queenie followed me into the house and watched while I put away the food Rochelle had sent with us.

For once, I walked upstairs fully dressed. I fell onto my bed and within seconds had crashed into a deep, dark sleep.

Chapter Twenty-Nine

My alarm wakened me from a half-sexy, half-scary Nick dream at five, and I was surprised to find myself in my clothes, lying diagonally across my bed. My first thought was of Howie, and I somehow made it to the bathroom before throwing up.

I walked out to the barn, looking straight ahead so I wouldn't see the garage, and did the entire milking myself for the first time since last week. It took much longer than I remembered.

As I worked, I wondered where everybody was. I mean, wasn't there anybody to help me? I suddenly felt the weight of Nick's words from our night under the stars, his questions about who would be with me when I'm old.

Nick, who was at that moment sleeping in his luxurious bed, anticipating a hot, gourmet breakfast and a soak in his room's private Jacuzzi.

But no matter what Nick was doing, or why he'd hidden his wealth, his prophesy was already coming true. Howie was gone and I was completely alone.

God, I missed him.

I stopped beside a cow, sadness threatening to envelop me, when I remembered there was a reason my closest friends were absent. People were sick. Kids were dying. It was five-thirty in the morning. I shook myself out of my stupor and started working again.

The cows' udders weren't as full as usual since they'd been milked late the night before, but I wanted to get them back on schedule before they got too screwed up. It was comforting to move among them, working without thinking. They were oblivious to all that had gone on around them—oblivious that Howie wasn't with me. It was nice to have something in my life that was consistent.

I had a hard moment when, by habit, I walked to the feed room, and saw the yellow police tape on the door. Without thinking, I turned right back around and was out the door to the feed barn before I could register what I'd seen.

Around eight I swept the last handful of lime onto the walkway, and had to either find something to do, or think. Not a hard decision to make. If I let myself think, I might as well just go in the house and shut myself in a closet. Forever.

I knew there were things around the farm that needed to be done. Things that couldn't be avoided even though Howie was gone. But being at the farm wasn't the solace it usually was, and I couldn't stomach being there without Howie. Wondering if I had somehow caused his death. Missing everything about him.

I also had something else to take care of.

I went into the house, changed my clothes, and got into my truck. Das Homestead was a mere five-minute drive away.

Nick's truck still sat between the Lexus and the chopper. Looked kind of funny, the little Ranger in the midst of luxury. I wondered what that said about Nick, but didn't have the wherewithal to try to figure it out at the moment.

I parked at the end of the row, distancing myself from the upper classes, and stared at the door for several minutes. Finally, I took a deep breath and stepped down from my truck.

A bell tinkled when I pushed open the front door, reminiscent of the Biker Barn. I felt out of place in this atmosphere, though— the antithesis of a motorcycle shop. Howie would've taken one look at the room and laughed at me, standing in the midst of all the frills. Candles, incense, potpourri. Gleaming hardwood floors and shiny antiques. Depression glass. Old pictures in frames. No smell of farm or garage or even fresh air. The overbearing scent was that of breakfast, making my stomach twist. A door to my left closed off a room which emitted the muffled sound of clanking silverware. The dining room, I guessed.

A woman in a dark blue dress and expertly applied make-up appeared through a door in the lobby. She attempted to hide her discomfort at my appearance, but wasn't quite successful. I could tell she was trying not to be overtly curious about the steer horns painted on the sides of my neck.

"Can I help you?" she asked, sounding like she doubted it.

"I'm looking for one of your guests. Nick Hathaway."

She raised her eyebrows.

"He's been working for me," I said. "I need to talk to him."

"Working…?" Her eyes flicked toward the door of the dining room. "He's eating breakfast. I'll check with him."

"That's okay," I said. "I'll just go in."

"But—"

I brushed by her and pushed open the door. Several people looked up as I entered, but only one of them interested me. Nick's mouth fell open, and he glanced at a stack of papers that sat alongside his plate.

I picked my way through the small room of tables and stood several feet away from his chair, studying him. He was freshly scrubbed and wore his usual outfit—jeans and a T-shirt. Red this time. He looked great.

"I'm so sorry, Mr. Hathaway." The woman from the lobby scooted past me and stood beside Nick, kneading her hands.

"It's okay, Janet," Nick said, keeping his eyes on me. "She's a friend."

Her face twisted with confusion. "So should I bring out another plate?"

I shook my head. At a normal time steak and eggs accompanied by a glass of fresh-squeezed orange juice would be heaven. Today it would just make me sick.

Still looking at me, Nick said, "Thanks, Janet, but no."

She left grudgingly, her expression daring me to make a fuss among her elite clientele. I pulled out the chair across from Nick and sat down without embarrassing anybody.

"Did you get any sleep?" he asked gently.

"Any."

We stared at each other.

"So," I finally said, gesturing to the room. "You're rich."

His eyes fell to the papers in front of him, and he stretched his fingers out over them. He sighed. "Yes. Yes, I am very rich."

A tremor started in my chin, and I clamped my teeth together. When the trembling stopped, I said, "Rich from what?"

He raised his eyes to meet mine, and my heart skipped a beat at the look in them. I was reminded of the sadness flitting across Howie's face during the past few days, and I wondered if the source was the same.

Nick picked up the papers and thoughtfully tapped them against the table to straighten them. He hesitated, then handed the entire stack across to me.

I took them, knowing whatever I saw would change our relationship forever. What hadn't already changed.

The header at the top of the first page said:

HATHAWAY DEVELOPMENT AND CONSTRUCTION
Harrisonburg, Virginia

The Board of Directors included Nicholas Patrick Hathaway, Jr.

I carefully placed the papers on the table, pushed myself off the chair, and left the building.

Chapter Thirty

"Hey, Wayne," I said.

It was eleven-thirty, and I had completely exhausted myself after returning from Das Homestead. The heifers in the lower pasture were fed and watered, the paddock was scraped, and the now-empty calf hutches were as clean as they could ever expect to be. Now the milk truck had arrived, and I had to try to behave naturally. Not an easy thing after seeing Howie's scribbled notes about our hauler.

Wayne jumped down from his cab and avoided my eyes. "Stella." He acted like a zombie, his movements slow and clunky. "Sorry to hear about…all that's been happening here."

"Yeah."

We stood silently, neither knowing what else to say.

"So how's Flo?" I finally asked. I worked to keep emotion from coloring my voice.

He gave a kind of hiccup. "Okay. Okay." He looked around. "Where's your new hired guy? I figured for sure he'd be here to help out this morning."

I took a shaky breath, and tried to hide it. "You mean Nick?"

"Is that his name?"

"He can't do much more work on the heifer barn."

Wayne managed a weak laugh.

"Well, I got some stuff to do," I said. "You can take it from here?"

"Like always. You do your thing, I'll do mine."

"I'll be in the office if you need me."

I really didn't want to be in my office, but I had to make sure I knew when Wayne left, and I could see the truck out of the office window. I dug my fingers into my temples and wished I could just go back to sleep. But Howie was dead and my farm was somehow responsible. Sleep just wasn't an option.

I knew it would take Wayne at least a half hour, so I rummaged through my files to find a number for the co-op. I had meant to call first thing in the morning, but chores and emotions had driven it from my mind. A few minutes later I was on the line with a secretary, and she was trying to look up my records on her computer.

"You're still producing milk?" she asked. I could hear her fingers clicking on her keyboard.

"Of course I am. I'm a member of the co-op. Have been for almost thirty years. Well, the farm has been, anyway."

"I'm not finding any records for you for the past year."

"You must be looking at the wrong place. What are you looking under?"

"Royalcrest."

"Try my name. See if they switched it to that."

I heard clicking again. "Sorry. Nothing there."

"So according to your computer, I stopped producing last year." Just as Howie had discovered.

"That's right."

"So why am I still getting a milk payment?"

"I really don't know. I'm sorry."

I sat back in my chair, completely thrown. "Can't you look it up on your payroll or something?"

"Our accountant would need to do that, and he's not here. Should I have him call you?"

"Yes, please. As soon as he can. And can you tell me why I got an invitation to the banquet if I'm not on the books anymore?"

"Oh, that's easy. We always send to past members. In case they want to rejoin."

I thanked her and hung up, confused. If the co-op hadn't been using my milk for the past year, where the hell was it going? And who was paying me? Howie's far-out theories may actually have had something to them.

Someone knocked on the door.

"Yeah?"

Wayne stuck his head in. "All done. See ya in two days?"

"See ya."

He closed the door behind him, and I watched as he shuffled out to his truck. He paused before getting into it to look back where the heifer barn had been, then to study the ground for a moment before stepping up into his cab. I let him get a head start before I bolted out to my truck. Once I saw which way he had turned, I gunned it down the lane and followed him.

I kept far enough behind him he wouldn't think about me—he knows my truck and I didn't want him to recognize it now. We went out Route 113 through Silverdale, through Blooming Glen, out to 313 in Dublin. We turned right and I followed him a few more miles until he turned off and started winding down a country road.

Again, I kept far enough behind he wouldn't see me, and when I saw him turn into a drive, I pulled off the road and parked in the irrigation row of a corn field. I was counting on the corn to shield my truck from view of the farm where Wayne was headed. The corn was about six feet tall, so I was confident it could do the job.

I hopped down from the truck and started making my way through the field toward the house. I crossed several rows until I couldn't see my truck anymore, then turned to walk down a row as far as I could without being seen. The field must've been irrigated recently, because my boots were sinking into the ground, and walking was tough work. I was glad I still had on my work boots.

When I got to the edge of the field I was still several hundred yards from the farm. I could see Wayne's truck and a couple of people talking and milling about. The only other vehicle was a shiny black Dodge Ram.

I went back into the corn several feet and began walking across the rows, trying to be as quiet as possible, which was hard, since the cornstalks rattled and crunched as I walked through them. By the time I got close to the barn, I was itchy and had a host of scratches on my arms and face. I went again to the edge of the field and peered out.

Wayne and whoever else had been there were no longer in sight, but the truck was now backed up to a small concrete building beside the barn. I made sure no one was around, then sprinted, staying low, to the back of the barn.

Once there, I caught my breath and crept to the corner, peering around the corner at the smaller building. Wayne was climbing into his tanker, having apparently emptied his load. He closed the door and drove away. I kept my fingers crossed hoping he wouldn't notice my truck.

After waiting a minute to make sure no one new was leaving or arriving, I hunched over and trotted the twenty or so feet to the side of the concrete building, where there was a window. Unfortunately, the window was blacked out and I couldn't see even a speck of light through it.

I crept around the back to the other side, only to find more blackened glass. The only other window was on the back wall, about eight feet off the ground. I looked around for something to stand on, but all I could see was overgrown grass—nothing to give me any height. I stared up at the window and tried to come up with a way to see in.

The window was set into the concrete about six inches, making a nice, wide sill, and the concrete on the wall was textured. Only one of my ideas could possibly work. I walked back several feet, took a few quick strides, and leapt up the side of the building, grabbing onto the windowsill. My hands and fingers received the brunt of the cement's roughness, but my boots got traction on the wall and I was able to pull myself high enough I could get my elbows onto the ledge. When I finally got up there, I was frustrated to find I couldn't see through the window because there was so much grime on it. At least it was regular dirt, and not black paint. I put all my weight onto my right arm and rubbed the heel of my left hand on a corner of the window, hoping no one inside suddenly decided to look up.

When I finally got a little circle cleared, my arms were starting to shake, but I gritted my teeth and leaned to look in.

An old milk processing plant took up the entire building. I could see each part of the system crammed into the space. On the end farthest from me, in front of one of the blacked-out windows, was the homogenizer, busily breaking cream into particles so the cream wouldn't float to the top of the milk jug. A separator sat close by, waiting to break the milk down even more, producing skim milk. I could see milk shooting through the tubes and could hear the machines working.

Directly in front of me was the pasteurizer, connected to the homogenizer by tubes, but it didn't look like it was in use.

On the wall closest to me was a control panel. There usually were four red lights, showing power for heating, cooling, pumping, and circulating. Only two were lit, which made sense if the pasteurizer wasn't heating up the milk. A fifth, bigger red light, showed the main power was on. Above the lights was a graph which shows that each batch has been heated to a high enough temperature and records it, in case of trouble. I was confused as to why they would need records, seeing as how nobody knew the milk was being processed here, but realized there was nothing being graphed on the temperature chart, anyway.

Finally, in the corner of the room across from me was a bottler, where I could see jugs from Rockefeller Dairy waiting to be filled. I was sure Robert Rockefeller would be surprised to see his logo on milk processed outside of his building.

Moving in the midst of all this equipment were two men, unrecognizable to me. They worked as a team, obviously having done this many times before. They talked while they worked, apparently sharing stories and jokes, for they were laughing and gesturing animatedly. I wondered who the hell they were.

My arms finally went numb, and I pushed away from the building and let myself drop. Now that I knew what was going on inside, I wasn't afraid they'd hear me. Processing milk is a noisy business. I peeked around the corner, not wanting to get caught by some latecomer, but no one else was there, so I ran behind the barn and found a spot to sit in the corn and watch.

I squatted behind a clump of weeds about three feet from the edge of the field. Milk processing takes a couple of hours, at least, and I knew for a fact they'd just started when Wayne had arrived. Without the heating cycle, it should take maybe half the time. I also knew there were only two guys in the building. There was a chance they'd go away and I'd have an opportunity to snoop. So I'd wait.

An hour and a half later my legs were sore and my jeans had mud on the knees and butt from necessary changes of position. I was beginning to wonder if the men would ever come out and had just shifted my weight another time when the door opened. I held my breath and ducked lower behind the weeds.

The men—both middle-aged white guys—were still talking, and didn't so much as glance my way. The taller of the two turned a key in the door, then poked his finger at what had to be an alarm pad. Great. So much for me snooping around.

The men headed straight for the Dodge Ram. As soon as they got in the cab they started it up and left, disappearing in a cloud of dust.

Seeing the alarm had stopped all thought I had of getting into the place. I knew I couldn't bypass a security system, so I was forced to leave empty-handed. Damn.

I picked my way back through the corn field and hesitated once I got close to the road, just in case Wayne had seen my truck. No one was waiting for me.

I got into the truck and sat for a minute, wondering what in the world I had just witnessed. Who were these people, what were they doing, and why was my milk hauler of ten years taking my milk to a plant no one knew existed? And why in heaven was I still getting a check from the co-op when they had no record of my production since last summer?

An answer started to surface in my convoluted thoughts, but it was so horrible that at first I couldn't allow myself to think about it. Eventually, though, I let it come.

People, kids mostly, were getting sick. They were getting sick from an ingested toxin, and no one could locate the source. Not on vegetables, not in the drinking water, not in the air.

My God. Had anyone thought to test the milk?

Chapter Thirty-One

I jammed the truck into gear and sped out of the irrigation lane, narrowly missing a passing car. Was I completely off-base? I mean, what were they doing? Poisoning milk—*my milk*—and distributing it? For what purpose?

A half-mile down the road I passed a woman out weeding in her front yard. Fifteen seconds later I braked the truck, did a three-point turn, and drove back to the little house.

The woman looked up when I pulled into the drive, her eyes half-curious, half-defensive. A baby lay on its stomach on a blanket beside the woman, slowly edging its way through a stash of toys toward the grass. I jumped out of the truck and tried to hide my anxiety.

"Can I help you?" the woman asked. She clapped her gloved hands together, spraying dirt over her shorts and the baby's blanket.

"I hope so. There's a farm about a half-mile down the road, looks empty, but has a barn and a couple of outbuildings that look in use. You know who owns it?"

"You mean the white house with the long driveway? Dark green shutters?"

I tried to remember. "I think so."

"We just moved here in May, so all I know is some older man owns it. About six months ago his wife died and he moved somewhere south to be near his daughters. Oh, Debbie, don't eat that!"

She lunged toward the baby, snatching a clump of dirt and weeds from the chubby fingers. She plopped the baby back on the blanket and the baby looked at the toys with disappointment.

"You know who's managing the property?" I asked.

The woman shook her head. "Sorry. The best I can do is that he had a brother living around here. Maybe he's taking care of it."

"Know his name?"

"Sorry. Can't help you with that, either."

I thanked the woman and left her to her weeds and her dirt-eating daughter, trying to wrap my mind around everything I knew. It wasn't much. I sat in the driveway long enough the woman stopped working again to look at me, so I waved and backed out of the drive.

As I drove toward home, my rage transferred itself to my foot, and I sped along the roads. Lord knew I didn't understand what exactly those folks were doing with my milk, or if it was even the substance poisoning people, but it didn't take a college grad to know they were up to something illegal. I had to call Willard.

I pulled into my drive, wheels skidding, and almost slammed into the back of Nick's truck. Nick was lying in the grass, wrestling with Queenie, but as soon as I pulled in the lane he was on his feet.

I got out of the truck.

"Hey, Stella," Nick said.

"Nick."

Queenie snuffled around my legs, probably smelling manure from the cornfield I'd been stomping through.

"How'd you get all those scratches on your face?" Nick asked.

I stared at him. "What do you want, Nick?"

He stepped toward me, then stopped and put his hands to his eyes. In a moment he dropped them, and the raw hurt on his face made me gasp.

"What I *want*," he said, "is a chance to do this over. To tell you the truth from the beginning."

I looked down at my boots. "How 'bout telling the truth now?"

He was silent for so long Queenie whined and trotted over to him. He knelt and rubbed her face. "You saw the letterhead. You know what I do."

"I know what you *are*."

He stood. "Goddamnit, Stella, you *don't* know that! You can't look at that one thing—the *business*—and think you know who I am inside."

"So why don't you tell me, Nick? Can you do that? You've spent the past several days picking *my* brain, getting all sorts of inside stuff from *me*. And what have I got? The false assumption that you're a guy who knows at least some of what farming life is about. Who knows a little of what I'm up against. Instead, I find out you *are* what I'm up against. You're the enemy."

He spun away, then back, and a fire I hadn't seen before lit his eyes. His voice was tight with anger. "I left my family in Virginia two months ago. My mother keeps threatening a nervous breakdown, and my sisters declare it's not all a ruse. All my life it's been assumed—*expected*—that sometime down the road, in the future, I would take over the business. I would take responsibility for developing the last remaining natural spaces of Virginia.

"But Stella, something in me has always been different. I look at those mountains and I see beauty. I see peace. I don't envision the high-priced condos with a view, the ski resorts, the retirement villages. I look at the farmland and I smell the fresh-cut hay and I see the animals and I think *this* is what it's all about. *This* is what Virginia is meant to be."

He stared out across the cornfield behind my house.

"Six months ago my dad was diagnosed with cancer. The doctors gave him a year. He got three months. All that kept him going those last painful weeks was the knowledge that the family business would be in my hands. I'd be in command. But I just can't...."

His voice shook, and he got it under control. "So I'm on a journey. I'm on a journey to find out just who it is I'd be buying out. Whose lives and land I'd be destroying. I couldn't do it in Virginia. Too many people know me. Know the Hathaway name. So I left the CFO in charge and traveled to Pennsylvania, where developers are just as aggressive as good old dad. And I came here, where I—"

He looked into my eyes. "I found you and I got to know you and...and I got to love you. I'd give anything to go back to that first night out in your field. I'd tell you at the first opportunity I had. And maybe then you'd be able to forgive me."

I turned away from him, realized I was looking at Howie's apartment, and spun completely around to rest my arms on my truck.

"We could've really had something," Nick said. "I felt it as soon as I walked into your office that first day."

I tried to breathe around the lump in my throat. "I felt it, too."

"I'm sorry, Stella."

I made myself look at him. "I'm sorry, too."

The distance between us evaporated when he took two quick strides toward me. He crushed me against the truck, his mouth finding mine, and I clutched him, my fingers digging into his back. I lost myself in the kiss, putting all of the emotion I'd been bottling up into this expression of anger, and betrayal, and love. Howie was dead, my farm was on the brink of bankruptcy, and this man had taken my heart and twisted it around my spine. It was a kiss full of a multitude of feelings. But absent of any joy.

Nick broke away and walked quickly to his truck, opened the door and got in.

"Nick," I said. "Nick, stay."

He closed the door, started down the drive, and was gone.

Chapter Thirty-Two

I called the police station. Willard wasn't in.

"Well, where is he?" I demanded.

"I'm sorry, I can't divulge that information, ma'am."

"Is this Officer Meadows?"

"Uh, no ma'am, this is Officer Wolfe. Do you want Officer Meadows?"

"Hell, no. Can you reach Willard?"

"I can try, but he's in the middle of something and can't really be disturbed."

"I've got to talk to him. It's urgent."

"Can you tell me?"

I thought about what I'd seen. "Someone's stealing my milk."

"Excuse me?"

"And I think it might have something to do with why people are getting sick. Can you tell him that?"

"Sure thing, ma'am. Um, what's your name?"

I told him, then punched in Jethro and Belle's number, getting the answering machine. Good grief. Didn't they ever answer the phone anymore? I left a message telling them not to drink any more milk, and to tell everybody else. They'd probably think I was crazy.

I stared at the phone for a long minute. I felt totally useless, and hoped Willard would call back soon. What else could I do?

Pulling out the phone book, I quickly found Pam's number and dialed. No answer, and no answering machine. Damn.

I called more of the Grangers. Jermaine. Jordan. The welding shop. Nobody was around. Where the hell were they?

I started to feel dizzy and realized I hadn't eaten lunch, so I hung up the phone and gazed into my refrigerator. There was nothing the slightest bit appetizing—even the food from Rochelle—so I drank a glass of orange juice and let it go at that. I stared at the milk carton for a moment before dumping it all down the drain. I didn't know if I'd ever look at milk the same way again.

I tried Pam's number once more, and still got no response. I'd have to go find her. But first I'd get the Grangers on board. And the best place to do that, seeing as how nobody was answering their phone, would be at Ma's.

I ran upstairs, jumped into my leathers, and jogged out to my Harley. I tried to ignore the fact that Howie's apartment, where the outside light still shone, was right over my shoulder.

The rumbling of the low-rider's pipes gave me an extra jolt of adrenaline, and I almost stalled the bike by letting out the clutch too quickly. Queenie yelped and trotted beside me to the end of the drive, then watched as I sped away.

As I rode, my brain was too free to wander to places I couldn't control. Howie. Nick. My milk poisoning children. I tried to concentrate on the feeling of the bike beneath me, the sound of the wind rushing past my face, the smell of the outside. But it took more effort to forget than to remember.

Das Homestead loomed up on my left, and I didn't have enough self-restraint to look away. There was an ugly, empty space between the Lexus and the chopper. No more Ranger. No more Nick.

I was about two miles from Ma's when I saw a different truck in my rearview mirror. I didn't think much about it until I was getting close to the part of the road that led into that nasty S curve. The truck wasn't slowing down, and I wanted to make sure I had enough room to take the curves at the slower speed they demanded. About two hundred yards from the curves, I put out my left arm and waved it up and down, signifying I was going to be slowing. The truck drifted back and I breathed easier until I noticed it was the same kind of truck I'd seen at the processing plant. It was a black Dodge Ram.

Oh, hell.

I focused on the road and leaned right, into the first curve. I had straightened out and was starting to lean the opposite way into the second curve when I heard the truck speeding up behind me. I glanced over my shoulder for a split second and saw the bumper only ten feet from my fender. I squeezed the handle bar, trying to stay out of the gravel that lay on the edge of the road.

The truck sped up and started to drift toward me. I straightened out to avoid getting hit. I couldn't brake, or the bike would completely slide out from under me. The truck came closer and when my wheels hit the gravel, I lost traction.

The bike fell on its side and started to slide, taking me with it. My left leg was trapped underneath six hundred pounds of moving steel, and my arm scraped on pavement and rocks. My pants ripped and I could feel the burning of stones and dirt tearing up my leg. Long grass whipped my face, lacerating my mouth and eyelids. My helmet whacked the ground, jarring my skull and neck. Finally, my body caught on something and the bike's weight pulled the machine over my ankle and foot and down into the ditch.

I lifted my head to make sure I was in one piece. When I saw that I was, I fainted.

Chapter Thirty-Three

When I regained consciousness, it was almost dark.

My first thought was that my bike must be completely destroyed, but when I tried to get up to look, the pain was so immense I forgot everything else. I lay back down and closed my eyes until the stars in my head went away.

My second thought was amazement that no one had stopped to help me. When I got my bearings I realized no one had stopped because no one could see me. The bike had pulled me down the steep hill and I was completely out of sight of the road. My Harley had continued down another ten feet to the bottom of the ditch, and when I raised my head a few inches I could see it crumpled and scratched, lying on its side like a dead animal. The red eyes of my new timing cover were somehow still glowing, and a cold shiver overtook me as I tried to comprehend what had just happened.

I took stock of my body as well as I could. My left arm and leg were torn up, my clothes completely ripped off of them. Oil coated my chest and what I could see of my jeans, and its metallic flavor tingled on my lips. The tattoo on my arm now said something like "hine own self be tr," with a lot of extra red and gravelly designs. Thankfully, my back had been spared by my leather vest, and my hands by my gloves. I moved each of my fingers, grateful none of them had been broken or ripped off.

I rotated my left ankle in a slow circle, and while this was very painful, it didn't seem to be broken. A miracle. The rest of my leg also seemed to be free of breaks. Many miracles. Ma's prayers must have been working.

I pushed myself into a sitting position, and when my head started to spin I put it in between my knees instead of lying down again. I had to get myself up and out of this ditch before I lost too much blood. There seemed to be a cut on my forehead that was dripping blood faster than I thought necessary.

Using my right leg and arm, with a little help from the left, I dragged myself up the hill to see where I was. There seemed to be something wrong with my ribs, because every time I put weight on my torso, pains shot through my chest.

I tried to stay out of sight of the road, not wanting to get hit by a car or make myself too visible, should the truck come back. This was probably irrelevant, because they could have come back during any of the hours I was unconscious and finished me off, but I wasn't going to take any chances with what body I had left.

I got to the top of the hill and stuck my head up over the top. From what I could see, I was about half a mile from Ma's house. Not very far if you're healthy, but a freaking marathon in my condition. I laid my head on the ground and muttered a small prayer of my own.

Slowly, I got to my knees, and then to my feet, trying to ignore the throbbing in my left limbs, my ribs, and my head. I took about five steps in the direction of Ma's house and fell onto my left knee, making me say many unladylike things. I dropped my head and blood ran into my eyes. I wiped it away and took deep breaths, trying to focus my energy.

It was getting darker by the minute, and I knew I either had to get myself noticed by a passing car, or make my way to Ma's. I pushed myself to my feet, gritting my teeth and clenching my hands.

This time I made it about twenty feet before falling. I was either overcoming the pain, or doing so much damage to my nerves I couldn't feel much anymore. I kept on with this rhythm, pushing myself to my feet, going as far as possible, and then falling and wiping the blood from my eyes, until I wasn't thinking—just moving.

I'd spent so much time in the past years complaining about housing developments and increased traffic, I guessed it was God's joke that no traffic passed to rescue me. If I hadn't been in such bad shape, I would have laughed.

About twenty minutes into my trek, when I started to see Ma's house in detail, I saw headlights coming toward me. They looked like car lights, as opposed to truck ones, so I stood straight and tried to wave my arms. The next thing I knew, I was waking up again, and it was almost dark. So much for an SOS.

I didn't know if I could go any further, but when I started to think about poisoned milk, and Howie, I got enough adrenaline pumping to get myself up and moving again. I kept Zach and all the other kids I needed to save up front in my mind as a sort of carrot, and by the time I thought I couldn't go another step, I was falling painfully onto Ma's front steps.

I lay there for a few minutes, amazed I had made it so far, and furious I had somehow been so stupid I hadn't seen the truck coming. I did my best to pound on the steps, hoping to rouse someone from supper or whatever they were doing, but could barely lift my fist to do it. Where was that stupid Missy when I finally needed her?

I grabbed at the railing and made my way up the steps one at a time, pausing to rest once I got over each. I pulled myself onto my knees to try to get onto the top step, but this was too much for my body to handle. I got my hands out and caught myself before I fell face first, but I landed on my left arm and collapsed face down, anyway. Several bright red drops landed on the wooden floor. I reached up with my left hand to wipe my eyes and my hand came away covered with blood.

I lay with my upper body on the porch floor, my left arm underneath me, my legs bent up on the stairs, and tried to focus on breathing—in through the nose and out through the mouth. Pain hit me in waves, but now that I'd made it to Ma's, I could feel consciousness gently slipping away.

The screen door was in front of me and I could hear Ma rattling around in the kitchen. She was humming as she worked—an old tune I recognized from Sundays when I was younger and she used to drag me to church. A hazy image floated into my head of me squashed between Abe and Ma, in my one frilly pink dress that Ma had made herself. She hadn't minded making it. What mattered was that I got my Bible learnin'.

"*'Tis so sweet to trust in Jesus,*" she sang now. "*And to take him at his word.*"

Fighting the cloud that was descending over my brain, I tried to push my body up with my right arm. I pulled my left arm until it came free and I crashed onto the floor again, slamming my chin. Blood splashed onto the wood from my forehead, and my head shook from my teeth banging together.

"*Just to rest upon his promise, and to know 'Thus saith the Lord.'*"

I heard myself moan as I pushed with my good leg. I scooted half a foot closer to the door and if I stretched I could just touch it. My foot slipped on the step and my thigh banged onto the lip of the porch. I fell onto the floor, tasting dirt.

"*Jesus, Jesus how I trust him, how I've proved him o'er and o'er!*"

I rolled onto my right side, daggers of pain shooting through my chest, and looked up at the porch light, moths dancing around it. The light was reassuring, somehow, and I decided it was too much work to get to the door. If I could just rest, I'd try again soon. I closed my eyes and my head lolled against the floor. Ma's singing was soft and gentle, and I let myself melt into it.

"*Jesus, Jesus, precious Jesus! Oh, for grace to trust him more!*"

I must have lost consciousness, because I was awakened by the pounding of feet.

"Stella? Stella! Oh my God!"

Vaguely I heard voices and felt fingers probing my face and bones.

"Is anything broken? Is she okay?"

"Don't feel around too much. Did someone call the ambulance?"

"I'm awake," I said. Or tried to say.

"Go call now," the second voice—a woman—said.

"Hey," I said, and they heard me this time.

"Stella?"

I opened my eyes, and when the blurring stopped the first thing I saw was Missy. I started to giggle. "Did you…are you…." I giggled some more.

She was pushed aside and suddenly Abe was there, staring down at me, a look in his eyes I couldn't describe.

"Stella," he said sternly. "What happened? Who did this?"

I sobered up. "I don't know. A truck."

"A truck? You crashed your truck?"

I shook my head. And blacked out.

Chapter Thirty-Four

When I woke up, I was surprised to see it was still dark. I was also surprised to see I was in a hospital bed. The last thing I remembered was seeing Abe's face above me, worried and scared. Not an unpleasant memory, surprisingly, and one of the only recollections I had of the last day. Since I'd lost Howie.

I was hooked up to an IV with two bags hanging on it—one with clear liquid, one with dark. I had bandages wrapped around my left leg and arm, and my forehead felt tight. I reached up to touch it and felt a bandage there, too. If the snugness around my chest was real and not imagined, I was wrapped up like a mummy. I wasn't sure how long I'd been sleeping or what had woken me. I began to suspect the throbbing in my arm and chest had something to do with it. Not to mention the nightmares I'd been having about Howie coming to pull me up from a ditch, only to reveal a bowling ball-sized hole through his torso.

I lay there for what felt like an eternity, trying to breathe through the pain, when the door opened and a nurse came in. She looked like a high schooler.

"You're awake!" she said. "How are you feeling?"

"Like I was run over by a truck." My voice sounded foggy and slurred. Like my brain felt.

The nurse gave a bubbly laugh. "It's time for your pain medicine, if you want it."

I didn't know why I hadn't thought of it earlier. "Fill me up."

She smiled, like I was a good student giving the right answers, and helped me wash down a couple of pills with some water by my bed. "That should do you till morning. Let me know if you need anything else. The button is by your right hand."

I glanced down and saw the button with a line drawing of a nurse.

"What's up with me?" I asked.

She suddenly got serious. "Your leg is very beaten up. Lots of blood loss, lots of skin taken off. Same with your arm, only worse, since you weren't wearing long sleeves. Your forehead got twelve stitches. And you have two fractured ribs."

"Wow," I said, and promptly fell back asleep.

The next time I woke it was completely light, and Abe was sitting in the chair at the foot of my bed. I studied him as he paged through some magazine, his foot crossed over his ankle, a Styrofoam cup in his hand.

"What time is it?" I asked, my voice clogged with gunk.

His head snapped up and his face went through a variety of expressions until it finally settled on a non-committal one.

"So, you decided to rejoin us, after all." He glanced at his watch. "It's about ten."

"What day?"

"You just got run down yesterday."

"Oh, God!" I said. "My cows!"

"All taken care of. Marty's been milking them, with help from whatever Granger kids can make it over."

"The heifers?"

"Fed and watered."

"I guess they're all right, then."

"Of course they are." He put down his magazine and came over to the bed. He reached out his hand, but pulled it back and crossed his arms without touching me. "You remember anything?"

"Howie's dead."

He blinked. "Yes."

"And a truck ran me off the road."

He nodded.

"My bike?"

"Jethro and Jermaine hauled it to their shop. What's left of it."

I turned and looked out the window, utterly exhausted. An overwhelming desire to cry washed over me, but I suppressed it.

"That detective wants to see you," Abe said.

"Willard?"

He nodded. "Probably wants to hear about your accident."

"Okay."

Abe picked up the phone and dialed a number from a business card. He gave someone a message for Detective Willard, and hung up. "He can't come now. He'll try to get here soon."

I nodded and closed my eyes, then opened them again when I remembered why Willard would want to see me. He didn't care about my accident. He wanted to know about the milk. I had just left him a message that my milk was being stolen before I ended up in a ditch. I opened my mouth to tell Abe, but he was talking.

"I was going to call Nick," he said, "but I don't have his number."

Grief exploded in my chest, and I had to labor to breathe.

"What's going on, Stella?"

I looked at him, unsure if he was talking about Nick, my accelerated breathing, or everything else. The seriousness on his face told me.

"I thought it was over," I said. "I found out who was doing the sabotage, and I thought I'd stopped it. But Howie…he left me…." My throat closed.

Abe came closer and took my hand in his. "Howie didn't leave you, Stella. He never would've left."

I shook my head painfully. "No. A notebook. He left me notes."

"Notes? About what?"

I was trying to form the words when the door opened and Missy walked in. She held out a sandwich encased in plastic wrap.

"Here, Abe. I got this for you in the cafeteria."

He kept a hold of my hand and inclined his head toward the table where his coffee and magazine sat. "Thanks. Can you set it there?"

Missy looked at Abe's hand holding mine, but didn't comment. She placed the sandwich on the table and sat in the chair.

Abe turned back to me. "I'm sorry. What were you saying?"

I cleared my throat. "I need a drink."

He got the cup from my bedside tray and angled the straw toward my lips. The water was warm, but soothed my throat anyway.

"Okay," I said. "Thanks." I tried to scoot up an inch, and my breath caught at the pain in my ribs.

Abe used the button on the side of the bed to make me a tad more upright. "Better?"

"Much. Thanks. Anyway, I was on the way to Ma's to try to find somebody to tell. I couldn't get anybody on the phone."

"To tell what?"

"That somebody's been stealing my milk."

He looked at me blankly. "What?"

"They've been taking it to a little processing plant and bottling it in Rockefeller bottles. I don't sell my milk to Rockefeller. I sell to the co-op."

"I don't understand," Abe said.

"Abe," Missy said. "Her milk is being stolen."

She spoke to me. "And what are they doing with it?"

I tried to look at her without moving too much. "I don't know for sure. But I'm afraid—"

The door swung open and a nurse came in.

"Sorry," she said. "It's time to take your vitals. Should I wait a minute?"

"Yes," I said.

My phone rang. I looked at Abe, and he answered it.

The nurse backed toward the door. "I'll come back."

Missy and I stared at each other.

When Abe hung up, he said to me, "That was the police. Someone will be coming by soon to take your statement."

"Not Willard?"

"Didn't say."

My eyes closed briefly of their own accord, and I almost drifted off.

"You okay?" Abe asked.

Missy stood up and walked to his side. "Come on. Let her sleep. We have to get going, anyway, remember? We're supposed to watch Jacob and Nina's kids, and we're already late."

"But how do we know she'll be safe? Maybe whoever was in the truck will try to come back and finish the job."

I thought about that. "I don't think so, Abe. If they really wanted me dead, they would've come back and made sure while I was lying in the ditch."

His forehead creased with doubt.

"The nurses will keep an eye out," Missy said.

"You think?" Abe asked.

I nodded. "Sure. You guys go do what you need to do."

"I'll be back," Abe said to me, "so you can finish your story. You'll tell the cops about your milk?"

I nodded.

Missy pinched her lips together. "I'm really sorry about Howie, Stella." She wavered there for a moment, but walked toward the door when I had nothing to say.

Abe squeezed my hand, then scooped up his coffee, magazine, and sandwich before joining Missy in the hallway.

The nurse came back a minute later, waking me from a doze. She was about the age my mother would've been. "Cute visitor." She waggled her eyebrows, and I had a flashback to Carla doing that when she saw Nick.

I snorted, trying to ease the sudden ache in my heart. "Cute, maybe. But taken."

She laughed. "All the good ones are, sweetheart. All the good ones are. Now lie back and try to relax. Your blood pressure is out of this world."

Chapter Thirty-Five

The nurse had just finished poking and prodding when Pam stuck her head in the door. "Up for a visitor?"

The nurse patted my arm. "Don't wear yourself out now. You look exhausted."

"I promise I'll be good."

Pam pulled a chair up to the side of the bed. "I'll make sure she behaves."

The nurse laughed and pushed through the door.

Pam's eyes roved over my face and arms, studying the bandages. She sat forward, rested her elbows on her knees, and said, "So. How are you doing?"

"I'll survive."

She looked at me with pity in her eyes. "I don't mean your accident."

I turned toward the TV and wished it were on.

"I mean Howie," Pam said.

"I know what you mean."

She focused her gaze on her shoes.

I sighed, and wished I could go to sleep for several days. I knew people would be asking how I was holding up. Knew I had a funeral to plan. An apartment to clean out. A friend to mourn, and avenge. But dammit, I didn't want to *talk* about it.

Pam sneaked another look at me, and I noticed that the bags under her eyes had grown.

"You sure *you* shouldn't be in here?" I asked.

She grimaced. "That bad, huh?"

"Not if gray is your natural color."

"Ha ha." She sank into the chair and rubbed her eyes. "I haven't gotten much sleep this week." She looked troubled.

"And?"

"*And*…Dad just got turned down for his loan. The bank will be 'more than happy' to give him money. But only half of what he asked for. With the Bergeys selling out for that new development—what's it going to be called, Orchard Hill or something—Dad lost a third of the land he farms. There's no way he could make payments on the original loan amount."

I shook my head. "What's he gonna do?"

"Play the lottery, I guess. Like you suggested." She closed her eyes. "It's so damned exhausting."

I studied her face and thought about all the knowledge in her head. "Pam. Let me run something by you and see what you think."

She looked at me. "Do I need to put my town council hat on?"

"Don't think so. But I need your doctor regalia."

"Oh. Okay. What?"

"Someone's stealing my milk."

Her face went from gray to white. "How do you know?"

"Followed the driver. On a tip from Howie."

"But—"

The door opened and a uniformed police officer stepped in, looking none too happy about it.

I groaned. "What do you want, Meadows?"

He stood at the foot of the bed. "Ms. Moyer."

She turned her head toward him. "Mister Meadows."

He took out a notebook and didn't bother to erase the boredom from his face. "So what happened, Ms. Crown?"

"What *happened*," I said, "was that I got run off the road. By people who *happen* to be stealing my milk."

He raised his eyebrows. "And you have proof of this? Or something that might point that direction?"

If I would've been able to move, I would've decked him. "Remember my farmhand? Who was *murdered?* I believe you were there?"

"Yeah, but—"

"I think the aflatoxin illness is being spread through my milk, and Howie knew it."

"What?" Pam said.

Meadows froze for a second, then smirked. "They're taking your farm's milk and infusing it with a fungus? For what purpose?"

"How the hell am I supposed to know? All I know is they're taking the milk to an abandoned farm and putting it into Rockefeller bottles. I don't know where they're taking it from there, or how. Or why."

He scribbled in his notebook, shaking his head and laughing to himself.

"Where's Willard?" I demanded.

"With his son. Where else would he be?"

"You need to let him know what I've found out."

"Brady's pretty critical. I don't think I should interrupt for just anything."

"Listen, Meadows. If this is what I think it is, this isn't 'just anything.' It could save Brady's life. Don't you think Willard would be interested in *that?*"

He wrote a few more notes. "I'll give him your message, okay? Now, about the accident. You think it was related to your milk getting stolen?"

"I *know* it was. It was the same truck I saw at the processing plant."

"Make?"

"Dodge Ram. A new one. Black."

"What'd the driver look like?"

"Didn't see him close enough for details. White guy, though."

"I don't suppose you saw the license plate."

"Oh, no. As I was sliding off the road, getting ripped to shreds, head slamming the ground, I made sure I got a good view of the clear numbers while the truck was speeding away."

Irritation flashed across his face. "Fine."

"Come on, Meadows. How was I supposed to read a plate?"

He flipped his notebook closed and pocketed it. "I'll get in touch with Willard and inform him of your theories. If there isn't anything else?"

I glared at him. He glared back.

Pam stood. "How about I show you out, Officer Meadows? I have to be going, too." She looked at me. "Meeting with Sonny Turner."

Meadows bristled. "I'll be fine without an escort, thank you."

Pam held up her hands. "No offense meant."

He grunted and left.

"You call Willard first thing!" I yelled after him.

Pam scooted her chair back to the little table.

"So what do you think?" I asked.

"About what?"

"My milk. Could they be poisoning people with it?"

She straightened the chair. "I don't know, Stella. Why would they do that?"

"Well, what would be the purpose of stealing it otherwise? It's not like they're not paying me for it. I'm getting money." I frowned. I was getting money, but the co-op knew nothing about it. I'd have to check with my bank about exactly where the deposits were coming from.

Pam crossed her arms. "Your sure it's just *your* milk they've got?"

I thought about it. "Don't know. Would it matter?"

"Well, maybe it's just a little plant Rockefeller's using."

"But I don't sell my milk to Rockefeller. I sell it to the co-op."

She pursed her lips. "Did you actually see them infusing it with something?"

"Couldn't tell. I was hanging by my elbows on an outside window ledge."

She shook her head, laughing quietly. "You are something else. Okay. Tell you what. I'll come up with some scenarios for you. Try to figure out how your milk could possibly be poisoning the neighborhood."

"You sound like you don't believe it."

"Well, think about it. There are lots of problems. Distribution. Cost. The number of people who would have to be involved. And the aflatoxin source would have to be considerable."

"But it's possible."

"Sure. Anything's possible."

She glanced at the clock. "Whoops. Gotta go."

"One more favor?" I said.

"Shoot."

"Check up on Officer Crabby Pants and make sure he actually contacts Willard?"

"No problem. How about I stop by later? Check in, see how you're doing. I can give you ideas by then, and hopefully let you know when the detective might be by."

"Sounds great. But I might not be here."

"What? Where would you be?"

"Home."

She stared at me. "You're kidding, right?"

I smiled. "What do you think?"

Chapter Thirty-Six

"You are such a stubborn ass!"

"Why, thank you, Jethro. That's kind of you to say."

He harrumphed and dropped into the chair where my other visitors had sat earlier. I hadn't wanted to call him. Unfortunately, I didn't have my wallet, since it was in the saddlebag of my bike, so I couldn't get a taxi, and had to enlist help. Jethro and Belle were the obvious ones to call. Jethro thought I was being…well…stubborn.

"Come on, Belle," I said. "Give me a hand, will you?"

She held out her arm and I slowly moved my legs off the bed. I sat for a moment to let my head get back to my shoulders before attempting to stand. Belle gripped my elbow like a vice.

"You're cutting off my circulation, Belle."

"Sorry. I just don't want you to fall."

"Let her fall," Jethro said. "Her head's too hard to hurt it, anyway."

"Now, Jethro," Belle said.

"Now, Jethro," I said.

"Sure," Jethro said. "She leaves some freaked out message that her milk's poisoning the neighborhood, but no one *else* knows anything about it."

"Jethro," Belle said. "Leave her alone."

Eventually we got into the bathroom, where I took a break by sitting on the toilet seat. Belle went back out to get the underwear, extra large T-shirt, and shorts she had picked up at my house. Together we were able to get my hospital gown off and my other clothes on without more than a few swear words on my part. On Jethro's part, at each sound of pain I could hear him jump up, like he was going to come rushing into the bathroom to save me. Belle just clamped her teeth and got through it, like a champ.

I was hobbling back into the room when a woman came in, her white physician's coat flapping behind her. I didn't recognize her, because she hadn't been in to see me yet.

"I hear our newest guest is going to be the first to leave," she said.

I lowered myself carefully onto a chair. "When I didn't have a welcoming party I figured I wasn't invited."

She smiled. "Just because you didn't see me doesn't mean I wasn't here. You're on some pretty strong painkillers. And you look very angelic when you're asleep."

"Ha," Jethro said.

"You here to chain me to the bed?" I asked.

She shook her head. "I would prefer that you stay, but seeing as how we're not in the military, I can't order you to."

"You could try," Jethro grumbled.

"Wouldn't work on Ms. Crown. I can tell just by looking at her."

"Thanks, Doc," I said. "And your name is?"

"Rachel Peterson. Remember it. You're going to see me every day until I tell you not to anymore."

"I am?"

"You are. Unless you want your insurance to completely disown you. Then you can pay for any hospitalization that has to do with skin grafts, infections, or those broken ribs." She blinked, feigning innocence. "But, of course, it's up to you."

"I'll bring her myself," Jethro said, "if I have to put her over my shoulder and carry her in."

I looked at Belle and she shrugged.

"I guess I'm outnumbered," I told the doctor. "Tell me where to go, and when."

She smiled and gave me her business card with an appointment already written on the back.

The ride home was uneventful, except for the few times we hit a pothole and I shrieked with pain. Jethro didn't go above thirty the whole way, so it took forever. Once we got to the farm I was exhausted, but fought Jethro off or he would've carried me across the threshold.

I got out of the truck and Queenie snuffled around my legs, inspecting the bandages. I kneaded my fingers through her fur and stared at the garage.

"Hard to believe he ain't there," Jethro said softly.

I silently turned toward the house, while what I really wanted to do was go up to Howie's apartment, lie in the middle of the floor, and wail.

Belle got a little suitcase out of the truck bed and started to follow me inside.

"Whoa, Nellie," I said. "What are you doing?"

"Staying overnight with you."

"I don't think so."

"Oh, I do." Her smile was reinforced with steel.

"What about Zach and Mallory? Don't they need you?"

"What am I?" Jethro said. "Chopped liver?"

"Jethro will take care of the kids," Belle said, "while I take care of you. Neither of them is getting any worse—in fact, Mallory is distinctly better—and neither of them has asthma, like poor Toby and that other little boy." Her voice wobbled.

"I don't need a baby-sitter," I said.

But she was already halfway up the walk, ignoring me.

"Jethro—" I said.

"Someone *did* run you off the road, you know. Belle can keep an eye out for unwanted intruders."

"And she'll fight them off? With what? An iron skillet?"

"No need for sarcasm. She can hold her own." He grinned. "And she can call 911 as quick as the next person. Besides, you've got Queenie for an early warning signal."

He patted my shoulder, got in his truck, and drove off. I did my best to walk with dignity up the sidewalk to the house. Queenie followed me in, coming through the hole in the screen door after it slapped shut behind me.

First off, I listened to my messages. Bart, Lenny, Jermaine, Carla. Nothing from Willard. Or Nick.

Belle fluttered around all evening, getting me things to eat or drink, cleaning, answering the phone, and basically doing so many housewifely things I thought I was going to scream. Instead, I sneaked out of the house while she was scrubbing the downstairs bathroom and made my way to my office. It took a while, but I got there, eventually.

I sat in my chair and swiveled it toward the aerial photo. So much had changed since it was taken. Besides the main thing—losing Howie—a neighbor boy was dead, the heifer barn was gone, my Harley was scrap metal, and I had made and lost a friend in Nick. And that didn't even count my milk being used as a biological weapon.

I gazed out of the window, letting my body sink into the chair. The garage glowed eerily in the circle of the dusk-to-dawn light, and I couldn't tear my eyes away from it. Howie was dead.

My arm throbbed, along with my head, and my pills were in the house. Crap.

"Ah, here you are." Belle stood in the doorway, one hand on her hip, the other holding a tray. "I went to tell you I made brownies, but you weren't there. I figured you were tired of me mothering you."

I opened my mouth to protest, but she grinned.

"I know you, remember. No use your lying about it."

"Okay."

"So, anyway, here they are. Along with a glass of milk and your next helping of pain medicine."

I wrinkled my nose at the milk.

"You don't really think your milk is poisoning people?" Belle said.

"Why else would they be stealing it?"

"But it tastes fine."

"Maybe aflatoxin doesn't taste like anything."

She frowned. "It's a fungus, isn't it? That can't taste good."

I sighed. Maybe I *was* putting two unrelated things together. It just seemed like too much of a coincidence.

"Now," Belle said, "when you're done with those brownies you want to get ready for bed?"

I looked back out at Howie's apartment. "I guess."

"Okay. I'll come in a little while and help you get inside."

"You can stay and eat some with me."

She patted my good arm before heading for the door. "I know you need your space."

"Belle? How's Jude?"

She turned back, her face pained. "As good as can be expected." She paused. "We just can't believe it was one of *us* that did those things to you."

"No, Belle. It wasn't. Marianne never was one of you."

She sniffled, and left.

My phone rang. It was Detective Willard.

"Officer Meadows says you have a theory about the poisoning. He thinks it's nuts, but I want to hear it."

"Where are you?"

"The hospital lobby."

"Brady okay?"

"Hanging on. Now what did you want to tell me?"

I told him about my milk.

"So where is this plant? You didn't tell Meadows."

"I was drugged up. I guess I forgot."

"Yes, but he wasn't. He should've asked. Anyway, the location?"

I gave him the road name and described the place. "You're going there now?"

"Soon as I can get a warrant. Anything else you need to tell me?"

"Yes. Thanks for believing me. You're the first one to take me seriously."

"Well," he said. "It's a serious business."

Chapter Thirty-Seven

As soon as I hung up, I saw lights in my driveway. Queenie was going nuts, so I leaned forward carefully to see out the window. It was Pam. I knocked on the glass before she went up to the house.

She came into the office, where she shut the door and leaned against it, hugging a briefcase to her chest. "I see you managed to get out of the hospital."

I shrugged a shoulder.

"How are you feeling?"

"Just took some painkillers, so I'm better than ten minutes ago. A little high, but less miserable."

"Good."

"How was your meeting with Sonny?"

"What? Oh. Okay." She was sweating, and her eyes were bloodshot.

"God, Pam, you look like hell. You need to go to the doctor."

"No. No, I don't think so."

I shook my head. "Whatever. So you have some ideas for me?"

"About your milk?"

"Yeah. About whether it could be poisoning people."

She dropped her briefcase, put her hands to her face, and burst into tears.

I raised my eyebrows, wondering what I'd said. "Pam?"

She pounded on the door behind her. "Goddamnit, Stella, why couldn't you just be dumb? You were *supposed* to be dumb."

I stared at her.

"That farm in Dublin was a secret. Wayne was ordered to watch his back, make sure he was never followed."

"Dublin?" I froze. "But I didn't say anything about Dublin."

She shook her head. Tears poured down her face. "You didn't have to."

"You mean—"

"Yes! Yes, dammit, I know about your milk. I know about the plant. I know how it's poisoning the neighborhood!"

I gaped at her. She picked up her briefcase, slammed it onto my desk, and thrust her hand into it. She pulled out a thick stack of papers. And threw them at me.

"Here! It's all here! God forgive me, it's all here."

She staggered back against the office door and slid down to the floor, hugging her knees to her chest. I watched her for a moment before forcing my eyes to the mess of papers scattered over the desktop, the floor, and me.

Numb, I picked one up. Then another. And another. Typed on the pages were equations, symbols, and vocabulary that were foreign to me. Lots of stuff about proteins, DNA, and other scientific garble. All this was mixed in with words I did recognize, like silage, grain, and corn.

I glanced at Pam. She was still crying, rocking and banging her head rhythmically against the door.

I picked up another page. More of the same, although there was something else I recognized. My name.

I scrabbled through the papers, looking for anything more that made sense. I began to see other familiar things. Jude's name, the dates he'd filled my silo and my granary. Good God, I was lucky if *I* kept track of those things.

The next page I picked up was even odder than what I'd already seen. The entire page was filled with a block of letters, reading "GCTAGGCTACGTAGGCTAC..." and so on. No breaks, no other characters, no punctuation.

Something clicked in my brain and I remembered reading articles about artificial insemination and gene pools. I recognized the babble on the paper.

"This DNA sequence," I said.

Pam turned glazed eyes to me.

"It's the genetics of Jude's corn, isn't it?" My stomach twisted, and I knew what I'd thought before was the truth. "My milk really is poisoning all those people. Somehow Jude's grain is making the milk toxic."

Pam's eyes filled again.

I stared her down. "Tell me."

She focused on something beyond my shoulder. My aerial photograph, probably. Ironically. She cleared her throat. "I engineered a seed. A seed that would grow corn with a poison in its core."

"But Marianne buys GM seeds meant to resist drought. She told me so herself, just the other day."

"Marianne has no idea. She thinks she's using a legitimate test seed. The clincher was when she was told it had only a fifty-fifty chance of working. She was counting on failure."

"And how was it you knew to approach her?"

Pam sat up, life beginning to return to her eyes. "Come on, Stella. The entire farming community knows Marianne hates the farming life. It's not exactly a secret. She'll do anything to sabotage Jude's crops. And it was perfect since Jude's crops almost exclusively feed your herd."

I swallowed, trying to breathe. *My herd.*

Queenie began barking outside, and I craned my neck to see what was going on. Before anything came into view she was quiet again. I turned back to Pam. "And it's making people sick how, exactly?"

"I've added a gene to the corn's DNA that's engineered to express potent aflatoxin."

I shook my head. "But that would make my cows sick, too."

She pushed herself up from the floor and stepped toward me. "No. I made sure it wouldn't. The fungal gene is programmed in such a way it's dormant until eaten by the cows. A protein from one of the natural bacteria in the cow's first stomach generates an inactive gene. Digestive acids are nasty, you know. They wreak havoc on DNA molecules. Anyway, once that gene gets to the udder, the oxytocin—a milk producing hormone—switches on the aflatoxin gene. It's out of the cow's digestive system by that time. And the level of oxytocin is highest during milking—meaning it's being immediately expelled from the cow. It's amazing, really."

Amazing.

"I didn't want people getting sick from other secretions, either," she said. "Otherwise you'd probably be dead from all the manure you shovel around every day. The aflatoxin gene was targeted to the mammary tissue in the udder so it would be in the milk but not in the cow's other discharge. It took a little doing, but from what I can see, I got it right."

I breathed through my mouth. "So that's why you weren't pasteurizing the milk."

She nodded. "Would've killed the aflatoxin along with all the other bacteria. Separating the cream from the milk was enough. No one knew the difference."

I studied my hands, gripping the edge of my desk. "But Pam, *why?*"

She laughed harshly. "*Why?* You want to know *why?*" She laughed some more. "The money I'm going to make, it's…it's astounding."

Money. Money to save her dad. Her dad's farm. *Her* farm.

"But Pam, people *died.*"

Expressions warred on her face, and her eyes began to water again. "No one was supposed to die," she whispered.

"So what went wrong?"

"I…I hadn't taken into account the ones who were already sick."

I looked at the ceiling, the cabinet, anything but her. "So where's the money coming from, Pam?"

She lowered her eyes.

"Pam. *Where?*"

She rounded on me. "Where do you think, Stella? Who's had an iron grip on my life for the past seven years? Who has enough money to save us all—every farmer—if he wanted to?"

My mouth dropped open. "*Sonny?*"

She closed her eyes.

"But *why?*"

She put her hands over her face briefly, then dropped them. "You know what they say. You can never have enough money."

I stared at her. "Sonny has enough."

"Tell him that." She wrapped her arms around herself and walked to the window to look out. "He knew all about my work at Penn, being my sponsor. You know he paid for every minute of my schooling? He considered it his right to follow my progress through every report and exam. He might as well have taken the courses himself."

She turned toward me, and I waited, paralyzed by shock.

"So he came to me. Said he wanted me to create a GM crop that would make a community sick. Assured me he didn't want something lethal. Just something he could control."

"But—"

"Then, when all the farmers were convinced the land was poison, and no one wanted to build a house in this town for fear of getting sick, he'd buy it all. Beat Hubert Purcell and the rest of the vultures at their own game." She stopped.

"Don't quit now, Pam."

She turned back to the window. "But people started dying. He hadn't expected that. Hadn't *wanted* that. He…he completely freaked out. Decided to change tactics. Figured we'd move on to other towns with the poison milk, and later he could ride in as the hero, dispensing medicine and wisdom. Took his cue from the anthrax scare, thought he could become a local legend."

I struggled to my feet, but she put out her hand.

"I knew it wouldn't work. He's going to go down, and I'm going with him. But no one else is going to die." She gestured at the papers. "You have what you need to stop it."

My arms trembled from supporting my weight. "How could you *do* this? How could you *possibly* say yes?"

Fire flashed in her eyes. "How could I possibly say no? If it hadn't been for Sonny, I'd be in your shoes, or worse. Trying to save a farm that was doomed for failure."

I lunged across the desk and grabbed her shirt, pulling her across the desk toward me. "So help me, if you killed Howie—"

The office door slapped open. I threw Pam away from me and dropped behind the desk, the pain in my ribs so intense I could hardly breathe. Sonny stood there, smiling his charismatic smile, holding a shotgun.

"Of course Pam didn't kill Howie," he said. "She doesn't have the guts for that."

"*You*—"

"Of course, me." His wild, red-rimmed eyes betrayed his smile, and his gaze flicked from Pam to me and back again.

I glanced out the window, wondering where Belle was, and what I had to do to get her to call 911.

"Oh," Sonny said. "Don't bother looking for that darling dog of yours."

"Oh, God. You didn't—"

He waved his hand. "Of course not. A good kick to the head knocked her right out. It's not like she can ID me later. After you're dead."

So he didn't know about Belle.

I spoke through my rage, my voice sounding strangled. "Why didn't you just finish me off when I was lying in the ditch yesterday?"

"Incompetent fools." The gun jerked in his hands, and I ducked my head behind the desk. "Should've just done it myself. They saw all the blood on your head and didn't know enough to remember head wounds bleed like crazy, but aren't necessarily fatal. '*But there was so much of it, Mr. Turner.*' Idiots assumed you were bleeding to death and left you to die."

"Instead of putting a bullet in my head."

"No. They should've just bashed your head a little more. Made it look like part of the accident." His eyes bored into mine. "Instead, you got to live an extra day." He shook his head sadly. "When your friends find you here tomorrow they'll feel so bad. What a shame you had to shoot yourself. You just couldn't take the fact that Howie was dead."

I couldn't. But I wasn't about to kill myself. I jerked my chin toward his gun. "They'll know I didn't shoot myself with *that*."

He licked his lips, having apparently forgotten that part of the equation. I wondered how quickly I could get to my rifle, but knew it wouldn't be quick enough. I had to play for time and hope Belle was on the phone with the police. Hope she saw Queenie lying in the yard, and was smart enough not to come storming out here.

"Howie figured out what you were doing, didn't he?" I said.

Sonny licked his lips and gripped the shotgun tighter. "He'd made too many connections. When Wayne told Pam Howie had been asking about milk distribution, I knew he was onto us. I sent Pam to find out how much he'd discovered, but I followed her, knowing she wouldn't be able to kill him if she needed to. We found nothing when we searched his apartment, but it seems something was missed...." He looked at me.

"He hid it here in the office. An envelope with everything he'd discovered."

"Ah. A pity we didn't have more time to search."

I swallowed. "So, if I had been at home that evening, as usual?"

"Pam would've simply done her charm routine and wormed things out on her own."

My heart plummeted. So Howie would still be alive if I hadn't been out chasing down Hubert and Marianne. Damn them.

"But don't feel guilty," Sonny said. "We would've come back later to get him."

I edged my way around the desk, putting on more of a show of injury than I actually felt. Those painkillers were really kicking in.

"Not too close, Stella," Sonny said. His voice wavered.

Pam caught my eye and subtly shook her head.

I leaned my hip on the corner of the desk. "I want to know about Wayne. What was in this for him?"

"Oh, he didn't have much of a choice," Sonny said. "His wife Flo is home alone all day while he's working. She'd never have the ability to protect herself from an intruder."

I digested that. "So Flo's MS didn't really take a turn for the worse?"

Sonny gave a high-pitched giggle. "God, no. Is that the story he gave you? No. We promised him a lot of money. More than enough to get Flo the treatment she needs. I had to have someone inside the hauling company, and Wayne was the logical choice, since he collects your milk. It wasn't hard to convince him. He simply emptied his tank at the storage facility after his morning run and came to get your milk over his lunch hour."

I shifted position so my weight was on my good leg.

Sonny waved the gun at me, and his voice went flat. "No more moving."

I rested my butt against the desk, wondering if the cops were coming, or if Belle was oblivious to what was happening out here. *Stall, stall,* I told myself. "One more thing. How come I was still getting money from the co-op, when they have no record of getting my milk since last summer?"

Sonny showed me a good portion of his dentures. "You *are* smarter than we thought, aren't you?"

I glanced at Pam, and she flushed bright red. She spoke softly. "It was Billy."

My mouth dropped. "Billy? Marty and Rochelle's *nephew?*"

She nodded miserably.

Sonny giggled again. "William's the accountant at Rockefeller, you know. Been on board from the beginning. He had a couple—shall we say, *laundry*, problems—that could be overlooked if he helped out. Besides being an old school chum of Pam's, of course. Oh, and yours." He smiled a wolfish smile. "William retrieved your banking numbers from the co-op, and after stopping your account on their computers, he paid you from an untraceable source we set up."

A slow burn sizzled in my stomach. I should've broken Billy's neck back in high school, instead of his arm.

Sonny cocked his head and raised the gun even with my chest. "Well, Ms. Crown, if all of your questions have been answered, I'm afraid we have to be going. Pam and I have some cleaning up to do, and some children to save. I'm going to be a hero."

"Pam?" I said.

She looked at me, sadness and fear pulsing in her eyes.

I lunged toward Sonny, knocking the gun barrel aside with my elbow. It fired by my head, making a sound like two trucks hitting head-on. The echo slammed my eardrums.

I collapsed to the floor, and Sonny swung his foot back to kick me. I shot out my leg, catching the ankle of his still-grounded foot. His leg gave out, and I hooked my foot behind his, pulling as hard as I could. He fell backwards, crashing into the chair, then onto the floor, and the gun went skittering from his hand. I pushed off with my right arm and leg and fell on him just as he was scrambling up. I screamed and body-slammed him onto the floor.

He squirmed onto his back, punching at my face and throat.

I banged his head against the floor. "You." *Bang.* "Killed...." *Bang.* "Howie." *Bang.* He went limp.

I sighed, letting my face fall onto his chest while I caught my breath.

I turned my head to see if Pam was coming after me. She wasn't. She lay crumpled against the wall, surrounded by a spatter of blood. Lots of it. It came from the hole where her throat used to be. I took a moment to steady myself, then forced myself to move.

Afraid Sonny would wake up, I gritted my teeth and limped behind the desk, where I yanked cords from the surge protector and the back of the computer. I worked as quickly as I could. In a couple of minutes Sonny lay face-down on the linoleum, his ankles tied and pulled up to be connected to his wrists. He was oblivious to it all. I squatted beside him and examined my handiwork. He wasn't going anywhere soon. Except to jail.

I turned and grabbed the edge of the desk, balancing myself on my knees. The phone was just within reach, and I knocked the receiver off the cradle and drew it toward me. The 911 dispatcher took my call with the usual calm of emergency experts, and I slowly sank to the floor and lay all the way down on my back. I didn't look at Pam again.

Before long I heard sirens. And I allowed the world to go black.

Chapter Thirty-Eight

The hospital room was peaceful, with occasional sounds of nurses going by the door, and random snores from my roommate. The curtain was pulled in between us, and I stared out the darkened window. It was almost dawn.

"Knock, knock." A nurse peeked around the curtain.

"Vitals *again*?" I said.

"Not this time. There's a Detective Willard who wants to see you. I told him I'd check if you were awake."

"I'm awake."

"So I should send him in?"

"Please."

Willard came in and sank onto the visitor's chair. He leaned an elbow on the chair's arm and rested his chin on his fist. "Sonny Turner's behind bars. And I don't care who he gets as his lawyer, I'm never letting him out."

"You'd better not," I said. "For his sake."

Willard met my eyes for a moment, then looked away.

"How's Brady?" I asked.

"Going to be okay, thanks to you. We've confirmed everything we found in the processing plant, so the docs know better how to counteract it. The sick kids had stopped drinking milk, of course, just with the regular clear liquids diet, but the damage the aflatoxin had done was too great for that to cure them completely. Same with the antidote." He paused. "Now we just pray all these people don't have permanent liver and kidney damage."

I remembered seeing that possibility on the aflatoxin web site. "For real?"

"The consequences of long-term exposure." Anger tightened his face. "Damn them."

My mind flashed to the image of Pam slumped against the office wall. Perhaps she already was damned. Somehow I couldn't find it in my heart to be in any way glad about that.

"So how did you check out the DNA sequence?" I asked.

"Woke up a Temple University geneticist. She ran the gene strand through an on-line database that analyzes DNA sequences and compares them to other DNA. The geneticist was pretty skeptical, though. Said it would take millions, if not *billions*, of dollars to perfect such a gene."

Which Sonny probably had in his wallet on a daily basis.

"Well, it worked, didn't it?" I said.

"Can't argue with that." He sighed. "Got a little good news for you."

"Yeah? I could use some."

"Hubert Purcell and Marianne Granger are falling all over themselves blaming each other for the sabotage on your farm. Marianne tried to be tight-lipped, but once I told her she was going to be charged with accessory to murder for the aflatoxin poisonings, she started gushing information."

"Like the manure she had sent pouring from my lagoon."

Willard managed a small smile. "And Hubert will be paying a hefty fine for letting your herd loose the other night. I did find his fingerprints on the lock you left out for me."

I closed my eyes, exhaustion reminding me of its presence.

I heard Willard stand, and I looked up at him. "One more thing I don't understand."

"Just one?"

"For now. Why was it just our borough? Why no other towns?"

He sat down again. "Sonny paid off the two Rockefeller drivers that delivered to all the milk markets in town. Every gallon of your milk went directly to local shelves. If someone from out of town bought a gallon here now and then, they'd never know the difference. It was those of us who bought here on a regular basis that felt the effects, since the symptoms only started showing up after months of ingestion."

My stomach turned. I still couldn't grasp that it was my milk that had sickened an entire population. Had killed people. "Sounds like an iffy process."

He shrugged. "Didn't matter to them, apparently. The whole thing was pretty much of an experiment. An experiment that worked far too well."

I closed my eyes, this time to shut out the world.

Willard stood again, but I could feel him hovering by the bed. "I'm real sorry about Pam."

"Yeah." I didn't open my eyes. "Me, too."

A few hours later I woke up with my arm and ribs throbbing. After pounding the nurse button and getting a hit of morphine, I tried to down my breakfast. Thankfully, the phone rang in the middle of my scrambled eggs. I got it on the third ring, my body not happy about the twisting, and had to catch my breath before answering.

"Yeah?"

"Hey, Stella."

"Zach. How are you?"

"Okay, I guess."

I waited, not sure what to say.

Zach spoke again. "I, uh, know it wasn't your fault about Gus."

"Thanks, bud."

More silence.

"I'm sorry I was so mad at you."

A smile made my forehead stitches ache. "Forget about it, Zach. It's over. How are you feeling?"

"Much better."

"Really?"

"Mom keeps saying I have color back in my cheeks."

"That's great. Mallory?"

"Bossing me around."

I laughed. "Glad to hear it."

"Anyway, Mom said I needed to call and let you know. Seems like…we're going to be okay."

"Yes, Zach. We are." I didn't have the heart to tell him what health problems he could face in the future. He was a teen-ager. Tomorrow wasn't important. "You tell your mom thanks—"

"She wants to talk to you."

"Oh, okay. I'll see you soon."

"Stella?"

"Hey, Belle."

She was quiet for a second. "I feel really stupid."

"No need to."

"When I saw Pam arrive I thought you'd be taken care of for a bit. I never heard anything over the vacuum cleaner."

"Belle, it's okay."

"You could've been *killed*."

"But I wasn't."

"No. No, you weren't."

We had a moment of silence.

"Well," she finally said, "at least now you'll go home to a clean house."

Chapter Thirty-Nine

Pam's dad sold out to a developer the very next day. Last I heard he bought a one-way ticket to Florida.

I sat on the side steps of my house staring at the barn, trying to decide how I could possibly go on doing what I'd done every day I could remember. Instead of a haven of family and hard work, my farm had now adopted an aura of tragedy. Howie—*oh, Howie*—had died because he tried to save it. Toby and the other boy died because they drank its product. Pam died because she had used it for evil. Who knew how many other people would be permanently affected.

I watched yet another vehicle drive down my lane and disappear. The county waste truck had emptied my feed barn of every kernel of grain in sight. They would be back later to empty my silo. I had already contacted a local granary that had never bought grain from Jude, and they would be coming to replace what I'd lost. The granaries that had bought grain from him were being cleaned out, as well, even though the amount of toxic grain would've been too small to affect anyone once it got mixed in with all the other. But the government wasn't taking any chances.

When I had gotten home from the hospital that morning, I had to run off several reporters wanting to tape interviews, then went on a slow tour of the farm, trying desperately not to cry at everything that reminded me of Howie. Marty was almost finished milking my cows. Carla—who had heard the news and made a sudden change to another company's milk—was performing an impromptu herd check. And there was a message on my answering machine from Brigham Bergey, my brand-new lawyer. I called him back immediately, and he gave me the first good news I'd had since Nick had first walked into my office.

But I couldn't let myself think about Nick.

Bergey had convinced the insurance home office I was entitled to the money for my heifer barn. Once Marianne confessed, there wasn't much more the company could do. But despite his success with the heifer barn, he wasn't sure the insurance company would pay for the grain I'd lost. There seemed to be some clause denying me coverage for any act of war or terrorism, and they viewed it as such. Cheap bastards.

I heard a cow moo in the paddock and had something else to be thankful for. The cows were completely unaware of what had happened around them. Carla said she couldn't see anything to tell her they'd been harmed. If they had been momentarily affected, they had adjusted or forgotten by now. Blissful ignorance.

Queenie, fully recovered from Sonny's kick except for the bump on her head, started to bark, and a car pulled up the drive. A glance told me it was Abe's Camry. I turned my head away, looking out at the fields. I took in my lush green acres, soon to be barren, stripped and sanitized by the EPA. Abe's car got closer, but I ignored it. I didn't think I would be able to stomach the pity that would surely be in Missy's eyes.

The car stopped and a car door slammed. Just one. I took another peek and saw Abe standing by the sedan, gazing at me over the top of it. No one was in the passenger seat. I tried to read his face. He had attempted to visit me in the hospital, but the nurses had acted as much like guards as caregivers. Willard had been the only person allowed in.

Gravel crunched under Abe's feet as he made his way to where I was sitting. He paused when he got to me, then sat on the step. We stayed that way for several minutes, silent, staring toward the barn.

"How's Jude?" I finally asked.

"Not good. Marianne's locked up, at least for now, and who knows what will happen if she gets out? Belle and Jethro insisted Jude come and stay with them for a little while. He fought it, but you know how they are. God, I'm sorry about all that, Stella."

"And I'm sorry for the little baby that's going to be born into all of it."

We lapsed into silence again, and did more staring.

"Queenie bust through that screen door?" he asked.

"The night of the fire. I'll get around to fixing it someday."

More silence. More staring.

"Where—" I said.

"I—" he said.

We both stopped.

"You first," we both said.

I gestured at him to go and he picked up a stick and started turning it around in his hands.

"I decided to move back in with Ma for a while."

I glanced at him, and he flushed. I didn't say anything.

"I figured with all that happened you could use a little help around here. Might as well be me. And it seems Rockefeller has an opening for an accountant."

I stared even harder at the barn, trying to digest what he was saying. "I can't see Missy and Ma getting along in that close quarters."

Abe threw the stick into the driveway. "Missy's already back in New York."

I looked at him. He jumped up and stood, his back to me. His shoulders rose, hesitated, fell. "She seemed to think I had the woman I loved right here at home. Said she's giving me some time to figure out what my heart is telling me."

I sat, stunned.

Abe turned around. "I thought about that for a while. Finally decided she was right. No matter how stubborn you are, or hard-headed, or downright bitchy, you seem to be the woman I want."

I stood up as abruptly as I was able and limped into the house, where I leaned on the counter, my head against a cupboard. I looked out of the window and saw Abe standing with his back to me again, rubbing his eyes. I splashed some water on my face and dried it off with a paper towel, then went back out and stood on the top step.

Abe lifted his head, but kept his back to me. "I guess with Nick around that kind of complicates things, but I feel like a teen-ager with all our arguing. I won't get in the way if he's who you need right now."

"Nick's gone." I tried to ignore the pain those words caused.

Abe stuffed his hands in his pockets and slowly turned to look at me.

I crossed my arms and looked down at my feet, at the barn, anywhere but him. "He's been gone since before my accident."

We stood like that for what seemed like an hour but was probably only a few seconds.

"So where are we?" he asked.

I closed my eyes and shrugged. "I don't know, Abe. What we're talking about would change everything."

"And that would be bad?"

"I'm not ready. Too much has changed. I'm already starting new."

"So why not try it now? Make it part of the new life?" He took his hands out of his pockets and walked up to me, but I backed away, wrapping my arms around myself. He looked at me for a long time, studying my face.

"I'll be around to help," he said. "Whether you want me to or not."

I took a deep breath. "I think you should go now, Abe."

His face reflected disappointment, but he was going to have to get used to it, if he expected too much, too fast.

"I'll be calling," he said.

I nodded.

He took a last look at my face and walked across the yard to his car. He opened his door, then stopped. "Know how long I'm going to be here for you, Stella?"

I closed my eyes, knowing what was coming, but not wanting to hear it if Howie wasn't there to say it.

"I'll be with you till the cows come home."

He got into his car, turned it around, and drove out the lane, not looking back. I sat down on the steps and held out my hand to Queenie.

"C'mere, girl." She trotted over and sat, leaning on my knees. I worked my fingers into her coat until I felt the warmth of her skin.

"Oh, Queenie," I said. "I miss him."

She rolled her eyes to look up at me, and I rubbed the silky hair on her nose. I knew I should get up and do something productive, but also knew I didn't have the strength. I leaned over and nuzzled my face into Queenie's fur.

And I wept.

To receive a free catalog of other Poisoned Pen Press titles, please contact us in one of the following ways:

Phone: 1-800-421-3976
Facsimile: 1-480-949-1707
Email: info@poisonedpenpress.com
Website: www.poisonedpenpress.com

Poisoned Pen Press
6962 E. First Ave. Ste 103
Scottsdale, AZ 85251